BIJOU ROY

RONICA DHAR

BIJOU ROY

ST. MARTIN'S PRESS

NEW YORK

This is a work of fiction. All of the characters, organizations, and events portrayed in this novel are either products of the author's imagination or are used fictitiously.

BIJOU ROY. Copyright © 2010 by Ronica Dhar. All rights reserved. Printed in the United States of America. For information, address St. Martin's Press, 175 Fifth Avenue, New York, NY 10010.

Book design by Jonathan Bennett

Library of Congress Cataloging-in-Publication Data

Dhar, Ronica.
    Bijou Roy / Ronica Dhar. — 1st ed.
        p. cm.
    ISBN 978-0-312-55101-8
    1. East Indian American women—Fiction.   2. Fathers and daughters—
Fiction.   3. Communists—India—Fiction.   4. Family secrets—
Fiction.   5. India—Social life and customs—Fiction.   6. Calcutta
(India)—Fiction.   I. Title.
    PS3604.H37B55   2010
    813'.6—dc22   2009045703

First Edition: July 2010

10   9   8   7   6   5   4   3   2   1

For Papa, Mummie, Didi, Arvind, and Rajiv

ACKNOWLEDGMENTS

With profoundest thanks to Emily Forland—at every step—and the Wendy Weil Agency; Regina Scarpa and all at St. Martin's; the New York Foundation for the Arts; my teachers, especially Richard Stern. And for such love: thank you, friends, family, and students, my stars.

BIJOU ROY

ONE

They are driving to the banks of the Hooghly River. It is the middle of the night, and she is struck by the darkness, so few lights on the roads, so few on the horizon. In the car (an old diesel Ambassador with bulky leather bench seats the color of ox blood), the driver turns on the headlights only sporadically, seemingly at his whim. She sits beside him, in what would not be the passenger's side in America, back home. Her sister sits pressed between their mother and aunt in the backseat, their windows rolled down. The air hardly moves. The humidity, she's overheard, has settled over Calcutta earlier than usual this year. When people rouse the energy for conversation, they grumble and recite: *It's never been this hot, this soon;* or, with monsoons still months away, *Think of it. We are prisoners of this leech until September at best.* They wait daily for sunset, some remission, but at that time the heat retraces its steps, unspooling from the ground like wool, and nets the body in polluted tropical steam. The songs sung here beg the gods to lift sorrows from the human heart, flirt with mynah birds and blue jays, detachment, illusion, but mostly they are about rain—the relief it gives with one hand and takes with the other. The rains separate lovers, after all, when roads become rivers.

Since midnight her family had waited for her outside the

airport. Her father had known it as Dum Dum Airport, but now it was named for a president, just as National now memorialized Ronald Reagan back in D.C., back home. Palm trees stood cocked in the distance, beyond the darkened parking lot, and the night smelled of burned rubber and lemon leaves. Her younger sister had spotted her at once and sprinted toward her, ahead of the others. They embraced and walked together, unsteadily, entangled, back to their mother and aunt. Kisses, tears, quivering smiles.

"Oh my, look at you. You're a grown woman." Her aunt held her gingerly, kissed her cheek again, then withdrew as though from a ghost. "Looks just like her father." A whisper, loud enough. Then she spoke to no one, to everyone, to her, encouraging introductions with the driver, saying something about *the last six years he is working for us* and *he knows more about these things* and *done this before.*

"Yes, this is our elder daughter," her mother told the driver. "Her name is Bijoya. We call her Bijou."

He nodded. His hands were clasped behind his back. He is about as tall as her mother, but darker, stouter, and at least a few years younger. While he waited for them to settle into the car, out of the corner of her eye Bijou saw him whisk a handkerchief across his forehead and upper lip. She already can't remember if her aunt, if anyone, has mentioned his name.

Bijoya, said to be her name because it is the closest in Bengali to what her father had already decided to nickname her. Her father, Nitish, lived in France in his youth—it is where he met the girls' mother—and in Paris he picked up the word "*bijou*," polished it, grew fond of it, as though the word itself were a jewel, a trinket, too.

Her father had made a habit of collecting intangible things. Material possessions led to the wrong kind of attachment, made it impossible to move quickly from one place to another. Why weigh down your life with houses, tables, beds, and cupboard goods? Better to furnish your mind. With? Truth. Justice. Love. Friendship. There was no fear of overcrowding your mind with abstracts, he told Bijou. Same principle applied to the heart.

Bijou hears his voice now, a baritone crusted with laughter, asking her if she remembers. *"Mone aache?"*

What can she tell him? *"Hai. Mone aache." Yes. I remember.* Literally: *It is in my heart.*

They had left the airport quickly. Now her sister says, "It is so, so hot," her voice thin and high. The only one in the car who speaks English exclusively, she is thirteen years old.

"*Phir se,* Pari? There is nothing we can do about it," their mother says. "*Goram to hobe.* It *will* be hot. Announcing it again and again will not change the temperature." She, like the rest of them, uses a functional patois of English, Bengali, Hindi.

Hitting a pothole, the car bounces her on its knee for a flash of a second, bringing Bijou back. The driver's profile is almost familiar. *Almost.* He is almost every driver in America who has ferried her away from an airport in a hired car. But he is not. She stares through the windshield into the nothing of road she trusts is ahead of them, a slim lane of scabrous asphalt over which they must be moving forward, she thinks, despite her suspicion that the car is running in place in the black landscape, petroleum fumes in the air, dust, shadows, the canter of a bullock cart's wheels as it comes toward and then passes the Ambassador, filaments of straw falling, yellow, onto the seat. The bull had been chewing what looked like a broom. She takes a deep breath. It smells as hot as forest fires.

It is the middle of March and you are out of your country.

In her country, a few days prior, there had been a blizzard, unseasonable, defining the stubborn end of a mid-Atlantic winter. Just the day before, everything had taken twice as long to get done: she had to trudge and plod across the research institute's broad campus to return books to the Library of Medicine, the deep snow glistening under the lampposts' peach-colored light. Another eternity spent crawling homeward on Wisconsin Avenue in her car, out of Maryland and into the District, behind a van marked THE BEST IN CELL CULTURE SUPPLIES, watching cars skid and recover, marveling over how no one in D.C. could handle winter driving, half-listening to a radio report on Yehudi Menuhin, the gifted violinist now dead at eighty-two in Berlin. And she imagined the month away from this rut, the phone calls she would not have to think twice about leaving unreturned, the problems she would not be taking with her. The institute, where she was a second-year fellow, had initially inquired if she could limit her leave to two weeks. In the end, they'd insisted she go for four. *Get some rest.*

Now she sits in this Ambassador with a parcel in her lap, a burgundy velvet bag, its tasseled silk drawstring pulled taut, knotted, dangling over her knees. Inside the bag is the box. The tops of her thighs ache from the weight. Smaller than a breadbox, about the size of one for shoes, so heavy it could be filled with granite for all she knows, really, for all she is resigned to believe these days. She harbored the thing thousands of miles to Calcutta just the way she'd received it six months earlier—she has neither tested the drawstring nor ever looked inside the satchel—and now she brushes a few bits of straw off the parcel, then rests her hands flat upon it the way a woman might lay her hand upon a sleeping child's back.

Six months, she'd lived with this box already. Six months.

"Perhaps we should let Bijou rest tonight," her aunt says. "Poor girl. We could do this tomorrow. Miserable circumstances for seeing Calcutta the first time. Unquestionably."

"There is no use in waiting," her mother says. She unsnaps the latch on her purse, then snaps it shut quickly. "If we must do it here, then let us finish it."

Bijou wonders why her mother has brought along a purse at all. Will they need it?

"Why make it worse by waiting, Anuja?" her mother says. "Why?"

"After such a long flight, she needs to rest, I thought. She looks so tired."

"No," her mother says, "it's the fashion to look like that now."

The fashion? Bijou wanted to say, but she was in no mood to argue; her mother, despite everything, had expected her to make an effort at appearances. This would be, after all, the first time the family in India would set eyes on the woman her first daughter had become. The messy hair, the lack of rouge, the boyish fit of the T-shirt and sweatpants that had suffered twenty-four hours on an airplane, the winter boots—yes, Bijou knew all of it had upset her mother. She had meant to change, was the sad part. Arriving in Delhi off a connecting flight from Paris, she had actually made a mental note to freshen up, but she swiftly forgot it in the commotion of immigration lines there, of coolies—sunburned porters lurking at the baggage carousel five at a time, offering to drag off her luggage—of checking in for Calcutta. Appearances were the last thing on her mind during that last flight, and certainly not as they made their final descent, when all she could do was clutch the box in her lap, concealed by the airline blanket, almost singing to it: *Here we are, then. Here we are.*

Here, there are conventions for a daughter's homecoming, fit for the goddess Durga herself returning to earth for a visit with blood-tied kin. And daughter she is, but no immortal warrior; this city never her home. She keeps telling herself to be steady, but this is only her father's terrain, the birthplace he had escaped once. Never revisited. She is the daughter of that deserter. His escort now on a trip he'd postponed his whole life. It is *his* homecoming.

"Is it okay if I ask to put the AC on?" Pari asks. She is attentive to the heat in that way anyone is when first encountering a cliché, before learning the statement is overused, out of favor. In time, Bijou muses, she will discuss the weather without listening to herself, to fill conversational gaps, but for now it is still a spectacle.

The driver adjusts the air vents.

Her aunt reports that the worst is yet to come, as goes this weather. There have been earthquakes elsewhere; flash floods, droughts, famines, too. "It's as though the world is coming to an end."

Bijou's mother murmurs in agreement, then asks why anyone would doubt it.

"Poor girl," her aunt repeats after a while. She may have been holding back tears. "This is not how things should be done. But these girls understand, can understand, everything. They are *raised* as Indian. Doesn't matter where, isn't it so?"

"We have two wonderful daughters. We couldn't imagine our lives without them."

It is unheard of, Bijou knows, what they are about to do, this many women involved in what is traditionally men's business. But such are the options: limited. If they'd been faithful to tradition, this night would not be this night. This night would have occurred six months ago. Right away. If they'd been faithful to tradition—well.

Her aunt's voice is deepening with concern. "She looks like him. *Pukka,* ditto," she says. "I can't believe it. Just like the photos you sent."

"Mmm. Everyone says the same. That was another life," her mother responds.

6

"She has that same profile. Same."

It is true. Despite the traces of her mother's influence in the hazel eyes and a complexion like linen, despite breasts and juglike hips, she is her father's daughter down to the cleft in her chin. There are times she thinks her mother hates this about her.

Her aunt sighs heavily. "Shankar will be shocked. Shocked." Referring to her husband, a man married into this family.

"Where is Shankar Uncle?" Bijou asks her.

"He wanted to come—"

"He's waiting for us at home," her mother says. "There is no reason he should have had to come with all of us, after all."

From the rearview mirror hangs a small relic, a burnished idol of Durga tied to a length of what appears to be fishing line. Bijou watches it sway like a pendulum, myriad arms splayed, weapons held in every hand: thunderbolt, trident, discus, dagger. She reaches out to steady it, wraps her fingers around its sharp points and unpolished edges. When she withdraws her hand, her palm burns as though branded.

The driver stops the car, kills the ignition, and disembarks. He comes around to the passenger side and opens the door. Bijou turns halfway around in her seat, rests her feet on the ground outside. *It is the middle of March and you have arrived in Calcutta.* She glances into the backseat. Her aunt, mother, and sister look back at her: six fixed eyes, three faces beaded with sweat.

They do not move.

"*Ki hoche?* Aren't you coming?" Bijou asks her mother. "Can't you come with me?"

Her mother's expression is the same as when the telephone or doorbell at home rang at an odd time, the look she would exchange with her daughters in practiced silence—*Don't make a sound.*

Finally her mother says, "Of course, Bijou. We're all coming."

"We can't stay in here; we'll suffocate," Pari says, rotating her shoulders in their sockets, agitated marionette movements that exaggerate the twiglike structure of her arms.

Her aunt's sandals grate against the gravel as she dismounts from the car, her hair in complete disarray from the ride, fallen from the security of clips. She takes charge, sliding away, speaks like one forest ranger to another: "Which way are we going, Ramesh? Let's not waste any time."

The driver leads them all away from the car. He is carrying a small burlap bag in one hand, a burning candle in the other, held out at the side of his head.

Bijou follows close behind, carrying her parcel like a bouquet of cut flowers now. The corner of the box is sharp against her flesh, and she wonders how it hasn't torn through the velvet bag when it feels as if it might, at any moment, puncture her breast.

Since September, she had kept the box untouched and alone on a shelf in her bedroom closet. No one knew where, under the circumstances, to store it. So it came into her care with the idea that it belonged there. Bijou had addressed it daily: *Where are you? Do you mind that I'm your only company? Can you see me? Any news for us?* Soon into her interrogation, however, she would catch herself, shut the closet door, leave the room. *Don't,* she would say aloud, shaking her head, frowning. *This is not what you do.* But at night, alone in her small, creaky apartment, twisted up in her bedsheets, things caught up with her. A couple of hours before daybreak, she could be easily convinced that someone was in the kitchen, stirring a teaspoon in a ceramic cup. She heard water running in the kitchen sink, or a window pulled shut and locked against a draft. She would slip out of the bedroom, into the snowy blue and orange lights of the living room, and see books there that she hadn't touched in months, books taken from the shelves and piled on the coffee table in uneven towers. Pillows punched and bent over like sacks of flour into the back crevice of the love seat, where someone had made themselves comfortable. In the kitchen, the fridge hums nervously; the faucet leaks in two different drips. Grains of sugar stick to the countertop; a tea bag has been throttled in a telltale way. She runs to the window above the sofa, climbs out on the ledge, and balances four stories above parked cars, leafless sycamores, a sidewalk scattered with rock salt and dirt. Molded in the snow-crusted ledge are footprints too large to be her own or any woman's. She steps into them, barefoot, follows them past curtained windows of the building's other apartments to where the trail ends near an ice-glazed gutter pipe. She steps off the ledge, dives toward the street, spinning, hands held above head, a pirouette.

"I've had a hard time sleeping through the night," she told a curious coworker several weeks earlier. "Strange dreams. I don't know. An adrenaline dysfunction, maybe. Maybe I should drink more milk. Or less juice."

"Well, whatever it is, Bijou, you might think about taking a break. You don't look so good; you look like you've been in the desert or something."

The desert? The desert? The desert.

The driver is humming a low tune Bijou thinks she recognizes as an Urdu *ghazal* from an old film sound track that her mother used to listen to some evenings; it is a sad kind of song, crossing the blues with a dirge. He keeps his arm bent at a ninety-degree angle, the candle steady in his fist. His thumb presses parallel to the candle, and the flame of it curves upward. She keeps mistaking the flame for his thumbnail. They pass by a group of busy people gathered around a small fire, a pot suspended from sticks that frame the butter-colored blaze. Imagine cooking in this heat, she thinks. Strange campsite. Like prehistoric people. These are the human figures who populate memories of her other trip to India, fifteen years earlier, four winter weeks in and around Delhi with her mother. (Her father had not come with them, claiming they couldn't afford three tickets.) She was almost ten then. Her mother's family had shepherded her away from the so-called beggars: crippled legless boys rowing by on square skateboards, slow-moving women with snake eyes and burned lips, keening for rupees. *Ignore them,* her family had said. Someone had likened the life of poverty to a lion's cage. Yet even her mother, despite some spoken sympathies, did not give the beggars coin so much as half-throw it at them without slowing down too much.

"In this direction is the way down to the ghat," the driver says, lowering the candle. He tells her to be careful, to watch every step, as this provisional staircase is unsturdy and may be slick.

It is difficult to decipher the way. *The ghat. Does it mean "dock"? "Pier"?* She worries how her aunt and mother will negotiate the stairs. She turns and sees their silhouettes not far behind her—the two women enveloped in stiff cotton saris, her sister trailing at the end of her mother's hand—and she calls out to them, repeating the driver's precaution. Her mother tells her to remove her shoes, to carry them, and to go on, that they will do the same.

Bijou hunkers down to undo the laces of her lumberjack boots, keeps the box safe by balancing it in the hollow between her chin and her knees. A frail breeze hardly cools the perspiring skin above her eyes and lips. *Unprepared,* she tells herself. *You've come here unprepared.* With one free hand, she unlaces her shoes. Her wool socks, removed, she tucks in the toes of the boots. *Should have changed everything on the plane.* She rises and follows the driver again. He is still humming.

The steps are long enough now for at least twenty people to descend them simultaneously, narrow planks made of stone, it seems, tough yet damp and cool like dough under her feet. She moves carefully down a dozen of them, then another dozen or so, boots clasped in one arm and box in the other. She glances at the candle's flame, then down toward the steps, back again, until the driver tells her she can stop. They are near the water now, he explains. She must put her shoes down behind her and come into the river. She stations her boots near the candle, then works on rolling up the cuffs of her pants.

A moment passes before he says, "Not too much is necessary. As long as you will be a little, little bit immersed in the water. Come."

She turns around, away from him. Her mother and sister are standing on one of the steps behind her, some six feet away.

"Already?" she mumbles.

"Now," the driver says.

She looks at him. "Now," Bijou repeats.

Her common sense has lost its purchase on issues of time. Yesterday could be last year. A tragedy six months old, twelve years old, begins this second.

It is the middle of March and you have arrived here. You have come from there, where it was cold.

Now snow seems something of a riddle, aberrant; she can see it in her mind but forgets everything about it except a color like milk or eggshells.

"Come," the driver repeats.

She walks until she is ankle-deep in the river. The water is tepid, and the mud, adhesive. She flinches. Her left eyelid begins to tremble of its own accord. When she tries to still it with her hand, she loses her grip on the box. She tells herself to snap out of it. She takes note of a long bridge perhaps half a mile off to her left, providing no light directly. It must be the Howrah Bridge, she thinks. It is like an American bridge. It is like an unfolded crown studded with lights. It could be the Golden Gate. Or even the Ambassador Bridge—they used to cross it into Canada when she was young.

"Please stop now and look here," the driver says. "You stay at the very edge, please; it is fine."

She stays at the edge of the river, which is supposedly sacred enough, by association with the westerly Ganges, where these rituals are meant to be performed. They have altered all the rules for her, in strange ways. By their logic, wouldn't it have been just as sufficient, then, since they couldn't get to the Ganges, to have done this on the Potomac? Others—men—would have waded into the river until submerged to their hearts. She is to stay at the edge; she is a daughter, here for lack of a son. Not one allowance they make for her, ironically, has made anything easier; in fact, with so many exceptions, how can this still accomplish its purpose? For something like this, she wonders, shouldn't there be entirely new rules?

There have been prerequisite rituals before today, through which she stumbled. She could not properly pronounce the Sanskrit, and therefore made a poor mimic. When snippets of ceremony were translated—*Do you understand, you are doing this so he has what he needs on his journey now*—she heard nothing but the thalassic roar in her mind, keeping time with her short, shallow breathing. She echoed the pandits as directed, but only in a hoarse, low voice, worried about making critical mistakes. Oh, but these are *formalities,* rites, customs, they told her. Do the best you can, they keep telling her.

The river is heavy around her ankles, as though a pair of thin hands has cuffed her legs, anchoring her to the spot. There is much the river has seen, much she has been fed by force. Bijou cannot see the water except for dimly moonlit crests on ripples, mercury-colored against black. Her night vision is weak; she thinks her pupils must be dilated to the size of dinner plates.

"This could be the Potomac," she says aloud before she can stop herself, and louder than she means to at that. She looks over her shoulder. Her mother and sister have edged closer, but her aunt is seated, a blot, toward the top of the steps. Beyond this, she can make out the saffron breath of the beggars' fire, and swears she smells rice burning, or sugar, perhaps, carbon, sooty and thick. *For all I know,* she wants to scream.

The driver opens his bag and extracts from it a small bowl, a short switch of wick, a bottle. He stoops over the water, running his hands under the mirrorlike surface. He does this for a while. The river smells of brass, fish, kelp. The driver's arms are thick, his gnarled muscles wrapped in copper sheen and shadows, oil. Sweat dapples his mustache; his cheeks are riddled with motley dents and pits.

When he rises, it is with a handful of mud or clay, glossy like taffy. He pats some of this into the bowl, adds the contents of the bottle—ghee, the buttery scent of it nauseating her—then installs the wick. He looks at her. She realizes she must summon a language to her tongue and form the same question she has been asking all along:

"What am I supposed to do?"

"You open," he replies, gesturing toward the box. "Can't keep it closed."

She turns to find her mother a few feet behind her, eyes shut, lips pursed, chest rising and falling in a deliberate pace. Her sister is leaning against their mother's arm, staring out over the river. What is her mother remembering? What is she trying to forget?

Her own mother has never had to do this.

None of the women in the family, as far back as the history went, have ever had to do this.

What comes next, she tells herself, is easy. The last six months? The next six decades? Difficult, those. This is nothing, nothing to nothing.

The water has risen to encircle her mid-calf. She thinks, *Have I moved or am I sinking?* The appeal of making strides forward into the river—the feeling that she could do so—momentarily lifts Bijou's spirits. She will walk with the weight of the box mooring her to the Hooghly floor, and live forever in the depths of this river, a swell of putrid holy water stagnant above her. It wouldn't feel unfamiliar.

The driver is waiting. He places the bowl on the ground. She unties the velvet bag, then attempts to pull it off of the box, but it snags; she looks at him. He helps her, efficient but not hasty, and hands her the empty bag.

"Throw," he says, pantomiming for her. "Into the river."

She looks at her mother again, who moves her lips in what can only be prayer. Her sister is crying the way the women in this family always cry, without sound, lips and nostrils twitching. They are two broken bits of mirror.

Bijou lets the bag fall from her hand. It makes no sound as it hits the water, and she cannot see whether it floats off or is engulfed. She wants to know. Will it reach the other side of the river? Will it disappear? Will some vagrant stranger come tomorrow and fish it from the water?

The driver passes the box to Bijou. It is wrapped in thick white paper. Securely taped to the casing is a label with a black border and typewritten text. She adjusts the angle in order to catch a bit of candlelight.

She reads: *Cremation Record.* She reads her father's name.

Not true, she thinks. *This cannot contain you.*

The driver tells her to unwrap it. As though it were a gift. She finds the seams and tears through the paper, is astonished when she sees the box is made not of wood but of a black sort of plastic, something designed to be light in weight.

You are not here. This is not you.

The paper falls into the river.

—*Who will do everything?* they'd said in America. *There is no son.*

—*A daughter will have to do, I suppose. No male relations on the father's side are available, they're saying. They say he has no ties to them. The older one . . . She isn't married, is she? Then? There is no choice. Let her do it, finish the matter.*

—*Yes, because the wife is in pieces. She isn't thinking clearly. What Indian, what Brahmin, would not want his ashes immersed in the Ganga?*

The driver tells her to open the box. She cannot. He takes it from her and unsnaps the lid, then hands it back.

His directions are delivered in a tender tone. *He is kind to help me,* Bijou thinks. Perhaps he does this often. Or perhaps the knowledge of this is innate to those who know this country as natives know it, as she never will. Or perhaps it is that she—young, female—is not meant to know these customs of burial. Women were meant to be protected from all this. That was the smartest rule of all.

Bijou thinks of the wizened face of the funeral director in America, his filmy blue eyes and charcoal brow. In her misery, she'd sat with him. Family and friends discussed arrangements for the funeral. Everything they wanted—open casket, open viewing, an altogether too-public service—she did not want. She wanted dignity, and felt privacy would ensure it. She disagreed with the others, was subsequently hushed by them. Each time, the funeral director, quietly assessing the conversation from behind his desk, had met her with his gaze. And in the end, as she was leaving, feeling at once entitled to and embarrassed by her temper, it was he who held her back in the foyer and said to her, "With all respect, Miss Roy, wouldn't it be more noble this way? You saw him through all the years of his illness. Let everyone see him now, just that same way. There's no shame in it, no shame at all. On the contrary, you should be proud. He fought the good fight."

"I shouldn't have said anything. I didn't expect these questions to come up, that's all. I don't know about these things. I've never been to a Hindu—I don't even know the word they use for it. I have no idea."

"Well, then, let those who know do what they wish," he'd concluded. "In the long run, you will understand that it is the only way it could have been done."

Now the driver is clearing his throat.

A plastic bag inside the box. These endless layers, like a trick. *But those who know seem to have discarded all common sense.* She draws out the bag. Here, then, is the core, the pit. The driver takes the box and tosses it into the river. The bag weighs only five pounds, at most, full of ash, the dust of bones, coffin, carnation garlands she had threaded herself with a long thick needle the morning of the funeral.

A bag of sand. The driver tears a small hole in it with his fingernails, and tells her to slowly pour out the contents. A bag of ashes, nothing, nobody, no favorite music, no characteristic gesture, no needs, no desires. This is the center, and she is being told to empty it. She obeys. Hovers now, just as she'd watched herself anoint her father's body lying in an American casket, a sickening similarity between the coffin wood and his flesh against her fingers. Someone had dressed him in a raw silk kurta at the funeral home, the kurta with gold embroidery around the neckline, the same kurta he'd worn for her tenth birthday party. Someone had sculpted his lips into a suggestion of a smile, infused them with color, and his cheeks, too.

No one had said, *Maybe the girl should not go through this*. No one had said, *There are no facilities here for doing this exactly right*.

There was a pandit there, a high priest from the metropolitan area Hindu temple, who led her through the cremation rites. A game of placing sprigs of some sanctified straw matter around the body, then pouring jar after jar of ghee into the casket, the nausea rising again as she wept, watching herself, thinking, *You are enabling a body to burn rapidly*. The oils, the straw, the hours of fire, chant, and ritual. Was it not enough to lose someone?

Men carrying the casket through heavy doors to the crematorium chamber. And she goes with them? She goes with them. Her hand guided toward a button. Her finger pressing the button, and then the sound of pilot-lit gas and flames, her father scorched, her hands belonging to another body, out of her control. There was no use keeping these hands. They should cut her hands off for this crime. How would she use them to eat, to wash, to soothe lovers and the sick?

And then she was led out, out, outside, and the pandit gently directed her to stare into the sun. She looked up, found it, a white disk, and she heard, "Look, and keep looking. The sun will dry your tears. No more crying now, okay? You must let him go."

Let what go?

The driver is motioning for her to pour the ashes into the river. In the bag she holds now there is bone and tendon and the cinders of a man's skin and hair. She proceeds to empty it, cautiously, and the finest powders converge in a thin cloud around her knees. No one has told her how to pace these rituals. She looks at the driver.

"All at once," he says.

All at once, then she nearly loses her footing. The driver catches her at the elbow. He picks up the clay bowl, takes a matchbook from his shirt pocket. A flare of fire, then, with which he lights the wick.

"You're doing fine, Bijou," she hears her mother say.

"It's very dark," she responds, wiping her cheeks with her shirt-sleeve. She smells the salt in her tears before she tastes them, dry and vinegary.

The driver hands her the *diya*, and she cradles it in her palm. He tells her to set it afloat in the river. It is meant to be a beautiful sight—the flame drifting the great distance downriver into the hereafter. A massacre might yield the spectacle of a thousand candles sailing; all those souls liberated.

She holds her other hand over the flame. Her father called them *her majesty's hands*. Clear as day, Bijou sees him wrapping a bandage around a razor cut on her index finger, as her mother encourages him not to get so nervous about these little injuries. He had been a caring father. A good man.

The streak of flame in the *diya*, the more she stares into it, begins to resemble a peacock feather. When she blinks, it becomes a violet petal. She remembers something about violets—didn't her father like them?—before setting the *diya* down at last, her fingers submerged in the water for a moment before she lets go. The clay lamp bobs and rocks like a toy, going nowhere. She urges it forward with her thumb, and within seconds, when it is just out of her reach, the flame is snuffed. She lunges to bring it back, falling.

But the driver catches her, again, this time pulling her gently toward him, and low enough that only she can hear him, he tells her, "I am also a father. He is happy it is you doing this for him. Believe me. You both have good fortune."

The bridge glitters in the distance. An unfolded crown of lights, all smudged and bright. She hears her own cries like an animal. When she looks down for the *diya*, she cannot see it.

"It's okay, it's complete now," the driver adds. He points toward the darkness behind her. Then, addressing her in formal language again, deferential, he says, "You can go back."

She wades out of the river slowly, long resistant steps through her own modest undertow. *And will he not come again? And will he not come again?* Empty-handed and gasping, she crosses her arms over her chest and stumbles on the ghat toward her mother and sister. In their arms, she is stiff. In the distance, from above and behind them, she hears dull laughter and chatter, the noise of people who call this site their home tonight. Her shirt is streaked with river water; the legs of her sweatpants are sopping, heavy. In the heat, naturally, these things will dry considerably by the time she finds herself in the car again, hurtling through the night. She could have drowned herself back there, she will think, but she didn't.

Two

Her mother was trying to tell her something. *It's late. People have come for dinner. Get ready; come meet them. They knew your father. It doesn't look good. Everyone thinks you are hiding.* Sounds of people talking, her aunt shouting at a servant come from the second floor of the house. Chairs scraping the floor, footsteps.

"Bijou, please get up. Aren't you hungry? Almost three days now." A fluorescent light flickered on.

She sat up slowly, the white bedsheet falling from her shoulder to expose her in a black chemise and thin blue cotton pajama bottoms into which she didn't remember changing. On a small chair beside the window, she saw her pants and sweater neatly folded, obviously laundered. Her boots under the chair.

"Did you put those there?" she asked her mother.

"Are you listening to me?"

"Who put my clothes there?" Her voice brittle. "Was it you or Pari?" She didn't like the idea that she had been seen here, sleeping, by strangers.

"They won't let me do anything myself here. The maidservant must have done it. You won't wear those now, anyway. Find something light, but that . . . that covers you. I wish you girls wouldn't dress like you belong in the army. Why did you have to wear those Nazi boots here?"

"The snow."

"In Calcutta?"

"Yeah, Ma, because of the snow in Calcutta." She looked away from her mother's pursed lips to the windows, and sensed nothing but darkness behind the thin curtains and metal bars. The air in the bedroom smelled of tar and sweat, night. "What time is it? Can I eat in here instead of moving?" she said, returning her head to the pillow.

"*Beta*, I don't want to do this any more than you do."

Pari walked into the room; she was wearing flared jeans under a gray dress that hung from her skinny frame like a dishcloth. She crawled onto the bed next to Bijou.

"Don't do this to me," their mother said, shaking her head. She crossed the room to the window and peered behind the curtain. "The two of you will not hide up here together! Why can't you understand? There are *people* here."

Pari shrugged her shoulders elaborately, and the pop of a bone into or out of its socket resounded like a gunshot.

"They don't care, Ma," Pari said. "They're talking about nothing." To Bijou, she said, "I have never been so bored. Nobody knows who I am until Ma points me out, which is, like, after they've been talking for half an hour. About *nothing*. Or about you."

"Who's there?" Bijou said. Silver minnows darted across her eyelids as she rubbed them with her palms. "Not Daddy's family?" She frowned.

"*We're* his family," Pari said. "I don't know who the hell these people are."

"Behave yourselves," their mother said, irritated. She had turned from the window and stood at the foot of the bed now, arms crossed over her breasts, dark swollen circles under her eyes. "Pari, show your *didi* where the shower is. I will see you both downstairs in twenty minutes." She left the room.

Pari sat up and crossed her legs underneath her. She took a *Rolling Stone* magazine from the bedside table and flipped the pages somewhat aggressively. "Sheela's been like this ever since we got here," she said, using their mother's given name as she always did behind her back. "All I meant was that I don't recognize anyone here, which anyone would think was weird, considering the circumstances. Right? Right or wrong?" She was pouting. "Do you know them?"

"How would I?"

"Well, you might. There's this one guy who keeps *asking* about you."

"I'm sorry you've had to put up with them."

"They're so weird."

Bijou looked over at her sister, who had paused over an article. Pari had a full mouth, a round face, and black pearl-like eyes, vaguely Nepalese features allegedly issued from the paternal side, anciently. She wore her hair in two tight braids, the part between them dividing her scalp like a painted line on a highway. Though she had recently given up a love of body glitter and beaded jewelry, she still wore a gold stud in her nose, and was currently sporting a paisley-shaped bindi between her eyebrows. At thirteen, she appeared much frailer than she behaved. She was playful unless pushed too far, too quickly, at which point (like their father) she could be quiet for days into weeks: the opposite of a tantrum, and worse to watch.

"We never lived here," Bijou said indifferently. "We're not really from here."

"Yeah, Didi, we're not."

"I think it explains everything. Always has, always will."

"Do you think Daddy's family will come see us?"

"What?"

"His family? Wouldn't they want to?"

"It's not like they would even know what's happened. Or that we're here."

"Then why'd you ask? And why don't they know?"

"I don't know, Pari. They've held on to their grudge. I don't understand it."

From her yellow courier bag, Pari pulled out what she referred to as her "lifesavers": a tube of Odomos mosquito repellant, a box of Pop-Tarts, her Walkman, a handful of cassettes. Bijou recognized them as music salvaged from her own early high school collection: The Police, U2, Kylie Minogue. "Did you bring any music, Didi?"

Bijou had brought exactly one tape. The yellowing sticky label on the cassette was lettered in the tidy handwriting of her father: *Billie Holiday*. It was the only album he had gone to the trouble of recording off of vinyl years ago. "You wouldn't like it," she told her sister. "No synthesizers."

"As long as it's in English," said Pari, "I don't really give a shit." She took a bite of her frosted Pop-Tart. "You should go down, make an appearance. The shower's right underneath us, by Massi's bedroom."

"Shouldn't you toast those before you eat them?" Bijou said. She sat up and stared at her sister's bare feet poking out from her jeans like hockey sticks. For the first time, she took in the room: a perfectly square space with two windows in one of the stucco walls. The floor was tiled in a patchwork of mottled orange and white, and mostly concealed by the king-sized bed. "Goddamn, it's hot."

"It's hot *all* the *time*." Pari began to rub the chartreuse bug-repellant cream onto her arms. "I've been trying to get Sheela to take us somewhere, anywhere, I don't care. The sooner the better. There's nothing to do here. Shouldn't I see the Taj Mahal? You've seen it. Now you have to show me."

"I'm not up for sightseeing, Pari. But you can still go. Agra's not exactly a day trip from here, though, you know."

"What would you do without us here?" Pari said. "I can't believe it's only been two weeks. Feels like *forever*. I got over my jet lag so much quicker than you are, Didi." She smiled. "Finally, I do something before you do."

"It's not jet lag," Bijou said. She turned from her sister and put her head back on the pillow, closed her eyes again.

"You've been half-dead for the last two nights. Just go down for five minutes."

"I will, I will."

"They seem eager to meet you, Didi. Especially this one guy—dude, what's his name? I keep thinking it's Novocain. He has this really, really big Adam's apple. When he talks, it's all I notice, it's so weird, like a *chicken* or something. I thought maybe *he* might be from Daddy's family. He seems to, like, know things."

"Pari, I'm telling you: no one from Dad's family would care."

"But he was their brother."

"I know," she exclaimed. "I'm sorry, Pari, I really am. I don't get it either. They just sound like mean people. The way Dad talked about them, they always sounded mean. From what I remember . . ."

Their father had been born Shantinath Chattopadhyay, the youngest son of an orthodox Hindu family that, over the centuries, had lived strictly by Vedic rules. They were descendents of priests. According to their father, the Chattopadhyays had money, they had morals. They were eternally pious, *appropriate,* and the alliances they forged via marriages with like-minded Bengalis were invariably a source of pride. Modern times had brought some outward changes, of course—men went to work in offices, wore Western clothes in public, more or less blended in with society at large. But concealed under their Oxford shirts was a red thread running across the chest, the ceremonial string every boy wore with respect to his initiation as a Brahmin pupil. Concealed, perhaps, but *there,* like the sense of entitlement itself.

From a family such as this, their father would conclude, it was scientifically inevitable that a rebel should eventually surface. At nineteen, Shantinath Chattopadhyay touched his father's feet in a moment of mixed atonement for what he was about to do, and left home for good. At the time, it seemed the only option. He had been in college a few months and had become closely involved with some people who shared his ideals—people whom Bijou would best understand, he'd once explained, if he called them social activists.

Within days of leaving home, Shantinath changed his name to Nitish Roy. It was more than a rebirth, he said. It was as if he were repossessing an identity he should have rightfully had from the start.

"This was long ago, Bijou. It was 1967, and the world was a very different place. Think of it: just twenty years after the Britishers had left India. They did their damage, and left it in ruined straits. When I began to realize what it would take to set our country on its proper course . . . I think what vexed me more than anything was how not one man in my family had ever lifted a finger to fight. I was not the sort who could leave work to the others, not even caring who the others were or if they had the means to carry out the work."

What kind of work? Bijou wonders, imagining jobs in tall buildings of mostly glass, or as mail deliverers or auto mechanics or cashiers at supermarkets. That was all work.

"No, Bijou. I mean something of a political nature. At any rate, it didn't end well. A good friend of mine passed away suddenly, and it upset me so much that I had to leave Calcutta for good."

Is Calcutta like Delhi?

"Nothing like it."

In the course of retelling the story, he will build on it. Gradually, the social activists he speaks of become political activists become Communists become Naxalites. They acquire names: Ashok, Kamla, Sanjoy. They all have clear roles in what sounds like a fairy tale.

Bijou listens because her father has said, "Listen to me."

Where is her mother? Sitting in the corner of the hospital room, talking to a nurse, reading a news magazine, or fallen asleep with Pari napping in her arms. And her father, sitting in the hospital bed cranked up almost ninety degrees, sometimes asking Bijou to reset his pillow because it's slipping out from under him—her father is speaking softly of a time she can never experience and a city where she has never been.

She learns that the good friend who died suddenly is Ashok, the same Ashok who appears in another story as her father's very intelligent friend—no, more his brother than a mere friend—and Kamla is actually Ashok's wife. Bijou learns that the three of them worked in and around Calcutta, with other friends from their college. Work of a political nature becomes educating villagers and peasants; later, that becomes defending the rights of the masses against those in power using any means necessary.

It all sounds very heroic. And then it gets bigger. Her father's story relocates to Paris and becomes her parents' romance. They meet there and fall in love so colossal it doesn't all fit in one place. It budges, then bolts.

In the hospital, her parents speak of the past with zeal. *Remember those last few days in Paris, the rain? Remember our first week in Detroit? Do you remember? Of course I remember.* And they turn to Bijou, opening the tale of their romance with a brief introduction for her benefit.

"I was in Paris because my brother—Padam, your *mamaji*—was studying there, and so I went to visit. Originally, he had gone to London, but he hated it there and found something in Paris. Anyway, he was living in this slum—"

"It wasn't a slum, Bijou," her father clarifies. "For the record, it was a boardinghouse for students from abroad."

"—and your father had taken up lodgings there, too. Well, I was homesick, and these boys were such opportunists, they asked me to cook for them. I was still a girl, really; I had never been out of India, and what did I know? I *actually* cooked for them one day."

"And after that, Bijou, I took her out every evening for dinner at restaurants and brasseries. Because her food was not normal food, the kind that you want to eat—"

"*Joot!* Such lies! Because you were *courting* me. You had to *impress* me, didn't you?" Her mother laughs, then her laughter frizzles away. She picks up Pari, saying, "Just think if I'd never come. We wouldn't be in this mess right now."

"What mess? That our daughters can claim the privileges of both Bengali *and* Kashmiri madness in the blood?" He takes Bijou's hands in his and chuckles, all mischief. "There is some greater design to all this, Sheela. We're too stupid to see it."

If there is a design to the ensuing years, no one has much luck deciphering it. At any rate, there is no time to step back and look. After the diagnosis of multiple sclerosis, there is only the next day, behind which lurks another day. *How long will this last?* No one dares to answer. And after her father loses his speech, no one dares to ask.

Over the years, Bijou will often listen to her mother talk about the beginning. *What did we know? If we only knew then. In those days, who knew anything? Something we might have done, better care we should have sought in another place. If only we'd had the money, the money, the money. Never should have left India.* But it was this way now. They had to live with it. What's done is done.

An earlier diagnosis wouldn't have been much use, Bijou learns much later, long after she and her mother have agreed to hate that first doctor, the gatekeeper, despite and because of the fact that he is correct in his prognosis. Her father's MS is marked by a severity that confounds the doctors who treat him. One suggests drugs, another suggests holistics, another suggests drugs *and* holistics, another publishes his suggestions in a case study that appears in the *New England Journal of Medicine*. It is a too-rapid descent after the diagnosis, and some theorize that this particular patient doesn't want to fight for his life—that he has slid into a deep depression, far beyond the psychology of perseverance. Unlike many others affected by the illness, her father is in a wheelchair after three months. A year later, he moves into a state-run medical facility, twenty miles from the house he'd half-assembled. He will spend the next dozen years there, except during the holidays, when he might come home in an ambulance, the siren off. At home, just as at the hospital, he refuses visitors.

There will be a period of hope and remission—a plateau during the years Bijou spends in college an hour away—and then a hairpin turn, a three-year spiral of bouts with pneumonia, apnea, atrophy. Those last years, he is never conscious. He had lost his speech, his memory, and he was utterly lost to the sensations of his body, the nerves literally exposed. His spinal cord became a chain of multiple scars; his brain, a tomb of hardened cells.

One day Bijou is one way, and the next twelve years she visits a hospital at every opportunity, spends the school holidays volunteering there, learning the ropes of hospital administration. She lets teachers, classmates, and even friends assume her parents are divorced because she doesn't talk about her private life, much less her father. She doesn't tell anyone what it is like to try to leave that hospital room—how she walks out into the hallway and then back into the room dozens of times, ignoring the limitations of visiting hours, feeling her throat clench at the thought of leaving, of what might happen in her absence. She develops skills in changing the subject, seamlessly. After a few years, the sight of her mother tearing at her hair and weeping daily separates from its initial horror and becomes one part of a predictable cycle. Visits to psychics and clairvoyants, consultations by mail with astrologers and homeopathy doctors in India, hours at the public library looking for articles that would reveal miracle cures—it will all lead to nothing. When nurses suggest various support groups, her mother says, "And how will that cure my husband?"

The job of raising Pari is largely Bijou's duty, as their mother tends to their father's care. It is a job Bijou takes with such pleasure that other jobs will invariably fall short in comparison. As for a career, it has been decided by her parents, circumstances, and skills: she follows an affinity for science into medicine.

When she secures a postcollege research fellowship requiring her to move six hundred miles away, her mother tells her, "You will go. Do whatever it takes to see that others will never have to endure what we have."

The spirit of achieving this keeps Bijou sharp. On the off days, she also tells herself that if her father could, in *his* youth, devote himself to the struggles that he felt so strongly about, then her own cerebral chores in research labs are certainly manageable. She is book smart, a workhorse, good with rote memorization, with analysis of concrete problems, with microscopes, periodic elements, bones and muscles, the logical processes of enzymes and cells. Perhaps her father's ambitions were more intellectual, but what matters is that she is the daughter of someone who would not dare complain of a problem before exhausting a million possible solutions. Like him, she is persistent, and persistence generally leads to success.

But when he dies, this sensibility of hers no longer makes sense. In her grief, there is this feeling that he has failed. But at what? For all his words on the things that gave life meaning, she thought, he might have fought harder to be the one thing they still needed him to be: alive.

The fourth day in Calcutta brought hell. Bijou woke in a cyclone of itching. Her arms and legs were covered in tiny red wounds, the worst of them concentrated around both her ankles, the backs of her knees. She could feel the bumps on her face, as well, like stones sewn in under the thin skin.

Her mother, her aunt, her sister were all crowded around her on the bed.

"It's your own fault for lying here so long," her mother said, visibly put off by the sight of her daughter's skin, but gently wiping the bite marks with cotton balls soaked in calamine lotion. "Sweet blood. You should be flattered. Mosquitoes don't come after old dried-up women like me." Something in her tone went back twenty years, to a time when she nursed her daughter with cool towels and ginger ale, guiding her out of fever.

"I want to go home," Bijou cried. "This is all too much."

"Now, don't overreact."

No one had actually seen any mosquitoes, was the thing. Nevertheless, they called in an exterminator, who sprayed the rooms reluctantly. *"Kintu mosha nei,"* he kept saying. He looked at Bijou, scratching the back of his neck, and repeated, "It is a waste of poison."

"I can't believe that, sir," she said. "Look at this, sir." She lifted the bottom of her pajamas, exposing the now raisin-colored rash on her ankles. She held out her arms. "It's the work of the devil," she muttered.

The exterminator looked away immediately. He apologized and left the room. She followed him down the stairs. He turned to look over his shoulder nervously. She could not relax her brows.

On the second floor, her mother and aunt were sitting at the dining table, discussing train schedules and the least complicated way of getting out of Calcutta. Pari sat there, too, reading a film magazine, headphones on, though, Bijou noted, nothing was playing on her Walkman. The exterminator bid his farewell to her aunt, took a last glance at Bijou, scratching his chin, and left.

"I wouldn't mind going to Darjeeling," her mother was saying. "Although I still think it doesn't make sense to have come so far and *not* visit Delhi. Maybe even show the girls Jammu."

Anuja Massi shrugged her shoulders.

Pari stared at a page of her magazine, opened to an advertisement for Fair and Lovely face cream. Bijou sat down next to her sister and poured herself some tea. She presumed that this was not the first time the idea of visiting Delhi had been raised in conversation during this visit. Only extended family lived there, no one Bijou's mother was close to except one cousin, it seemed, from whom condolences were sent via telegram last September. Although she never went into details, it was generally clear that Bijou's mother had been more or less disowned upon marrying a non-Kashmiri.

"You are here for such a short time. I still don't think," Anuja Massi said cautiously, "that you should waste any energy."

"Why do you insist it would be a waste?" Bijou's mother snapped. "The girls should know something about their people, shouldn't they? What will they get from Calcutta now? I cannot show them Srinagar. How will they understand?"

Anuja Massi looked at her and Pari. "No one is left in Kashmir, you know that. Hindus couldn't stay."

"And I couldn't even come back to say good-bye to my birth-place," her mother interjected, shaking the train schedule in her fist. "Now you are telling me they still hold grudges? Nitish is gone. It's what they always wanted, *hai na?* My parents are gone, my husband—what can they do to me now? What I have seen since they . . . They can never imagine what I have seen. No one can describe it. At least here you have *people;* you have servants to clean your house, to make your food, to *talk* to. There is life on the streets. What do they think? Raising two daughters, working eight days a week, my husband being called a *vegetable* behind my back—was that the life I deserved? I wouldn't wish it on my worst enemy. I wouldn't wish it on any of them."

Anuja Massi stared into her teacup. "How can they understand?"

"I have no one to share my life with," Bijou's mother went on. "*They* do not know. No one can know. If it weren't for these girls, I would have killed myself long ago, believe me. And how much can daughters do, in the end? I worry all through the nights, sleepless. How will they marry? Who will counsel me? It is not something any woman should do on her own. Only their father would have cared as much as I do. I am alone."

Pari looked up at Bijou, eyes wide, lip chewed.

"You have us," Anuja Massi said. "You can come back—"

"*You are not by my side,*" her mother said. "You are as far from me as Nitish."

"I have always defended you. You can yell at me now, be angry, but I will still be on your side."

"I never expected anyone to do me any favors. Not then, not now. They think I was a foolish girl. Let them be happy, then. I've gotten what I deserved."

"Who are you talking about?" Pari said.

"You, be quiet." She scowled and gestured in disgust, flicking a hand away from her ear. In Kashmiri, she announced that everyone had (taken literally) eaten her head. "These girls deserve to see my home," she added. "I only do this and everything else for them."

No one said anything for a while. They went about drinking tea until Anuja Massi called for the maidservant to bring more tea biscuits. Then she added, "If you would like to see Darjeeling, it is easily arranged. But it may be cold there."

Bijou's mother set her cup down slowly against its saucer. "I prefer the cold now," she said. "You don't know what cold means, in *this* country."

"You're right," Anuja Massi said. "It's just that Darjeeling—you will be among tourists."

"And what else are we," Bijou's mother said, "if not tourists?"

Bijou felt a sharp pain in her thigh, and looked under the table. Pari was prodding her with a teaspoon. Historically, this was the sisterly code for *Change the subject*. Bijou grabbed the spoon. *No, it's your turn*. Pari coughed, rose from the table, and left the room with her magazine.

"Where is she going?" their mother asked, cocking her eyebrows toward Pari's back. "She is the one who started all this travel-planning business."

With some care, Bijou placed the teaspoon on the table. "Listen, Mom, I'm not in the mood to travel," she said. "I've been thinking, and I think I should go home. I'm going to change my ticket."

The storm clouding her mother's face gathered more pitch as she turned to Anuja Massi. "You see?" she said. "This is what I mean by *alone.*"

"But I've done what was required," Bijou added. "What more do you want?"

"Changing your ticket is not so easy as you might think," her mother said without much sympathy. "Not from here. Why are you doing this suddenly? We agreed: one month, we would stay together."

"I'll pay for it myself," Bijou said. "Besides, this makes sense. If I go back early now, I can use the vacation time to come home and be with you and Pari later. I could extend Memorial Day weekend by a whole week or two."

Her mother shrugged, mollified slightly, but not willing to say it.

"*Beta,* you've come all this way, after so long," Anuja Massi said. "Who knows when you'll come back again? You should—"

"She's an adult," Bijou's mother said. "If she wants to go, let her. Maybe she's right."

Anuja Massi began to cry. "You all haven't traveled halfway around the world just to stay for two minutes!"

"Good, Bijou, now see what you've done."

"If things were different," Bijou pleaded with her aunt, "maybe I'd stay. It's different for Pari. She deserves to see something good on her first trip. Please don't take this personally." She turned back to her mother. "You *know* I shouldn't be here; you *must* understand."

In the end, it was tediously agreed that her mother and sister would take the trip on their own, be gone for a week or so, while Bijou stayed with Anuja Massi and Shankar Uncle. After that, she would be free to return to Washington. Her mother didn't like it—changing a plan midway invited trouble; better to keep things as they were—but said she didn't have the strength to argue anymore. Let everyone do what they thought best, she declared, let them go their separate ways, let them go (the implication was) to hell, for all she cared.

Like a mother to all, Anuja Massi asserted that a good compromise had been met. "Calcutta is half Bijoya's hometown, after all. *Adhi-Bengali*, isn't she? She has more right to be here than we do." She smiled at Bijou. "The point is, you should have the time to see it. This way you will."

"I would like that," Bijou said quietly. She looked toward her mother. "Ma, please, don't get upset. I just want to be home."

"Nitish wouldn't have wanted it this way." Her mother was crying, a statue, eyes empty as though the irises once painted there in orange, gold, and olive had eroded over the years. "He should be here. I never imagined it this way. After the last trip . . . I vowed I would never return here without him. I made a promise. What the hell is happening?"

"How can we explain? But he will always be with you," Anuja Massi responded anxiously. "Be glad he is out of all that suffering. *Bechara.*"

"And my suffering?"

"I know you believe he is still present."

In fact, her aunt did not know even half of what her mother had come to believe, Bijou thought. Above all, there were the empty seats. Her mother had made a life from saving empty seats, filling the void beside her at dinner parties, receptions, Bijou's graduation ceremonies. She saved the seat with her purse and coat, kept one seat empty for Bijou's father, kept Pari on her lap if necessary. For years, Bijou had watched her mother protect those places beside her, the anxious look on her face. What this woman was capable of believing! That he would walk in through the door. That he would navigate his way through a crowd, and come to her—late, but there; apologetic, but present.

Occasionally, Bijou saw him there as well. She felt his proud gaze, saw his hand on his wife's arm, where it belonged, and she wished she could be the daughter who stayed in that moment forever, but another woman, too, who moved on, forward, lighter.

Six months and some days ago, the first sight of her father's stiff corpse: immobile on a metal gurney, covered to the shoulder in a thin sheet. She couldn't approach it. The nausea that had begun to plague her rose from her gut again, hit her chest in waves, one muscle contracting after another, her breast, her throat, her head aching, hands ascending to and then clamping her lips. Shaking her head, whispering in Bengali, *No, this I cannot do.* Friends of family there, pushing. Her mother crying, *How could they leave him like this?* Her mother at her father's side, as for years she'd kept vigil through his sickness, sobbing now, as she'd wept before, rage against science, faith against fire. It had all ended so badly.

He'd died without them. A call early in the morning. The news. She is home for the Labor Day holiday, sleeping beside her mother, who would be the one to answer the phone. Bijou wakes to her mother's voice trembling, unbelieving, a child's: *He's gone where? He's done what? He was fine yesterday. We were just there yesterday. He would not go without us by his side.* The news. *This can't be happening.* Then the hysteria. Running from her mother. Locking herself in the bathroom, hiding her face in a towel, biting down on it as though to release or relocate the pain, this raw, feral pain. Until Pari taps on the door, and then the three of them, wife, daughters, are being driven by a friend to the hospital. The news travels, and by the next day their house is overrun by others, not kin, half of whom had not seen her father in over a decade.

That decade during which her father has a private room, the walls painted blue like a robin's egg. A yellow curtain hangs from a track on the ceiling around the bed. Tape recorder and favorite music rest on a bedside table, next to his television and a stack of *Time* and *Golf Digest* magazines.

A corkboard is affixed to the wall above the table, upon which Bijou has created an ongoing project. Stapled to the board are thin cutout magazine pictures of Jack Nicklaus, Chi-Chi Rodríguez, and Greg Norman. Birthday cards. A calendar with bright landscape photography. Any picture Pari doodles goes up. Bijou's report cards; later, Pari's. Notes from friends with promises to visit or pray. In the middle of all this, as the centerpiece of her provisional altar, Bijou places a photograph of her parents embracing under the Eiffel Tower.

His nourishment drips through a tube sewn into his stomach. He loses a great deal of weight toward the end; his arms grow so stiff they seem snappable; his hands bloat. It makes them think *nostalgically* now of only a few years earlier, when he could still answer the phone, despite an unsteady reach, his arm moving in a quiver, in slow motion, involving one minute of every ounce of willpower and muscle he had left, one minute that would exhaust him for hours.

He doesn't recognize his daughters anymore, or his wife, or his own knee. A good day is defined as one he can sleep through, without seizures, without screaming. The only thing that truly calms him is when they leave the television tuned to golf tournaments, the sober voice of the commentator, the sound of breath held over a putt for birdie. As if somewhere locked inside his body, which had so thoroughly betrayed him, her father still dreamed of eighteen holes, the crunch of green under his cleats, driving a ball so far out it would seem to have been swallowed by the sky.

What keeps a man in this condition alive? They have weaned him off of drugs. Bijou studies the can of protein-rich formula on her father's bedside table. She knows the smell of it, repulsively sweet. Her father never liked sweets, often joked he was the only Bengali alive who didn't yearn for *mishti* of any sort. *Why should you have to live like this?* Bijou wonders, retying the knot of her father's hospital gown at the neck so it hangs loosely, comfortable. She kisses his warm forehead affectionately, once, then his cheek, then holds her head against him, her ear near his heart, in what will have to serve as an embrace. In those moments, she feels she can read his mind somehow; he makes clear what he wants to tell her: *I live for the three of you. Nothing else has ever meant more.*

Toward the end, Pari spends more time in the hospital cafeteria than in their father's room, reading books or taking naps during their visits. She tells Bijou she wants to see their dad, but she can't. Bijou assures her this is all right, on the condition that Pari must at least come with them when Bijou comes home—often—from Washington.

In what she does not know will be the final year of his life, she tells her father she understands. She understands that certain unions are timeless, and he has nothing to fear. If he is tired, he shouldn't live like this for their sake. She wipes his face clean with a white washcloth, traces his lips with a flavorless salve. When he sleeps like this and she talks to him, and his pulse beats steadily in his neck, no one watching would suspect the truth of the matter, that he is no longer capable of listening, that he has long since slipped away.

What keeps a man in this condition alive?

That year, Bijou's mother takes to staring out the window of the hospital room. "What can we do?" she says. "They would have us starve him to death? This is God's way of punishing me? Was I such a bad person in a previous life? Did I murder, did I steal, did I abandon all of you and run off to the hills?"

"Ma," Bijou says. "You don't believe in revenge."

"You have your whole life ahead of you," her mother says. "Don't lecture me. You should be thankful I didn't abandon you all. I could have left. Other women would have been selfish. Look at all those patients. No one touches them. What difference does it make?"

With that, she comes to her daughter, who holds her delicately while she weeps.

Her father has fallen asleep again; as Bijou gazes at him over her mother's shoulder, feels her mother's tears seeping through her blouse, she can see his eyes moving from side to side underneath his lids.

This, Bijou understands, is where love takes you.

THREE

The bloody last thing he needs right now is a broken record player. But at least this is a strictly mechanical malfunction, a problem he can solve. He holds up a small aluminum level in front of his eyes, checks to make sure the vials are intact. Orange paint is peeling off the frame to reveal a cheap iron color, but the bubbles look to be aligning properly. He removes an LP—Billie Holiday—from the top of a stack under his drafting table and places it with care on the platter. He adjusts the springs of the turntable until the platter is level. It doesn't take very long; five minutes at the most. He sets the level aside, puts the needle on the record, and pushes the dial, and his favorite noise quickly fills the basement: those first revolutions of slurpy static, full of promise, before the real music begins. It's not about getting the best sound—there is newer equipment upstairs for that—it's about honoring humble times, low-fidelity times. He crouches to watch the old record spin. Billie rotates without a warp or a dip. The machine is as good as new now; hard to believe it is . . . how old? Purchased for next to nothing in 1972; that makes it nine years old already, this little self-contained system of plastic and gears in its dirty, putty-colored case with a sturdy handle. The portability is what he still loves most about it. It has the feel of a briefcase.

He hears an abrupt drone and thinks it's the garage door open-ing, wonders if his wife has come home for lunch. Checks his watch. Only ten-thirty. He lifts the needle aside, letting the record spin without sound. The buzz is actually the furnace kicking up. It's early March, and although the snow is melting, the sun is dis-tant, weak, and pale through the small windows around the top perimeter of the basement walls, reminding him of cough loz-enges. He stands back, crosses his arms over his chest, and contem-plates taking the entire machine apart and putting it back together again. Because he has that kind of time, that's why.

Nearly thirty-four years old and recently laid off from a job he wasn't particularly fond of to begin with, Nitish Roy has all but moved into the poured concrete basement of the small three-bedroom house he has shared for six years with his wife and eight-year-old daughter. Underground, safe from the bright gray end of another Michigan winter, he talks to tools. Mutters to a drill bit, *You'll find something soon.* Declares to the swivel nails, *You have solid experience,* and he does, having clocked long hours with companies that satellite the automotive trinity. It has been nine years since he came to Detroit (and bought this record player)—longer since he left India—during which time he has managed to go so far as to procure a master's degree in civil engineering. *Something will give.* He has skills, credentials, even a little talent if he doesn't suppress it. *It could be worse. Just keep going. Remem-ber, you have always found a way.*

His wife, Sheela, is habitually telling him, "You could start your own company; why not!" and for a while he designs stationery and business cards for a company hypothetically named Roy Industry. The materials look very professional. Ultimately they are utilized for jotting down phone messages or to mark the page he's left off on in whatever he's reading. These days it's *The Right Stuff*.

He doesn't complain about unemployment, spends a few early mornings a week at a nearby Big Boy trapping want ads in red felt-tip nooses, dunking pecan rolls in black coffee. If there are résumés to mail, he schleps to the post office, where they call him Hey Roy.

"Hey, Roy. Another mail-forwarding request from the house next door to yours. You aren't scaring them away, are ya? This must be the third time in six years. Something wrong with that house?"

"My wife thinks so. She's very glad we didn't buy that one."

"New family nice? Think they'll stay?"

"Don't know anything about them except they aren't coming until the school year is through. I think they have three or four kids. Should be fine."

In the afternoons, he throws his burgundy leather golf bag into the hatchback of his Chevette and goes to an indoor driving range, where he whacks basket upon basket full of white wounded Titleists. With each satisfying *shhwippp* of the driver dividing the air, the *pop* as the ball hurtles toward an imagined green, he feels better. He loves practicing like this. It is the opposite, he believes these days, of life, which is only about performance, winners and losers. He did not consider himself an unlucky man when he was younger, but now it all seems up for grabs. He drives for his own private show.

Then he comes home and showers. If it's been three days, he'll shave: by the fourth day, the growth is impossible to manage, but on the third it qualifies as a fight he'll actually win. The scale informs him that his body is approaching one hundred seventy pounds with alarming speed. He vows to quit smoking, start jogging, *tomorrow*, then puts on the cleaner of his two pairs of Levi's, a white V-neck tee under a striped golfing polo, tube socks, and his wedding band. He saunters into the kitchen and grills and broils and steams (his specialty is shish kebab) while his little girl, Bijou, plays in the backyard with her giggly Korean friend from across the street. He watches them as if he is the child and they are the puppet theater. It is so much. He has so much.

His own father he remembers as materialistic, rigid, a neophobe and a coward. The news of his father's death, when it came to him by mail from an old friend in Calcutta, did not upset him. There hadn't been anything in their relationship but silence and ice for decades. When he wrote his friend back, he wrote, *Dear Kamla, Thank you for including in your last letter the news you did,* but the rest of it was devoted to the weather and *How are you? How is your son? The time really flies.* They are never very long, these letters, but he sends one each month. They are the last connection he has with India.

Sheela comes home later and later each evening from the lab where she works as a technician. She lets him massage her shoulders after dinner. Then he disappears into the basement to tinker in his studio again, until the dishwasher has been loaded and Bijou tucked in, and then he walks purposefully into the bedroom, changes into his pajamas, crawls into bed, and is relieved to find that Sheela is already sleeping. He slips his arms around her, just under her soft breasts, kisses her as she mumbles into his hands. *Jaan, jaan,* she calls him, *my life;* they nestle together, good night, and in the middle of his sleep he is grinding his teeth, tendons and muscles tight through his neck and back. He wakes tired and sore in the morning, Sheela's perfume lingering in the air, her good-bye kiss blotted on his cheek. Her notes for him on the kitchen counter, weighted down by a thermos of tea, written in her loose loopy script like ripples of water: *2% milk, eggs, dhanya patha/cilantro/ Chinese parsley, onion, Oscar Mayer only bologna, American cheese slices, whole chicken, potato, carrot, Indian apples/pomegranates, pepper, celeries, Cokes, orange juice frozen type, cereal corn flake, if on sale then the good fish otherwise leg of lamb from Yasser's store and Jordan almonds half pound but only if no fish!!!*

Sometimes in the basement a scene from the prior night's dreams will attack from nowhere—a nameless boy lost; his daughter lost; his wife shot; his father shooting—then disappear as quickly into the moans of an electric jigsaw, into the essence of wood stain. On any given day, there is new shelving in the den, a new mug rack in the kitchen, or a new mailbox at the curb. Bijou asks him if he knows how to make dollhouses. Within thirty-six hours there is a colonial residence like their own, hardly two feet high, off the front porch, with its own garden of violets. He says, "This is just a blueprint. A lawn ornament for your mother. I'll make a better one for you." And he does. It even has a garage. He watches from the doorway of Bijou's bedroom as she pushes her Barbie Corvette across the mottled green carpet from the dollhouse to what is evidently the gas station—a long drive to the closet, a fill-up from a shoelace she has taped to an old calculator. It seems she's developing an imagination like her mother's, rooted in practicality.

A few weeks into his full-time free time, with no job offers on the table, he does what prizefighters do when the outlook is bleak. acquires a completely new hobby.

"I'm thinking about putting a wood kiln in the backyard," he tells Sheela one night. "Just a small thing. For amateur pottery."

"We did some ceramics in art," Bijou says. "Me and Sally made boats, remember? But they wouldn't float."

Sheela says, "Don't set anything on fire. Watch out for the pines."

He tells them he has been to Pewabic Pottery downtown, where he watched tiles being pressed and fired in iridescent glazes he found astonishing. If things went well, he added, he would try his hand at raku.

"Maybe I will retile the bathroom floors," he adds.

"Downtown?" his wife repeats.

"Yes, Sheela. Just near, there on Jefferson Avenue."

"You call this looking for a job?"

"I call it a wise use of time," he says, "between interviews."

"We don't have to stay here. What about Chicago? What about Houston?"

"I like it here just fine."

"Since when? *Since when?*"

"Since I went to Pewabic Pottery."

Sheela shrugs, throws her hands in the air, and shakes her head like a toreador.

He builds a brick oven with a chimney. He builds a shed over the oven. It takes him two weeks, and on the last day, Sheela reads her verdict to him unknowingly. He is sitting under the kitchen window, about to smoke, when he hears her through the screen. "Oh God. There's a crematorium in our backyard."

But Nitish is focusing on survival. He is surreptitiously resourceful. He finds an old tabletop potter's wheel at a garage sale and begins throwing clay in the basement. He fills the workshop with empty vessels, greenware. He saws wood into tiny blocks for kindling. He makes some vases, some bowls, planter boxes for Sheela's kitchen garden of spearmint and succulents. He starts small and works hard, listening to records of Pannalal Ghosh, Ella Fitzgerald, sometimes Vilayat Khan, more often Marvin Gaye. But most often Billie Holiday, whom he began listening to in Paris.

"This is my favorite song," he tells Bijou, in the middle of "Strange Fruit." "I'll explain it to you when you're older."

"You say that about everything."

He crushes a cigarette in an amber ashtray. It's true. For the life of him, he doesn't believe he has stories appropriate for children. And she's just a child, hardly more than androgynous still. She resembles him so much—the same bowed legs, lopsided bite, thin lips, and Roman nose—that sometimes he worries she'll have his temper, his anxiety, his restlessness, too. So much trouble in the blood. What will her allotment be?

"You should make something, too," he says. "I can spare the clay. Does Sally want to come over? Run across the street and get her."

"She's at Bible school or something."

"Oh, I see. Well, we won't interfere with that." He hands her a hunk of clay and shows her how to wedge it and squeeze out the air bubbles. "My friend Ashok was very skilled with his hands. He taught me how to build things back in India. You know, if you take a train there, they sell you cups of tea from the station platforms during your journey. They come to your window. The cups are clay, see, so then you just toss them out on the platform."

"I think I'll make a spoon rest," Bijou says.

He smiles. "On the street, you know, in India, the poor people sit in front of their huts with their clay. Making cups, teapots, statues of the gods for our *pujas*. They fire everything in their own little kilns. It's how they live. I've always wanted to be like that."

His daughter smiles back and says, "I think when I grow up I'd like to be an astronaut." She positions her so-called spoon rest next to a Pringles can full of ceramics tools and paintbrushes on her father's workbench. "It's ugly," she declares. "It looks melted."

"*Na, sona,*" he insists, "it's just not finished."

She picks up his putter and hits a ball toward the plastic 7-Eleven cup he has positioned at the other end of the basement. It careens across the concrete floor. The putter is nearly as long as she is.

"Can I go to Bible school with Sally?" she asks earnestly. That sweet tone of voice, the clean slate of her gaze, the total fear of his refusal when all he wants to do is laugh and cry, *Yes, yes; anything for you!*

Instead he says, "Do you know what they do there?"

She shrugs. "Talk about the Bible. Jesus. Stuff like that."

"Jesus?"

"Yeah, he's their god. They have ice cream socials *every month.*"

After a while, he says, "We should ask your mother."

"She said, 'No way.'"

He smiles. He loves Sheela more than ever, and loves this kid they've created for giving him so many new and precious reasons to do so. He tells his wife this, in so many words, in bed that night, and they laugh as if *they* are eight again, over the things they are getting away with, namely parenthood.

The next day, Bijou and Sally get off the school bus and race each other down the street: ebony pageboy haircuts flying, reckless. Nitish is standing in the garage, smoking a cigarette. He watches his daughter run up the driveway, screaming, "Hello! Hello! Hello!"

He hushes her and points to the transistor radio on the shelf, next to a grimy can of motor oil. The voice filling the garage is static and flat in the pitch of AM news radio. He is wearing the same shirt and jeans as the day before, with a pair of flip-flops. He hasn't shaved, and she cries that the stubble tickles her as she kisses his cheek.

"What?" she asks, unhitching her backpack and dropping it on the floor. "What's going on? What are you listening to?"

He waits until the reporter finishes his sentence, then says, "The president was shot."

"Ronald Reagan? Is he dead?"

"Doesn't look like it."

Over the next several days, Nitish will be glued to his radio or television for news. Job searches and all other projects are on hold; the kiln, forgotten. They order pepperoni pizzas or Chinese take-out and eat shrimp fried rice off paper plates in wicker holders.

Nitish's refrain is "He says he forgot to duck. What kind of leader makes a mockery of this? It's no frivolous matter. This country stupefies me."

Even Sheela is taking root in front of the TV at news times. "What a madman this Hinckley is! Psychotic obsession."

"Madman, indeed. You need a better reason than his to use such violence against the state."

Sheela stares at him. "*He* thinks his reasons are just fine."

"How can the president like *jelly beans*?" says Bijou, grimacing. "They're so sticky."

By the end of May, Nitish has had fifteen fruitless interviews and fired approximately fifty pounds of clay. Much of it he recycles.

Sheela wants to visit her brother over Memorial Day, in Chicago, to celebrate his thirty-fifth birthday, which, at thirty-two, she seems to think is a milestone. She doesn't know what to get him for a gift.

Nitish says, "I have time, Sheela. Let me make something."

"*Na,*" she snaps. "*Tor ki matha kharap?* They'll think something is wrong."

He is standing with his back to the house. Fire weaves through the cracks of the kiln where the mortar is uneven. It creeps out in sheets and blazes of amethyst, topaz, ruby. "You think what I am doing is just a phase?"

"He is a grown man, Nitish." She squats down and plucks some dandelion weeds from the lawn. "What would he do with your potteries?"

"Padam would appreciate it. You all come from a family of

artisans, don't you? Kashmiri weavers and whatnot." He smiles complacently.

She sticks out her tongue like a kid. "My God, I pray you find a job soon." She throws the weeds into the kiln. "What the neighbors must think of us. Maybe that we don't know how to cook indoors like civilized people. That we can't afford to buy our own dinner plates!"

"I could always get a job at the hardware store. Just until something . . ."

But his wife is already halfway back to the house. If she wanted a man who worked in a hardware store, she would not have married him, now would she? She had begun to carry her own weight, too, working at the lab. The training she'd done was paying off, wasn't it? She knew the value of work. She knew what it would do to him if he never worked again. They weren't those kind of people.

She spends most of the ride to Chicago discussing what kind of mediocre cooking they can expect at the hands of her sister-in-law. "It is going to be very hard for you, Bijou, but just pretend. You won't like anything she makes, but you have to act as if you do. I will make sure you get plenty to eat, don't worry. I'm sure there's a McDonald's nearby."

"McDonald's! That sounds fine," Bijou says quickly. "Oh my God. This is going to be a great vacation."

Nitish turns around and winks at her.

Somewhere just past the Michigan state line, well into the evening, mortgage payments come up. Nitish's brown eyes are glossed by a band of light reflecting off the rearview mirror, while Sheela organizes the glove compartment for the fourth time. "Remember, we have to send Bijou to college," she is saying. "I don't think there's any market in this world for arts and crafts. It would be different if you were casting sinks and toilets."

"Would it?"

"By this age, my mother had had six children! Just one, just a brother for Bijou, or a sister. I can't stand to think she won't have *someone* to keep her company."

"I know," he responds, staring at the car ahead, one hand clutching the stick shift. "I'll find something soon."

"Sally's dad is an engineer, too," Bijou reminds them. "He gets to test all the DeLoreans. You could get a job with him."

"I'm not that kind of engineer, Bibi baby." He watches his daughter in the rearview as she lowers her head, letting hair drape over most of her face. Next to her is a large box wrapped in gold foil and ribbons. Inside the box is his gift for his brother-in-law: a large vase with intricately curved handles and a surface that glints from feldspar and iron shavings pulled to the surface by slow heat.

"You can't fight with them," Sheela says. "This is not our country, after all. Look what they do to the blacks, after all they have *done*. You have to be a politician. Think of Gandhi." She slams the glove compartment shut and checks the slack on her seat belt. "I would like to get out of this car."

"Why on earth would I want to be like Gandhi?" Nitish says. He is abruptly, openly angry now. "Ashok's ears would have bled to hear such nonsense."

"Ashok, Ashok," his wife mutters. "Can't you let bygones be bygones? How can you come to defend such a man, after all this time?"

"He was a good friend," he says. "You don't know."

"I know enough. Maybe I didn't when we met."

"You're having second thoughts? Ten years too late?"

"You know what I mean. We were leaving our families, our

friends, our whole lives in India. I just assumed we were leaving our problems behind, too."

In Chicago (Cicero, to be fair), the women disappear to the up-stairs bedrooms while the men sit at the kitchen table drinking. Padam has been drinking for a while, he tells Nitish in his raspy, optimistic way.

He says, "I was at the damn project site at six this morning. The *sala*-director bastard—he'd sell his own children, I'm telling you, if it meant maintaining his Mercedes—comes in at ten, spreads around his bullshit, and we all nod, *Yes, yes, correct, of course.* He runs off to catch a flight to the Kansas City plant." Padam shakes his head at his drink, as if it has been naughty. "But he trips on his way out and fractures his damn hip.

"Now who will take over for Judson? That's his name. I'm the only one who knows what the hell is happening, what needs to happen, but no one asks me to take over, so I don't say *any*thing. Why bother? By the end of the day, the whole job goes to some *sala chokra* Bihari who was just released from MIT. I came home at eight, and I have been drinking ever since. To celebrate. A long weekend, a happy birthday, and whatever excuses you have brought to the table, of course. Whatever!"

He laughs, refreshes their Scotch, and goes about shelling a few walnuts with what can only be called finesse.

Nitish doesn't tell his brother-in-law that he and Sheela are going into serious debt; he has made her promise that she won't ask for Padam's help. They talk instead about their projects at work, about American news, and then about the world. They talk about the young Turk who shot the pope in Rome several days earlier.

"He's just twenty-three years old," Padam says. "Fascist, fine, but totally insane, I think, is what he is. It's always these bad apples that spoil the whole crop."

Nitish raises an eyebrow, frowns. Swirls the ice cubes around in his Scotch.

"And such extremism. What is the difference anymore between far left and far right, Nitish? Who is to say? Hm? What is it? You're not usually this quiet."

"Nothing, nothing," he lies, wincing. "Hinckley. Twenty-five years old, wasn't he?"

"Was he?"

"When you're that age, you think you know everything. The question of sanity is a moot point."

"Son of a bitch—*arré*, here is Bijou. All fresh now? Had your bath? Ready for bed? She's growing up so fast! Looking so smart!"

Nitish jabs an unlit cigarette against the brown glass tabletop. "Doing well in school, too. Tell your uncle about the science-fair prizes you won, Bijou."

"Aha? We have an Einstein in the family?"

She accepts the invitation to sit in her uncle's lap. "Mom says you guys should make tea and I'll take it upstairs for them."

The men exchange a smirk. Padam says, "My sister never changes. Wasn't it just this way in Paris, Nitish?"

"Once a boss, always a boss."

"You lived in Paris, too, Mamaji?" Bijou asks her uncle.

"Of course! I am the one who introduced your mother to this fellow! *Kamaal hai.* Why doesn't she know this, Nitish? I think I'm offended. Yes, I have a right to be. After all, I deserve some credit!"

Nitish laughs. "Take all the credit, *bhai.* I can't think of a better way to repay you." He groans, and realizes he is starting to get a little drunk. He says with half-closed eyes, "Someday, Bijou, we'll have to take you to Paris. City of Lights."

"Forget lights, shites, and rabbit food," Padam says. "Let's take her to India. It's time we went for a visit. God knows how much longer it will be safe to go to Kashmir."

Nitish shifts uncomfortably in his seat and drums the side of his glass with his fingers. "But you know I could never," he says quietly, staring at the table.

He hears Padam sigh and rise from his chair, taking Bijou with him to make the tea. When it is ready, she takes it upstairs, and the men exit by way of the sliding door in the kitchen, equipped with their cigarettes, crispy snacks from Devon Street, and a fresh bottle of Black Label. They settle in the backyard, where they lounge on patio chairs under Midwestern constellations and the branches of a lone weeping willow. They will continue to talk politics (office and federal) all night, get fantastically drunk, get somewhat sober, and in the morning, after they have impressed their wives with couplets of Urdu poetry in exchange for a feast of tea, *parathas,* spicy omelets, and Italian sausages, they will go to the golf course. At the club there, they will meet someone who might be able to help Nitish find a new job. Indeed, it works out, and within days of returning to Michigan, he has started working again, at a company in Ann Arbor.

"You see?" he tells Sheela. "I told you not to worry."

All commutes being relative, the drive from Oakland County through Wayne to Washtenaw could be worse. He wishes they'd stayed in Detroit proper, rather than fleeing for the suburbs like the others. Until Bijou was born, they had rented an apartment near Eastern Market, not far from the Stroh's Brewery. But it was the early seventies; the city was broken by the riots, and decades of abhorrent urban politics. *Another Nitish,* he thinks, *would have stayed.*

A new family, named Dillingham, moves in next door. The

husband works for the FBI as an accountant; he travels a lot and talks very little. The wife introduces Sheela to new cosmetic products. There are four children, ages twelve to twenty-one. The youngest is a boy named Crane, who, just like his older brother, sports a short blond Mohawk, wears rolled-up trousers and suspenders, and rides a skateboard. Nitish has counseled Bijou not to be scared of them, but she is, very, until Crane wipes out on the sidewalk one day in front of her, breaks his wrist, and cries for his mother, and she thinks they're not *that* different.

One night in August, the crickets trilling slowly, Nitish sneaks outside for a cigarette. He has quit smoking, sort of. He doesn't smoke inside things anymore: not in houses, cars, offices, bars, or restaurants. Now, thanks to the new rules, he has come to love the outdoors. He strolls with forced casualness through the yard, kicking at invisible rocks, stops to light up in the grass between his house and the Dillinghams'. He hears a thump and a curse word as Crane stumbles into view. He is barefoot, wearing a sleeveless undershirt and torn sweatpants.

"Hi, Mr. Roy," he says.

Nitish nods. Fireflies blink behind the boy, whose face is lit blue by the moon. He seems sleepy and angry. "It's late," he says.

"You see my brother? He comes outside to smoke, too."

"No."

The boy yawns like a kitten, covering his face with his hands. He's written something on his fingers in black marker, between the knuckles. Nitish asks what.

"It spells out 'punk rock.' My brother did it for me. We're rebels."

"I could tell from your hair."

"He said you guys were Indian."

"That's true."

"What's India like? Hot, right? Like tonight. I hate it. I can't sleep. We used to spend our summers on Cape Cod when we lived in D.C."

Nitish drops his unfinished cigarette to the ground and grinds it out. "You miss D.C.?"

"Yeah. A lot. Our friends were cooler there. Here, everyone is a million years behind."

Nitish laughs. "I understand what you mean."

"Do you miss India?"

"Not on nights like this. I like that there's all this empty space."

"I hate it. It's so quiet. It's so boring. I hate this place."

"Well, maybe you should go to India. It would change your whole, um, attitude toward life in just a couple of weeks."

Crane looks up at him seriously, says, "I'll think about it, sir," and walks back to the house swiftly before Nitish can say, "But I was joking!"

He runs into the boy a few more times that fall, the same way, in the same place, and each time they hold a similar exchange of his adult blend of optimism and apathy for Crane's pubescent sense of rage and displacement. When the boy's English teacher assigns a Kipling story to read, they discuss that, too.

"The youngest son of those Dillinghams," Nitish says to Sheela, "is really going to get in trouble if they don't watch out."

"You told Bijou not to be afraid! You said you liked him!"

"I said he reminded me of myself at that age."

"Well, the mother is very nice. She's so patient. Can you imagine? Those crazy clothes and hairstyles like clowns. The older ones aren't that bad."

"What does it matter?" he cries.

"You're right. No one lives in that house longer than two years."

Over the next two years, he saw less of Crane and more of the brothers coming and going in their red Beretta; once or twice police lights flashing quietly in their driveway on a Friday night. And then, again, the FOR SALE sign was up one morning, but this time another just like it had sprung up across the street at Sally's house as well. DeLorean's cocaine trafficking charges had, in their wake, at least one victim on this one street. That the Dillinghams were moving back to D.C. because of the scandal, too, seemed implausible, but sometimes Nitish wondered.

When Sally moves back to Korea with her family, Bijou is lost. Nitish begins taking her to the driving range with him on Sundays. By the time she is eleven, he has taught her to define slice shots and side-hill lies when she sees them, but her command of the golf vernacular does not score points with her peers the way it does with her father. She develops a game called PGA Tag, but no one will play with her but him.

For three years in a row, however, life is calm from good money and the vacations it affords them. They go to Florida every Christmas save the one time Nitish can afford to send Sheela and Bijou to Delhi; Sheela has wanted it so badly. He refuses to go with them, but he spends the month they are away missing them so much, he vows to find a way to go with them the next time.

Then it's the end of April 1985, and Sheela is pregnant. This is unplanned only in the sense that they had, after countless failed efforts, given up the hope that planning involved. Now there is new excitement. Bijou prays for a sister. Sheela rests in bed much of the time, as she has been told to do. She has new preferences in appetite: refuses to drink tea, loathes the smell of meat, demands Bavarian cream donuts at all hours.

"I must be the oldest woman in history to get pregnant!" she declares.

One evening in the third trimester, she develops a yen for

roasted liver with béarnaise sauce. She gives her orders. Nitish must go to the supermarket and get all the ingredients, and if she is lucky it will taste exactly like a dish they shared in Paris more than fifteen years earlier.

Bijou buckles herself into the bucket seat of the Chevette, and they are on their way to Kroger's. Nitish turns the radio on for her. She sings along. He doesn't, though sometimes he does. Tonight, he'd rather listen to her.

In the meat aisle at Kroger's, he picks out a package of brick-red veal liver, plastic-wrapped in a Styrofoam tray. Bijou refuses to touch it, appears torn between throwing up and crying. He says, "You know, when she was pregnant with you she only ate eggplant. Ten times a day. That's why, when you were born, you were so fat and purple."

"I was not!" she says. "Was I?"

They stroll the aisles. He picks out a package of bacon, onions, lemons, parsley, then a box of King Dons (Bijou's favorite). Along with these he purchases a gold and white pack of cigarettes, three packs of peppermint Chiclets, and a magazine featuring Tom Kite blasting a sand trap on the cover.

On the walk back to the Chevy, he stops to help a woman who is trying to load the trunk of her Cutlass Sierra while balancing a baby in one arm.

"We're expecting another one soon," he tells her.

The woman thanks him. "I'm beginning to think one is really enough."

They have hardly moved a car beyond the Cutlass when he hears a man shouting. Bijou turns around. It is someone from the supermarket. A manager in a striped shirt and tie, no apron. Bijou pulls Nitish's arm.

The manager catches up to them.

"I'd like to see your receipt, please," he tells Nitish.

"What for?" In the bluish light of the lot, he shifts the paper bag of groceries from his right arm to his left.

"It's my job," the manager says. "Don't argue, okay, because I can call the police."

"As could I," Nitish says. He looks into the grocery bag, then back at the manager. "I have every right to know why—"

"Just show me the receipt, nigger," the manager says.

Nitish freezes. It seems years before he extracts the white slip of paper from the grocery sack and hands it over. The manager takes a long look at it, then tosses it back into the bag. "You can't be too careful these days," he says. He walks quickly back to the store.

The woman slams the trunk of the Cutlass shut and approaches. "You should sue him," she says. "I can't believe he did that. Right in front of your kid, too."

He nods.

He is silent on the drive home, his profile set in one blank expression the entire time. *Another Nitish would have said something. Another Nitish would have fought.*

Even at home he is quiet, braising the liver in a skillet. It is only after Sheela has come downstairs and eaten and after he has washed the dishes that he begins to describe what happened in the parking lot.

"I will pursue this," he says. "There was a woman in the lot. She gave me her phone number and address. I have a witness."

"Why draw attention, Nitish? That man is a hillbilly; he didn't know better. A million things like this happen every day. There's no helping it. Think of those who have been kind to us instead."

"It was not an accident. He accused me of something we both knew I had not done. And to use such words!"

"We are like untouchables to them. *Never* are we shopping

there again, Nitish. I am so sorry I made you go. This child inside is so—I'll bet you it is a boy."

"We won't stay," he says after a while. "We cannot raise our children in this provincial country. I don't want them to blame their father for bringing them here so they could have such people say such things to their faces! How dare they?"

"*We* might not fit, but why should we? *They* will adjust. See how Bijou talks and even looks like one of them now."

"But is that in our best interests, Sheela? What of our culture?"

"What culture? What of it?"

"We have nothing left."

"We *chose* to leave, mind you."

"We had no choice. We must get out."

"And go where, Nitish? To Calcutta? Your family doesn't know you anymore. To Delhi? My family is not much better."

"No! You know I can't go back. I'm not an idiot, Sheela."

"Well, what am I?" She reverts to a less sympathetic tone, businesslike. "Uprooting the children will only create more problems. We have a family. We have each other here."

He says, "Mark my words. This country will be the death of me."

He makes plans to sell the house, announces that they are going to move to France.

Sheela asks, "On what money?"

He shakes his head. He says, "It's time. I am sick and tired of fighting."

She says, "I am pregnant."

"I am sick," he repeats, "and tired of fighting."

But they do not move to France, nor—as her father has also considered—do they make it as far as Montreal, or even Toronto.

Sheela gives birth to another girl, Pari. Though late to the party, from day one she is like the best guest, self-reliant, an unfussy eater. As a newborn, she is given to bursts of laughter that Sheela ascribes to memories of a previous life. Nitish suggests, based on the baby's puglike nose, her rosebud mouth, that it could be his own mother who has come back to be with them.

"Although what memories she'd have to laugh about," he adds, "is beyond me."

"But your mother was beautiful, wasn't she?"

He nods.

Sheela beams with relief and pride. "And thank God they both got my color. So fair." She clears her throat. "But none of that matters. I want them to be healthy forever."

Nitish agrees.

Eventually, he quits his job in Ann Arbor for a better one, this one in Flint. He claims to enjoy his new work very much. He has a degree of leadership. There is some travel involved. His coworkers are jolly, enjoy sports, have personalities; he likes them.

"It is difficult to express what it feels like to have *job satisfaction*," he says at dinner one evening. "Every minute of the last fifteen years, I feel I have wasted. Sheela, I never imagined it could be so good."

"You talk like it's a love story," she says. "Lines like this I haven't heard in too long."

"But it is like that," he says. "A weight has been lifted."

Four months later, a numbness in his arms begins to bother him. He ignores it for a while. A doctor he meets at the golf course says it's probably a pinched nerve or a pulled muscle. But eventually it gets to the point where he can neither throw clay nor execute a trap shot. Worse, he has difficulty carrying Pari. He complains of feeling tired.

"You've never been sick in your life, *jaan*," Sheela reminds him. "You probably need more exercise, that's all."

He tries to break down the backyard kiln, intending to build a gazebo in its place. The job remains unfinished. The numbness interrupts everything. It travels through his arms like heavy electricity, at strange intervals, with increasing frequency, until finally he must seek medical attention.

"Don't worry," he tells Sheela after the first doctor's visit. "It's just a mechanical malfunction, right? The body is a machine, nothing more. I need a tune-up, let's say. I'm telling you not to worry." He looks at her for a long time, taking in every molecule of her, her beauty, which he has never taken for granted, this soul who has rescued him every day and every night since they met, and he looks at their kids: Pari in Sheela's lap, Bijou sitting next to him. A smile flutters across his lips. "You three," he says, with all the arrogance it takes a man to hide his fear of dying, "will carry me through."

Four

Lenin Sarani, Elgin, Southern Avenue, Red Road, Banerji, Ghosh, Ghalib, Bose, Ganguly, Burman, Sen, Strand Road, Eden Gardens. The cricket stadium is that way. Do you know what cricket is? Victoria Memorial is this way. Somewhere around here is Tipu Sultan's Mosque. Do you know who Tipu Sultan was? Eighteenth-century freedom fighter from Mysore, key to getting rid of the Britishers. We passed St. Thomas Church, did you see it? There is the Kali Temple. Salt Lake. Chetla. Taltala. *This* bazaar, *that* bazaar. The first underground subway in India. Rashbehari Avenue. Would you like to buy something? Someday you should learn more about the tribal peoples of India. Kols in Bengal. Shantals.

Shankar Uncle sat relaxed behind the wheel. Next to him, Anuja Massi narrated the trip. In the backseat, Bijou said nothing. It seemed to her that the gestalt of Calcutta was enough to shut up any newcomer.

"Did you know Chowringhee was once just paddy fields and bamboo groves? All this"—her aunt's rings clinked against the window as she gestured for Bijou to look about—"was not even a village. All this was jungle. All this was marsh."

Now, signs of civilization: rows of shops, tenement housing, banks, and restaurants. Billboards of assorted sizes hung from every facade possible, ungraceful urban ivy. Here, an old mansion with Corinthian pillars; there, high-rise offices clustered like a bar graph; and everywhere boxy concrete shops and homes with opaque shutterless windows, small doorways, fading pastel paintwork.

The traffic was staggering. Not just cars, not just diesel-heaving lorries, scooters, and rickshaws (auto, cycle, man-pulled), not just bulls lingering like silenced troubadours in the median islands, stray dogs and cats, chipmunks running in the streets, not just pigeons and ice cream carts, but also pedestrians in the hundreds by the smallest block, so many men propelled by forward momentum, a destination in each's mind that he evidently deemed more important than anyone else's, rules of yielding and road signals be damned. Were they fearless?

"I could *never* drive here," Bijou said. "I would get in so many accidents."

"You wouldn't have to," Shankar Uncle said. "It's not worth the tension."

"But I love to drive."

"Then you will adjust," her aunt said affectionately. "Lots of girls here are driving these days. If you love it so much, you will learn how to cope—think of the adversities as *extras*. Think that in America you have only standard features. Yes, lots of girls are driving these days. It's about time!"

"But they drive in constant fear. Like this." Shankar Uncle hunched his shoulders and pressed himself close to the steering wheel, looking about in exaggerated glances.

"Keep your eye on the road, Shankar!" Turning slightly toward Bijou, she added coyly over her shoulder: "He knows if I learned to drive, he would become dispensable."

Bijou laughed. "You're so different from Ma," she said. "She's always been so serious."

"No, not so! You didn't know her when she was young. She was quite a . . . Well, she always had us in stitches. She *loved* to play jokes." A long pause, then: "My sister is the last person who deserved the life the gods gave her."

From the backseat, Bijou considered her aunt's three-quarter profile. This was indeed her mother's sister; the same inflections in their speech had endured despite the distances, and though her features were drawn softer than her mother's, there was a pretty sweetness there that so many younger sisters boasted. *Someday, she supposed, this is where Pari and I will end up. My daughter bitching to her about how serious I am.* It felt a long, long way off, however.

Earlier in the morning, they had all gone to the Howrah rail station to drop off her mother and sister for their train to Darjeeling. Afterward, her uncle had thought it would be nice to drive around the city, since it was the only morning he would be able to steal away from teaching. It was generous of both her uncle and her aunt, and Bijou had agreed, her mother's parting words underscoring her concession: *You are their guest. Don't be moody.* And Pari, color in her cheeks again, added, *Don't leave until we're back, okay?*

Seeing Calcutta from the backseat of her uncle's Maruti, however, hardly counted as seeing Calcutta, Bijou believed. She stared at her hands, the fingernails she'd cut to the quick the night before. Her arms and legs, despite the creams her uncle had brought home for her, were still itching, and she had the sort of headache that she always suffered during a bout of flu.

Her aunt pointed out a few more street names, then lapsed into a commentary on P. C. Sorcar's circus.

Bijou hoped no one back home would quiz her on this city, for she would have little to offer them. This was her first trip abroad as an adult; friends of hers always returned from trips abroad with stories they loved to tell about strangers befriended, adventures on streets off the maps, delirium over fresh fish and unlikely fruits, romance and rebellion at dance clubs, bars, hostels, airports. This trip would never, she was sure, be fodder for droll conversation.

They were almost home, her uncle told her. He solicited her opinion of Calcutta.

"It's spectacular," she said. "Thank you so much." And she thought, *I am dizzy and possibly developing a peptic ulcer or dying of malaria. I have symptoms.*

"Did you know, Bijou," her aunt said, "that Park Street—all this is considered the *posh* area of town? Theater, culture, nightlife, et cetera. Wouldn't you agree, Shankar?"

"Historically, perhaps," Shankar Uncle said. "It's not what it used to be. Calcutta has changed, times have changed. A little hunger is good for a city. I fear the modern generation has no aspirations, as such. They are too easily satiated."

Anuja Massi was staring out her window. A small heap of garbage smoldered on the sidewalk.

"I wouldn't be so quick to pass judgment on the modern generation," she said. "All I'm saying is that Calcutta has a rich history—I agree with you, Shankar—but if society is in decline now, perhaps that's not disastrous either, as it started from such a great zenith."

Shankar Uncle shrugged.

"Sounds like Detroit," Bijou said.

Her aunt turned around to look at her sideways again. "Does it really?"

"Well, sort of," Bijou said, defensive of her birthplace out of habit. "It used to be quite a lively city. More like this."

"Oh," her aunt said, and turned away. "I always wonder, what did your parents *see* in that place? All alone out there."

Bijou laughed. "But if you saw it these days, it's like there are more Indians there than there are here. Seriously."

"Perhaps Columbus was the real prophet."

They all laughed, heartily.

It was afternoon by the time they returned to the house. After lunch, for which Bijou ate a bowl of *daal* and toasts spread with Amul cheese, the household settled into the silence of siesta. She took her teacup upstairs, up the curved narrow stairway that led from the third floor to the rooftop. The doors to the roof were unbolted, and she pushed them apart with her free hand. The maidservant was napping on the floor of the roof, sleeping in such twisted fashion she seemed thrown there, dropped from the hot sky. Though Anuja Massi insisted that the girl, whose name was Ketaki, at least sleep on a cot, she would not do it.

From her perch, Bijou watched South Calcutta below her like live theater, her fellow rooftop spectators limited to the clothesline and the ravens, who came by flapping their wings in a sheen of teal and purple, like oil spills. The vista here was cluttered with houses, buildings crammed together on the narrow haphazard lanes of neighborhoods, and trees—if only those trees could talk—ancient palms, ferns, conifers, and tamarind trees decked with heavy pods, peculiar fruit.

She sat in the chair she'd brought out the day before, an old wicker-seated iron-backed thing that had been left in the hallway by the kitchen, utilized—before she rescued it—as a receptacle for discarded newspapers. She sat near the edge of the roof for a while, finishing her tea.

Her aunt and uncle's house, tightly packed between the neighbors' homes, stood three stories high like a tower of cement blocks welded together. It had a narrow facade but was deep; either end of the house faced a street. The irregularly spaced windows had wooden shutters, and the outside of the house was painted a light blue. Like most of the city's buildings, it bore drab watermarks and patches from the soot and dust kicked up from the streets. Security measures were innumerable: locks, bolts, iron gates, colorful shards of broken glass bottles stuck upright in the cobblestone wall around the house. A small patio-sized garden had been left to some neglect in the backyard, where the lone inhabitant was a tree laden with champak flowers—those pale yellow petals spiraled exquisitely, blooming denser and even more fragrant than their magnolia cousins.

Her aunt and uncle had transplanted themselves from Kashmir to Calcutta a dozen years earlier, not entirely by choice. They were childless professors of Hindi and history, respectively. Both remarkably at home here, fluent in Bengali now.

In a letter to the States a month earlier, her aunt had written a phrase that haunted Bijou: "Here it is always lonely sometimes." That her sister and her sister's children would finally be able to visit—although in service of such terrible misfortune—made things seem finally worthwhile, for it affirmed what she had never really ceased to believe: that any place inhabited solely by men and women of the same generation was not fit to be called a home.

Bijou stood up and walked to the ledge, resting her empty cup on it.

A small child ran down the street below, his loose, dingy shorts falling to his knees. He stopped to tug them up, ran off. Within seconds, his shorts slid off again. After a few fits and starts like this, just when Bijou thought for sure he'd give up and walk, the boy let the shorts fall completely to the ground, calmly stepped out of them, and ran along half-naked, unfettered. She chuckled, appreciative, watching him disappear around a corner. A yellow-backed black auto scooter came buzzing up the street, caught the boy's discards on a wheel, and carried them off.

It was afternoon here, which meant people back home were likely still sleeping, deep in dream. She pictured them now, women spooned into the guard of their lovers, jaws slack at the hinges, a film of sweat like the silver leaf of fish scales gleaming between their backs and the chests of their men.

And what about her own, she thought. What about him?

Bijou could see him, stumbling from bed to bathroom, the gurgle of the coffeemaker occasionally rising above the talk of public radio. She saw him checking for rain out the bathroom window, checking if the trees on Fulton were swaying, checking his watch, checking the front page of the *Post*. Perhaps, while he made the bed, while he tapped a fork against a jar of marmalade, while he chose a tie from a collection she had been largely responsible for creating, he thought of her. Perhaps not.

He was Crane Dillingham, rediscovered in D.C. when she'd moved there more than fifteen years after they had, once upon a time, been neighbors in Detroit. Their meeting again, the way they had, seemed ultimately a thing of fate. He worked in her office building. She saw him her second week at the job. They shared an elevator a few times until one day he stage-whispered, "Listen, this might sound weird, but you've probably noticed that I stare at your ID badge a lot, and I don't want you to think I'm ... well, I'm not ... like that. But the thing is—and it's a weird thing, mind you—are you from Michigan? I swear to God, I think my family used to live in the house next door to you. I keep hearing your mother call out for you, whenever I see that badge!"

Then wows and oh my Gods and what a small world.

"What a coincidence, huh? My mom will love this story; she

lives for this stuff," Bijou said. "How crazy. I wouldn't have recognized you at all."

He grinned. "I was an angry kid back then. I've changed, believe me."

He had. Gone was the skinny nimble porcupine boy in faded black hand-me-downs, replaced now by a man with a runner's body and deep-ish lines defining his mouth and sea-like eyes. (When she told her mother that night on the phone, "Guess who I ran into," her mother responded just as anticipated: "Oh, that's such interesting kismet! What a small world. Does his hair still stick straight up like daggers?" And Bijou would find out later that he had not traded in his skateboard for a suit so much as stopped listening to the Circle Jerks and lost interest in safety pins as accessories.)

She smiled back at him as he leaned into the corner of the elevator, and she said, "I remember your brother wearing dog collars."

"He still does. He's in Prague these days, sculpting."

"Really? That's great. Wow. Well, wow!" And she'd gotten off the elevator with nothing short of an embarrassing, garbled goodbye, flustered as he called out that they should have lunch.

They did not have lunch, but over the next few months there was another meeting at a happy hour on Capitol Hill, a third at a video store on Wisconsin, a shared love for Julia's Empanadas in Adams Morgan, interest in seeing the same exhibit at the Freer. All this will be the Prelude.

One evening, they are walking in the snow. It is two years ago. It is not as cold as it can be in January, in Washington. They do not walk too close together or too far apart, and in the careful distance between them there is an energy. An invitation. She is telling herself, *There is nothing between us*. They walk in the foggy lights through a neighborhood of New England houses with wrapped porches and clapboard siding. Rosebushes are burlap-encased for the winter. The trees are barren, as though their roots suckle brine. They have parked six blocks from the movie theater that they are heading toward. She thinks of what might fit between them: a broomstick, a parking meter, a baby stroller. What wouldn't fit: a house, another woman, an old, old sycamore.

The marquee lights outside the theater are bright. Their shades remind her of gum-ball machines. The pavement is wet with melted snow around the ticket booth, and the light is tonic, warm; it refreshes her after the doleful lights en route.

There is nothing between us.

Crane tells her he gave up working on the Hill after the '96 election, and then he'd gotten the NIH gig, administrative work, on a lark.

"A lark?"

"Well. My dad's friend."

"Didn't your dad work for the FBI or something?"

"He retired. And yours? Wasn't he an engineer?"

"Yes," she says, leaving it at that.

"Cool dude, your dad. If it weren't for him, I'd never have gone abroad. Yeah, I totally went to India for three months when I took a semester off from undergrad. I was in the south, Kerala and Tamil Nadu. Your dad was so right. That country changes your life."

"That's crazy. I haven't been back in, like, I don't know, almost ten years."

"Remind me where your parents are from. Isn't Roy a South Indian name?"

No, well, her mother, she explains, was from Kashmir, the north, but her father was from the east, Calcutta. Different though not opposite places. It was unusual-ish.

"It's like I've been cut in half," she says. "Or maybe quartered."

She does not mention that her father had chosen their last name of his own accord; why bring the Chattopadhyay name up, anyway? That tribe was only full of strangers.

"At least you're interesting. Man, I'm dying to go back there." But what else about her? Does she enjoy research? Does she leap out of bed every morning?

It isn't like that exactly. Work is work. Yes, she feels lucky to have the fellowship. But a lifetime of research? She is skeptical. Not that she knows how to do anything else. She has plans for medical school. Science has always been her forte.

"I love the idea of that," he says. "Stability. My dad is a believer in rock-solid stability."

She nods. Doesn't say her own father is unstable. Thinks of rocks turning to stones, to sand. Thinks she is eight years old again and afraid to walk to Sally's because Crane is in his driveway setting off firecrackers and throwing them at squirrels. She hands her ticket to the usher, who swiftly tears it in half. *This is what the usher does all evening,* she thinks. *Tears things in half. Perhaps you should be dating an usher.*

"I would hate to work here," she tells Crane as he waits to buy a soft drink.

"Fuck that. Think of all the movies you could see," he says. "For free. And I'd sneak you in. I would."

The theater is not cold, but she is not warm. When they sit, just in the middle of the middle row, she says, "I'm sorry. I'm cold. I should have worn a heavier coat." He gives her his scarf, which she coils around her neck. She is not as utterly naive as she used to be. She is breathing the scent of his scarf and thinking of his skin. When the movie begins, she feels less a member of the audience, and more the actress on-screen who is pretending to be unaware of the camera. The woman on-screen who fools everyone. Bijou lets the side of her arm from elbow to shoulder move against his, flush. He knows so little about her. She can be anyone she wants; she can be someone with a different history. He glances at her, she sees it in her periphery; she turns to him, and his eyes are back on the screen. The woman on-screen walks the dirt roads of a village in the south of France. Out of the corner of her eye, Bijou studies Crane's profile. She thinks, *Did I come here for you?*

Later, he will make soup for her, and feed her bread with his hands. In bed, he will tell her how white the skin around her navel is, sing to her how sweet it tastes, and then it will have been weeks like this, then months, her complete secret, her first *lover.* She will think how odd and wonderful it is that he wants to be with her, how their bodies fit together.

She doesn't tell her mother any of it. Her mother would not understand, has always insisted Bijou keep her career the priority, not dating blond boys, and certainly not having sex with them.

But with Crane working where she does, it's technically part of her career, isn't it? They trade office gossip with exaggerated zeal. They run together up the Potomac, ride the carousel in Glen Echo Park, are known by their first names at what they refer to as "the microbrewery *we* go to." He virtually moves in with her because his roommates are toys. In the evening, they pack identical lunches for the next day. For a while he calls her Cannibal Roy. It is a joke funny to no one but them, and like this there are many. The new ones always have a way of killing off the old; a month after he stops calling her Cannibal, neither of them remembers why he ever began. She meets his friends, learns their names and idio-syncrasies, but they are just watercolors, baseball caps and beat-up button-down boys who compete to regurgitate lines from stoner-comedy flicks in clever ways; they pale next to Crane, who is all flesh and bone and hers alone.

He finds a picture of himself in his youth, from when she knew him in Michigan, but now she swears he could have been the boy from the cover of U2's *War* album, minus the split lip. She's seen him set his mouth in the same sad anger sometimes, when he doesn't like the news he reads in the paper.

On several occasions, the one weekend a month she flies or drives home to Detroit, she almost tells him about her father's health, the reasons she goes home so often, the hospital. She never does. It is easy to let him come up with his own explanations. He believes she goes home because her family misses her, and this is not false.

They spend the summer working through each week, treat themselves to a few nights here and there on the Maryland shore. Then she is home for Labor Day weekend, thinking she might tell her mother she has met a boy, and there have been forays into the marriage topic. But everything changes.

When she returns to Washington after the funeral, lost to her senses, Crane tries to understand. She stares through him. He slides his hand down her back, into her jeans. She tells him she needs time.

Like most people, he stopped trying after a while. All those unreturned phone calls, her silences. *I'm going to disappear,* she'd thought, weeks after her father's death, days after returning to Washington. She'd turned away from her friends, then from family friends, and then even from family, with their words about weather and current events, presuming she'd gotten on with life, that Father Time would take care of her now, ultimately. *They should know better,* she would tell herself. *They should know me.* Those moments, standing like a fool in the middle of her apartment, rooted in front of a window watching a neighbor's calico cat sleep, stir to stare down a wren, sleep again. Hours could pass like that, a whole weekend. *I am not well,* she told no one. *I am making a ghost of myself.*

But something was botched in the execution. Practical life got in the way—pleasantries exchanged in the office, the car needing an oil change, the bills due for payment. Eventually you got thirsty, eventually you could swallow solid food again, eventually you wanted to hear a bit of music. The strategy of disappearing more or less failed, and gave way instead to misappearing. Bijou was no martyr. She laughed. She went out wearing lipstick, spent her workday gratefully lost among computers, lab charts, and petri dishes, scouring for aberrations, plotting variant numbers of T-cells on grids. She was polite to strangers. Yet all the while she was semiconscious of a thing that wrapped its pincers around her throat. Just when she thought she had gained some ground on it, this visceral squeeze that was not quite guilt, or jealousy—at least neither of these things alone—all it would take for her to rebefriend the sadness was the simple event of standing in line at a drugstore, overhearing a man discuss chewing gum with his daughter. What they said never mattered. Simply that they could speak, and to each other. Images amassed like this could haunt her for days, taunt her: *This is what you are missing, and this, and this. . . . This is what you are missing, and this, and this. . . .*

From the house next door came the sound of a Hindi pop song on the radio, the melody a peculiar sister to an old Madonna tune. The words and lines Bijou could translate melted together: *Me, I have lost myself, you, if you knew, since our first meeting, this is first love, come here, in your gaze I feel a kiss.*

The air felt like a steam bath, the Bay of Bengal boiling over.

Spring would be in full swing when she got back to Washington—Bijou told herself, as though taking dictation, to look forward to cherry blossoms. Maybe she would ask Crane to accompany her to the Tidal Basin. Maybe he would agree to just that much, and then leave her be, no asking to spend the night, no asking about the next day, and above all no asking whether or not she was going to stay with him forever. Who could guarantee anything? Everything could change in the next instant. She knew.

Across the street, the ironing man arrived at his shacklike stall on the curb. He stoked a stack of coals, placed a hulky iron over them, and unpacked dusty parcels of clothes, bundled and tied in old cotton sheets. Her aunt had given him such a bundle from the house just this morning. Eventually, he pulled out a white dress of Bijou's. He shook it out, laid it flat on his board, and pressed it. First the length of the skirt, then the bodice, then the sleeves. Not once did he look up while he worked.

She'd seen Crane last on the second anniversary of their meeting—he'd wanted to celebrate; she'd refused—and remembered now the back of his head and the stiff angle of his shoulders as he walked away from her, the snow collecting on his scarf and hair. The texture of that yellow-brown hair like tinsel. *You've rejected me.* He didn't know how she wept in his absence. *No, no, can't you see? You've been freed.*

"I'll make you crazy, too," she says. "I don't want to watch that happen."

They are sitting on cement steps in the park near her apartment. She hears a fire truck wailing down U Street as a child walking by trips on the stairs, stubs her toe, begins to cry, is scooped up into the arms and coos of her parents. Although summer is waning, it is humid tonight.

"I know you, Bee," Crane says, calm calm calm. "You can handle this."

"I'm not the same."

"Stop saying that." He sets his mouth in sad anger. "Why didn't you tell me before?"

"I don't know." She is going to cry. "Our family is really private about these things. I don't know." She leans into the brick banister, slips an arm gingerly through the slim space between two concrete spindles. "I don't like to tell people. Everyone acts like you're something to be pitied then."

"Oh my God. How can you be so wrong?" he is saying. "Not to mention, you can't make these decisions without me. You can't say, 'Go,' and expect me to run."

"But this isn't about you." She wraps her arm around a spindle, holds it. Turns away from Crane, sees dry scratches forming all over her arm, and knows they will deepen, bleed.

"If it's about you, then it's about me."

"That doesn't make sense."

"Look at me. You can't let this consume you."

She yanks her arm back in, one searing, painful motion. "I didn't choose to be consumed, Crane. It's going to take time, or something; it will take *something*. Nothing's like we thought it would be. Everything has to be replanned now. It's not simple. I don't even know how much I'm going to have to do. I swear to God, this world—at least my family's world—is not cut out to handle this. You have no idea. We're an aberration. People don't say we're unlucky, but it's clear what they think."

She isn't sure she knows what she's talking about anymore. Words skid and burn as they leave her lips. Were it her in his place, Bijou believes, she would comfort him by keeping her distance. Were it her in his place, she would stay out of his business, never dare to simplify his feelings.

He says, "You'll waste your time being sad."

She stares at him. "I'm sorry. I'm sorry I'm not you, and I can't be talking about marriage like it's easy. You think everything's easy. Things come easily to you."

"You don't. Not at all."

"Crane—"

"I just wish you'd at least let me come to Michigan."

"You never wanted to go before. I didn't think—anyway, it wouldn't have helped anything. Don't frown at me like that." She takes a deep breath. "Some time. It's still not over; we have to go to India."

"So we'll go to India."

She starts to tell him he won't, but says instead, "I have to go to India so that I can put his ashes in the Ganges." Her throat tightens. *How am I supposed to survive that?* she doesn't ask aloud. Her voice crackles: "The ceremony—it's a ritual—is just for family. For men, actually, but there aren't any men left. My mother isn't even sure that this is what he would have wanted—my father, that is—but she's more superstitious than ever."

Whatever he says next, Bijou won't remember; she is listening to another approaching fire truck. The wail of the siren speaks to her. *Emergency. Emergency.*

Still, with Crane, she tries. At night, she cries while he sleeps. When she wakes in the morning (if she has even slept) and sees his arm around her waist, where it must find its way in the middle of the night, when she looks at his hand, the fine hairs on his knuckles, she tries to want this, to forget everything else but this. He tries to arouse her, sulks when she cannot respond; she feels he loathes her, and so loathes herself.

If only it were her in his place, the easy place, all loved ones intact, a realistic sense of proportion.

If we got married . . . Let's get married, Bee. Will you marry me? I'll come to India.

Everything feels wrong. No one will ever understand. She cannot find the right words. She cannot find "yes."

She asks Crane to leave, explicitly this time. She takes back the extra set of keys. She repeats, *We'll see, we'll see. Let me get through India. We'll see then.*

As soon as he's gone, she starts sleeping better, really resting, dreaming again. She meets her father in the kitchen. They stand in front of the refrigerator, conspirators in midnight snacking. He asks what she wants to eat, holds out a handmade ceramic plate with violets and a transistor radio on it. He is wearing his hospital gown and pajamas, his plastic identification bracelet with the sharp edges that are apt to dig into his skin.

"No one listens to me," she says.

Her father cries and cries. No one listens to his daughter. He cries because it is one way and not another. He cries because he does not know his daughter anymore, because he is exhausted, because it is his daughter's dream, the one in which he is the only one capable of hearing her voice. He crawls out of the kitchen and through the living room window.

She follows, flying.

A vendor rode his bicycle-rickshaw down the street, hawking corn and sugarcane in a loud slow tongue. Bijou turned from the road, saw that the maidservant had gotten up and was hanging saris and Oxford shirts from the clothesline. She was watching Bijou.

"You shouldn't be up here during the day, Didi," Ketaki said. "Very hot. Your color will go bad. Don't you want to go inside?" She spoke her Bengali quickly, her voice like birdsong. She was nearly a foot shorter than Bijou, with a frame as petite as Pari's but with strong shoulders and curves at every angle. She kept her hair wound in a knot at her nape. From what Bijou had witnessed, Ketaki didn't work herself to the bone, except perhaps in the living room when the television was on or when she dusted the bureau where Pari had left her lip gloss and barrettes.

"Don't think about it," Bijou responded in the elided Bengali dialect she improvised for communicating with the hired help. She went to the clothesline, picked up a towel from the wicker laundry basket, and began clipping it to the line.

"*Na, na,* Didi," Ketaki chirped, her mouth and pug nose contorted in distaste. "*Koro na! Aami korchi!*"

"But this is nothing!" Bijou said. She shook her head. "Over there? Over there we are our own workers. This is not new for me. Work. I do alone. All of it."

Ketaki nodded, though it was unclear if she followed, if her smile was not the abbreviation for laughter over Bijou's affected accent.

Bijou fastened the beige towel to the line, effectively pinning a curtain between herself and Ketaki.

"You should go inside, Didi," Ketaki called out. "It's very hot."

Bijou ducked under the red *anchal* of a cream-colored sari and joined the maidservant on the other side of the clothesline. "I know it's hot, Ketaki," she said. "I want to help you." But when she leaned over to choose another item from the wash, Ketaki slid a foot into the handle of the basket and pulled it away.

"This is my work, not yours," she said. "I'm telling you, it's too hot. *Go inside.*"

Feeling she had no choice, Bijou went inside. Her aunt told her to rest, and that later they would take a walk to the market if it wasn't too hot.

* * *

Marginally shielded from the glaring sun by infrequent store aw-
nings, Bijou followed her aunt along a narrow sidewalk, the two of
them not quite keeping pace with each other. She started to roll up
her sleeves, remembered the constellation of lesions there, and
stopped. Frustrated, she sighed. Why was it so hard to acclimate
to the heat? Shouldn't a high threshold for heat be in her nature?

"So, Bijou," her aunt said, "how is Washington? Have you met
any nice Indian boys?"

Bijou laughed sharply. "No," she said. "They prefer blondes."

"Perhaps you haven't met the right one."

"Anyway, I am so busy," she lied, "I hardly have time to date."

She kept her eyes on the heels of her aunt's sandaled feet. They
poked out from under her sari with each step.

"How old is Ketaki?" Bijou asked. "Does she have a family?"

Her aunt gestured to stop. A truck drove by, holding a heap of a
hundred light-green melons in its bed. Half a dozen working-class
men lounged on top of the melons, just like that, as though people
were transported on fruit all the time.

They crossed the street. "Anuja Massi?"

"Yes, *beta*?"

"Does her family live in the villages?"

"Who?"

"Ketaki."

"Yes, yes," her aunt replied. "She goes home in the spring for a
while. For holiday."

Bijou nodded. "Where *are* the villages, exactly? Anuja Massi?"

But her aunt was not listening, was waving to a woman who
called out to her from a veranda. "We were born in something of a
village ourselves, you know," she said to Bijou a minute later. "Your
mother, me, our brothers. When we were still in Kashmir. We are
not originally even middle-class, far from it." She flashed a look of

surprise, then added, "It really could be embarrassing, when I think what *you* would think of it! We hardly had plumbing!"

"Oh, no, I wouldn't—" Bijou began to say, then had to pull herself off to the side of the street in order to avoid a woman with her baby carriage. Consequently, she nearly collided with a group of young boys, who did nothing to get out of her way. "Excuse me," she said. They smirked. She felt her face flushing—the boys were at least ten years her junior, didn't they realize?—and scolded herself for speaking. In English, at that.

"She—Ketaki—seems very young. Anuja Massi? Do you know how old she is?"

"Ketaki? *Nahi,* she's probably Pari's age. I don't think she'll last with us much longer. There are rumors she is involved with someone who works nearby."

" 'Involved'?" Bijou repeated. "Are they getting married? Is he older?" She thought of the ironing man, the sugarcane vendor, the man in sunglasses who had been speaking to Ramesh earlier today. Who would Ketaki love?

Her aunt shrugged.

"I'm shocked. She's so young, she's just—"

"That's how they are. But what can you expect?"

"I don't know. Just not to throw her life away so soon."

"Well, I don't think she's ever had any ambition to go to school, to make something of herself, so . . ."

"Maybe she doesn't know it's an option."

"But these girls are not so innocent as they behave with us, believe me. Before you know it, she will have ten babies of her own to feed."

"Whose fault is that?"

"Well, of course. I suppose you can't blame anyone for being human," she replied, with what seemed like discomfort in the face of Bijou's inquisitiveness.

They crossed another street, and a thoroughfare. Here, apartment buildings rose from the boulevard. People were simply everywhere. This would be the perfect place to understand orders of magnitude, she told herself; this was experiencing the difference between an America of millions and this India of a billion. From above, Bijou thought, the city must look like a colony of desert insects, scrambling through paths they had worn. And in the midst of it, her: a girl in sunglasses, long sleeves, linen skirt, and tennis shoes, following her aunt in pure faith. She pulled her hair back with one hand and held it up to cool her neck. Strands of it stuck regardless, like wet yarn, to her skin.

Her aunt flagged down a three-wheeled scooter, and they rode the rest of the way to New Market.

Her father had sometimes mentioned this place, but only in asides: Such-and-such a friend of his used to live near New Market, or he and his college friends frequented a certain bookshop near New Market. Whether he had ever ventured inside or how frequently, Bijou didn't know. He had certainly never paused to describe the look of it—redbrick, Gothic, with towers bolting from the roof like arrowheads. A formidable clock tower. Clearly left over from the days of the British.

In the parking lot, they were immediately approached by men with cardboard trays of strawberries, plastic bangles, bottles of nail polish. Anuja Massi picked up a package of clothespins and asked how much they were in a terse voice, clearly braced for haggling. The vendor looked at her with disinterest, then passed the same gaze over Bijou, who looked away. As she fixed her eye on the clock tower, she heard the vendor quote a price. Her aunt snickered, then threw the package down and walked away. Bijou followed.

"You might make it difficult to get anything at a reasonable price," her aunt said. "Did you only bring Western clothes?"

"Don't lose me," Bijou said. She reached into her skirt pocket, making sure the few rupee notes she'd brought were still there. "I'd never find my way back."

Inside the market, stores and stalls and merchandise spilled out everywhere. Bijou pushed her sunglasses to the top of her head. There was another floor of the market above them.

Ready-made garments hung in a small glass-walled room, a sign near the entrance advertising CLOTHINGS FOR MENS. Inside, a tailor stretched a yellow tape measure across a man's back, then down his arms. Next door, leather bags and shoes. Then a stall of copper housewares, brass figurines of Shiva Nataraja on a shelf, carved lacquered furniture, then a stall of Tibetan curios, then a silk store, then a record store.

"They say this place is haunted by the ghost of the man who built it," Anuja Massi said. "That was over a hundred years ago. He was not Indian. Sir Something-or-other Hogg."

"It would certainly be easier for a ghost to move through here," Bijou said as she sidestepped the outstretched arm of another nearly robotic merchant, rapidly droning his demand for her to *Come see saris, come, madam, come see suits silk look here best silk try.*

"Oh, but he haunts it at night only," her aunt said breezily. "When the building is empty."

She led her through the market to the opposite end, to an area partially covered with a bright yellow tentlike awning. The tables under the awning were full of rings and earrings, cotton textiles, batik skirts, the stuff of big export to college towns in the States. Bijou smiled and shook her head at the man behind the table, who held out beaded bracelets toward her. Her aunt walked along farther, just beyond the market building, to where condiment stalls of imported food, sweets, and vegetables stood.

Bijou picked up a silver ring with a small gardenia-shaped flower painted white on it. She tried it on, noticed the paint chipped off at the edge of the petals, and took it off. But she didn't put it down. It was the sort of ring that, decades ago, she would have bestowed with magical powers, Wonder Twins power. For no other reason than it was a ring, really.

Her aunt returned and said the vendor she had come to see had closed shop for the day. "I'll send Ketaki tomorrow."

"This is nice," Bijou said, holding out the ring in her palm. She turned to the man and asked how much it was.

Before the man could respond, her aunt pulled a two-rupee note from her pocketbook and handed it to the man. "She likes this trinket," she said, and pulled away Bijou, who mumbled a thank-you over her shoulder.

"In my opinion," her aunt said, "the shopping is better in Delhi. I do miss the emporiums there."

They passed a table decked in portable radios and wallets. From a wooden hat stand next to the stall hung several wigs, all of long black hair.

As they reached the entrance they'd come in by, her aunt ran into other acquaintances. Evidently mother and son. The latter had a plastic shopping bag out of which poked a stalk of chard. Bijou stood by, refocusing on her new ring. Perhaps it wasn't meant to look like a gardenia at all, she considered. It might have been designed as a white rose or one of those champak blossoms. The band was adjustable, and she readjusted the pinch. It was, she thought proudly, pretty. Where was the harm in calling it a gardenia?

"Yes, yes, this is Bijou," her aunt was saying with some pride. "My sister and Pari went to Darjeeling for a few days. Some peace, rest. Pari, also, wanted to see more of India."

Bijou looked up. The woman she was addressing replied, "That's good, Anuja! I agree, we must go on. What else to do?" She embraced Bijou. "My dear. My dear, how you look just like our old Nitish. How much we miss him, too."

The son held out his free hand and introduced himself as Naveen. She shook his hand. "I've heard so much about you," he said. "How nice to finally put a face to the name. You're just how I would have pictured. You'll be in Calcutta for a while now, won't you?"

"Naveen has just started teaching at the university this year," her aunt told her. "History, like your uncle."

"That's great." Mother and son both looked at her expectantly, and she wondered what she was missing. Who were these people?

"What do you think of our Calcutta?" Naveen asked. He cocked his head slightly and added: "I understand you haven't been here before. It's rather different from Delhi. Not to mention Detroit. You must find quite a number of contrasts."

"I'm not a stranger to contrast," she said dispassionately, "just because I'm American."

He had a roughly polished British accent, his words at once perfectly enunciated and perfectly slurred. Something in his tone put her on the defensive; his did not seem to be a benign, chit-chatty curiosity. He stood nearly two heads above his mother and Anuja Massi—one above Bijou—and was dressed in a short beige kurta and jeans. He had a sharp chin and a long neck, both stubbled, sideburns carefully trimmed, as was his wavy hair, slightly receding. A pair of pewter-framed glasses poked out of the breast pocket of his kurta. Quickly, he began to remind her of the Indian graduate students back home, the pool from which many of her college professors had drawn their assistants.

"I believe that Bijou would be quite happy here," Anuja Massi said. "This visit will be the first of many. There has to be something in these children that calls them back to their mother country, don't you think? After all, they are raised as Indian."

Bijou pulled down her sunglasses and looked out into the parking lot. Her arms were beginning to itch again.

"We must be going," Naveen's mother said amiably. "But you will come to our house for dinner. Come tomorrow, won't you? Okay? No formalities."

"Of course," her aunt said.

Naveen half-waved in farewell. "Looking forward," he said.

They parted ways.

Her aunt decided to buy some walnuts before they went home. As she purchased them, Bijou asked for some elaboration on the woman they'd just met.

"I thought you knew! She's one of your father's old friends, Dr. Mazumdar. Kamla Mazumdar."

"Oh! Ashok's wife?"

"Yes, yes! Have you never seen her before? I should have said something. I am so stupid sometimes. Kamla Di's clinic is not far from our house, actually. But she works all over the city. Doing such good things . . . You will like her. I've gotten to know them quite well since Naveen joined the college. He comes over often, and sometimes we go to their house."

"I don't really know them. Didn't Ashok pass away a long time ago?"

"Very early, very bad. Naveen was just a little boy. But Naveen studied at Oxford, and returned home only a few years back. It's funny, really," her aunt said. "I still think of him as sixteen years old. He was a rather unruly boy. Bright, but defiant. He has a black belt in karate."

"You're kidding," Bijou said, and giggled. "Oh, can we stop here, please?"

They were passing a sweets stall, and she wanted to purchase a Cadbury chocolate bar. "For Ketaki," she told her aunt. "Would you like one?"

"Too much will spoil her," she replied. "But thank you. I don't care for chocolates."

They walked the rest of the way in silence. At one point, a maidservant from a house just a few doors away emptied a bucket of water into the street. Bijou watched it trickle and die out yards before it had a chance to meet the nearest sewer grate.

"Kamla Di is a very good cook. You'll have a nice time there," her aunt said, when they'd reached home. "And Naveen is charming, but don't think we're setting up any funny meeting-dating business between you. I wouldn't do that, not without permission"— she opened the door—"from your mother. Of course, you might quite like each other, who knows? Perhaps—"

Bijou shook her head. "No *perhaps*. No. I'm fine the way things are, for now."

"Don't be so sure of everything at your age, *betiya*. 'I'm fine, I'm fine.' Naveen says the same thing. You sound like a very nice match to me."

Bijou let the matter drop. Later, after dinner, she handed the Cadbury bar to Ketaki.

"Enjoy it," she told her. "It's a small thing."

Ketaki seemed either puzzled or uninterested.

"For you," Bijou added. "From me. It's chocolate. It's good."

Ketaki raised her eyebrows, nodded, and said she would save it for later.

Bijou spent four hours of the following morning on the telephone, trying to change her ticket. The airline agents were not eager to help, and she passed a great deal of time on hold, twisting the gardenia ring around her middle finger. This telephone was kept in the receiving room on the first floor, next to the kitchen, from where she could hear Ketaki and the cook conversing, washing dishes, and rearranging the steel cookware.

In the end, the airline was able to locate a seat on a flight that would take her to Paris, then Newark, then Washington. The flight left the following week, two weeks earlier than her original booking. Would that do? It would. She replaced the receiver on its hook and stretched her neck and arms. From the direction of the front porch came honks from a passing vehicle. She slumped into her armchair. The ceiling fan spun like a propeller lost from its plane.

It struck Bijou that she was rushing back to a life she was not completely missing, and the thought of unlocking her apartment door to meet the silence of her bedroom, the scent of bleach and snuffed candles lingering in the air, the profound lack of company, momentarily filled her with a sense of aversion. She thumbed through her passport, studying the few inky stamps from immigration on the page opposite her tourist visa. It would not expire for ten years. She could come again.

FIVE

The Mazumdars lived in Alipur. On the drive over, Anuja Massi pointed out the National Library, and reminded Bijou that the Kali Temple was nearby. "We *could* go inside. It would take all day—so many people—but we could."

"Anuja, she's probably had enough."

"Bengalis are very devoted to their goddesses," her aunt continued. "You must come one year for Durga Puja. The preparations are fascinating. How they make the idols from clay and straw, then paint them, et cetera . . . Oh, it's a sight. Thousands of them. When the *puja* holidays are over, they set Durga to sail on the river—thousands of her in the river, thousands of Durga statues. They love their goddesses in Bengal!"

"You think the traffic is bad now, Bijou," her uncle said. "Come back at that time. You really should come, actually. The weather is nice then, too. Everyone should witness the *puja* chaos at least once. It's a *mela* unlike any other. That's true. I've seen many *pujas*."

Bijou wasn't listening to him carefully. Her aunt's words had set her off in another direction. "They put the statues in the river?" she said now. "In the Hooghly?"

Her aunt affirmed this. "Yes. The *murthis*."

"They just leave them there?"

"Well, it's all part of the greater ritual, you see," her uncle told her.

"But doesn't anyone worry about the water? You can't just go on dumping things in it; eventually it's going to be . . . I mean, no wonder it's unsafe and unclean. It isn't right. If it's supposed to be such a sacred place, then treat it with some respect."

Her uncle began to say something, but Anuja Massi shushed him.

"The *murthis* are made of *clay*," he said anyway. "Recycling, plain and simple. Nothing toxic as such, nothing—"

"I understand what you mean, Bijou," her aunt said. "It's true. But it's difficult to control what so many people will do. I know, it's frustrating."

Bijou kept quiet, imagining the silt of the Hooghly, her father's ashes commingling with pulverized remains of Durga idols and who knew what else, how many ghosts, abandoned there. Who knew how many vestiges of grief and devotion that riverbed held? *Puja* usually occurred in September or October, weeks before which the artisans would come to collect their share of clay, take it with them to their workshops, make it into something worthy of worship. Where would her father's remains be by then?

Where will you be?

Her aunt and uncle were talking to each other quietly about another professor at the university. Bijou closed her eyes and leaned back as if to nap.

Her uncle parked the car in front of a salmon-colored house. On a small plastic plaque by the front door was printed DOCTOR K. MAZUMDAR. They were greeted by a middle-aged maidservant, who led them up a circular stairway.

"They divided the house many years ago," her aunt told Bijou, "and another family has rented out the first floor ever since."

Upstairs, Kamla welcomed them. She wore a beige embroidered Lucknowi-style *salwaar kameez* with a silvery chiffon *dhupatta* that glistened like teardrops; the kurta was long and A-lined, and the pants stiff and wide, banded at the hem. She looked fresher than when they'd met at the market, her eyes bright and rimmed with black *kajal*. She was an attractive woman, Bijou noted, with a small, curvy nose, and a mouth, if not a disposition, like Faye Dunaway's and lacking, for better or for worse, any laugh lines.

They sat together at one end of a warmly lit room that appeared to take up most of the second floor. The furniture was carved of dark wood, with pink cushions, and under a long coffee table there lay an antique-looking Persian rug of gilt lavender chrysanthemums and ivy. Opposite the sofa were two armchairs that seemed plucked from a mod Hindi movie. Bookshelves lined the walls, punctuated with flower vases, hand-sewn dolls, and framed photographs. The largest picture was a black-and-white still of a young man Bijou assumed was Ashok: he wore thick black glasses, and a neatly trimmed beard enwrapped his jaw and neck. At the opposite end of the room there was a dining table, which had been set for five. A green curtain hung over a doorway that led to a small pantry, then the kitchen.

Naveen was nowhere in Bijou's sight. Kamla explained that he had called to say he would be late. She asked what she could get them to drink before dinner.

"How far away does he live, Kamla Auntie?"

"Oh, but he lives here, Bijou," she replied. "I should say he sleeps here. The bulk of his time he spends in his classroom, or in his office."

"We're trying to get rid of him already," Shankar Uncle said. "There are plenty of schools abroad that will take him for a visiting post."

"Leave it to your uncle," Kamla said to Bijou, "to drive a woman's only son out of the country."

"What can we do? If Naveen publishes just one more paper this year, the rest of us will have to pull up our socks." He spoke in a humdrum style, didactic yet good-natured. "We write books that no one reads. Your son, on the other hand, is invited to every major conference in the world. The academic world, but still."

"But isn't it time the next generation took the reins? At our age, our parents were retired," Kamla said. "We deserve the same respite, I should think. Let these adults, after all, take care of us now. Tell me, why else have children?"

"How are things at the clinic, Kamla Di?" Anuja Massi said sweetly. She was sitting in one of the armchairs and looked almost regal, her sari an attractive peach color with black accents, her legs crossed gracefully under the perfect pleats. How a woman could negotiate herself gracefully in a sari was beyond Bijou; the few times she had let her mother dress her in one, she felt acutely conscious of herself. One false step, she was sure, and all six yards of silk would puddle around her ankles, exposing the blouse that revealed much of her cleavage and a petticoat that burned rings around her waist from how tightly it was tied there. "You get used to it," her mother had said. "Thicken your skin."

Now, as Bijou gazed at her aunt, it was ever clearer that she had been spared her mother's hardening, the hardening that came from years of . . . perhaps from years of raising children, Bijou conceded.

"As usual, there are some successes and many fights," Kamla replied. "You should come next week, Bijou. Now, tell me about your work in Washington. Perhaps you can lend us some of your expertise."

"Well, I just help with research," Bijou said. "My preceptor specializes in the study of rare diseases. Specifically immune deficiencies. I spend most of my week thinking about T-cells. More or less."

Kamla was nodding appreciatively.

"Specifically," Bijou added, "our lab is researching certain immunoglobulins and glycoconjugates. What causes the stripping of myelin—" She glanced at her aunt and uncle, who seemed terrifically alienated. "Well, I was interested because of the multiple sclerosis angle. It seemed like the right lab for me. I haven't been working hard enough, though, lately. Maybe when I get back . . ."

"What do you want to specialize in? Neurology?" Kamla said. "Infectious disease?"

"I don't know. I deferred medical school for this program."

"Don't wait too long." She ran a hand over Bijou's head with affection. "Now, what will you have to drink?"

The front door slammed, and Bijou heard footsteps on the stairs. Naveen appeared, glasses on, a leather bag slung diagonally across his torso. His face glistened with sweat.

"*Namoskar, namoskar.* I'm so sorry," he said, holding his hands together in greeting to Bijou's aunt and uncle. "Would you believe my scooter is falling apart?"

"I would believe it to be a miracle," her uncle said, "if you didn't have to walk that death trap the *entire* way here."

"And where is your helmet?" Kamla asked.

Naveen was wiping his forehead with a white handkerchief. He grimaced, then looked toward the kitchen.

"Ma," he said, "why haven't you served dinner? I told you to begin without me."

"We are having a pleasant conversation," she said. "That happens when you are not around."

"Naveen, *beta*," Anuja Massi said, "we only just arrived five minutes ago. There's no rush."

He excused himself to put his things away. Bijou watched as he went back to the stairwell, and listened to his quick steps as he ascended to the floor above them.

At dinner, Naveen and Shankar Uncle sat at opposite ends of the table, while Bijou sat next to her aunt and across from Kamla. An empty chair stood between Naveen and his mother.

Kamla had brought out the food; the maidservant only came to the house once a week, Bijou was told. Kamla had cooked the meal herself: pilaf with cauliflower and cashew nuts, *dal makhni*, and a dry mutton dish. She didn't believe in making too much at once, she told her guests, but there was more of everything in the kitchen.

"You should feel special," Naveen said. "My mother rarely cooks for others, Bijou."

Bijou glanced at him as Kamla passed the platter of rice her way. "Thank you," she said.

"Do you cook?" Kamla asked her.

"I can."

"I bought the yogurt," Naveen said.

"Naveen bought the yogurt!" Shankar Uncle said with mock enthusiasm. "What can't this boy do?"

When everyone had been served, they ate without much conversation. Bijou focused on her fork, resisting the urge to bring up topics that might upset the enjoyment of what was certainly a fine meal. She wanted to ask about Ashok. The hush at the table annoyed her, when there was so much that might be said beyond the weather.

At last, after clearing his first servings, her uncle said, "What is the update on your plans, Naveen?"

Naveen looked up from his plate and sat up straighter. "I am leaning toward Chicago," he said. "But there is Columbia. It would be nice to spend a year in New York."

Bijou asked if he'd been there before, and he said he had.

"My elder brother lives in Chicago," Anuja Massi said. "It's very close to Detroit. It's good someone is near to our sister. If you go there, Naveen, you can visit all of them."

"Does your *mamaji* ever come to Detroit, Bijou?" her uncle asked her.

"Oohf. Of course they came in September, no?" her aunt told him, slightly irritated. "For Nitish Da."

Bijou nodded. She used her fork to chase a clove out of the rice, then stared at the rim of the plate. She suddenly felt quite full; the thought of another bite made her ill. She moved the food around the plate, as if dispersing it would have the same effect as making it disappear. Why hadn't she gone with her mother to Darjeeling? she thought. Why had her mother gone without her? It wasn't right, sitting here. If her mother were here, she'd have an anchor.

"Remind me how old you were, Bijou," Naveen said, "when he got sick?"

She looked at him. He had stopped eating, too. "Nearly fourteen, I guess," she said.

"That's what I figured," he said, grimacing again. "It seems like yesterday, doesn't it?" He returned to his food slowly.

Kamla excused herself from the table. She came back, through the green curtains, with a plate of chapatis. "Your father and my husband were good friends, Bijou," she said when she'd sat down again. "When they were young, they were not just *like* brothers, they were *closer than*. We were all very idealistic by nature, wrapped up in our beliefs."

"Daddy spoke so fondly of Ashok Uncle. He really did! That friendship was something he always held very, very dear." Her mood surged toward excitement, and she flushed as she felt the others' eyes on her, curious. "It's just that I've heard so much about you," she said. "I heard about the work you all did—such good work—in the villages, helping all those people. The Naxalite movement. Right? Naxalites?"

Naveen seemed to be twirling his fork in his rice, as did Shankar Uncle. Her aunt smiled nervously.

Kamla was the one to respond, at last. "Yes, we worked together, in a sense. We started out sharing good beliefs, at any rate. But too soon after Naveen was born, I lost my husband for those beliefs. Then there was the famine. And I went back to school, the smartest thing I ever did for myself." In her voice, there was neither nostalgia nor malice but a severed quality, as though she spoke of an event that had impacted a stranger. Her gaze wandered back to Bijou, and she said, "They still make the news. Sometimes you see reports about Naxalite activity in the paper. But it's no more a part of my life now than it is a part of your mother's life. We are left with nothing but our husbands' surnames."

"The children," Anuja Massi said firmly, "will keep them alive. God tests good people. Does it make any sense?"

Shankar Uncle shook his head. "We lost too many intelligent boys in those days," he said. "They are the real martyrs, I should think. The cost was too much, too much."

"One learns," Kamla said, "to move on. You're correct, Anuja. The children help." She turned to Naveen, somewhat reanimated. "I think we have photographs. Naveen? Where are the pictures? There was an album, no? Red?"

Naveen looked up and nodded.

"You must show them to her," Kamla said. She turned back to Bijou and added, "You understand, I never look at them. Or I would show you myself."

"Do you have photos of my father?" Bijou asked. She just managed to keep the excitement in her voice at a respectful level. "We do not have any that were taken before he was married."

Naveen cleared his throat. "They're in my office. I didn't think to bring them back, Bijou." He looked her in the eye. "I wasn't thinking. I should have."

"Then you'll take her to your office after dinner," his mother said. "Using *my* car. Her father would have wanted this. Nitish would insist."

Few people were on campus by the time Naveen and Bijou reached the university. They hadn't spoken much on the drive, and Bijou was startled by Naveen's voice when finally, as he unlocked his office door, he said, "We won't stay here. We can take the photos somewhere else to look at them."

She stayed back in the dimly lit hallway. The air smelled faintly of ginger, smoke, and mothballs. She shuddered to think of what medical school would involve. Memorization, insomnia, tests, all those tests, and more tests so that you could spend the rest of your life testing other people.

Postponing medical school had been an obvious effort to buy time; she was beginning to wonder, however, if her deferral was just a decision to quit. What else would she do with her life, though? Why couldn't she be making these decisions—without fear of judgment—when she was in her forties, instead?

She wandered to a nearby bulletin board, upon which hung layers of class announcements and calls for papers. One of the notices promoted a joint lecture given by the history and linguistics departments. On the list of panel participants, she read: *N. Mazumdar, "Repeat After Me: Dialect and Transcendental Dialectic in Contemporary West Bengal."*

She rolled her eyes. Where once academia and all its hard consonants had dazzled her, now it made her want to sprint in the opposite direction, as far as the moon. Why had she given up on her dream of being an astronaut?

A door latched closed behind her, and she turned to see Naveen looking at her, a sizeable scrapbook in hand.

"If you're ready," he said.

"Where is my uncle's office?"

"Upstairs."

He led her downstairs, and when they were back in the car, he gave her the book to hold on to. It was too dark to peruse it; she ran her fingers around the edges.

"I told your uncle I would bring you home," Naveen said. "We'll go to a coffeehouse near here. It's no use going all the way back to our house."

He was looking into the rearview mirror, backing the car out of the parking space.

"Thank you," she said. "This is not something I expected."

"Just remember, a few snapshots are not the entire truth."

She nodded, frowning, then looked at him. He was staring ahead into the street, his profile sharp as a paper cutout. She abruptly had the feeling of having sat in this car with him countless times before. She turned to look out the passenger window, and met her own reflection in the glass. She tucked her hair behind her ears, adjusted the neckline of her dress to conceal a bra strap, then rolled down the window.

Naveen took a right turn, and they had hardly driven a block when they were slowed by a procession in front of them. A batch of young men followed a small vehicle, decked in holiday lights, which at first Bijou thought was an ice cream truck. She raised her head to peer above the men, moving forward in her seat.

A speaker had been propped on the roof of the truck. She heard the metallic clank of thumb cymbals. The men were shouting unintelligible words over a recording of women chanting. As some of the men moved to the sides, she saw a life-sized *murthi* of Kali—another goddess, related to Durga, or another avatar, Bijou couldn't recall—propped inside the truck, the back door to which was slid open. Her face painted black, with wide-open black and white eyes and a bloodred tongue, Kali was dressed in a green sari. A garland of red hibiscus flowers hung around her neck.

"What's going on?" Bijou said. "What's that music?"

Their car had come to an almost complete stop, and the cars behind them began to press their horns. She rolled her window shut.

"What is this?" she said. "Is this common?"

"Puja," Naveen replied in a distracted manner. "A religious ceremony."

Bijou sat back and crossed her arms. "Kali Ma in the back there kind of gave that away, Professor."

"Madness," he said, fingers drumming on the steering wheel. He looked around, presumably for a way out.

"We don't have to do this," she said. "You can take me home."

He told her it probably wouldn't take too long for the procession to get where it was going. In the meantime, they would have to be patient.

"I say that more for my own benefit," he said. "This city will be the death of me."

"Don't say that," she said. "We don't have to go out."

"No, we don't," he said. "But we will. We will beat them."

The truck ahead of them had gained some speed, and the men were dancing now, some of them hanging on to the sides of the truck.

"You could always join them," she said.

"That would destroy the delicate balance," he said, "between us and them."

"Yeah, I've never really been religious," she said quietly. She ran her fingers around the edge of the book again. "Were you?"

"God, no; it wouldn't have been appropriate. Religion, opiate for the masses, so on. My parents kept Hinduism at arm's length, to say the least. Unless he changed his tune completely, your father must have been the same way."

"I don't remember us really talking about it," she concurred.

Naveen nodded. "All my flatmates and friends in England were pagans, so I can't say I had any spirituality then either. I wonder though, sometimes. If there isn't a large puppeteer behind all our lives."

He went on a little about what it had been like for him at Oxford, and made oblique references to a romantic relationship that had evidently defined those years as good while they were going, then bad after the relationship got rocky. It was unclear if he was still involved with someone, and Bijou didn't feel it was her place to ask for clarification. He seemed to her much older than he was, with his experiences abroad and his academic career.

He yanked the wheel to park the car off the side of the road, where men in cotton pants and old dress shirts unbuttoned halfway down their chests were directing vehicles into a tightly packed row, shouting and pointing.

When they were out of the car, he handed one of the men some money, which was quickly deposited in a shirt pocket before the man barked and waved his hands at another car, directing it into a space that hardly seemed large enough to contain a scooter, much less a car.

"It defies physics," she said, "how you guys deal with space in this city. Every law. How—I mean, how—"

"They just do it." Naveen looked at Bijou for a moment, then inhaled sharply and said, "You ready?"

She followed him across the street as he explained it wouldn't be a long walk. He walked quickly, and she struggled to keep up. Soon they overtook the boisterous *puja* procession (still ambling along strong), and she longed to press her hands against her ears, perhaps would have done so had it not been for the album in her grasp. They flew by a Chinese restaurant, a snack stand, two bookstores, and a barbershop, Naveen just slightly ahead of her, clearing the path.

Wary of the crowd, she gripped the book tight to her chest and moved closer to Naveen. He looked at her and smiled. His lips were thin, and his smile had an upward turn like a child would draw. He seemed gentle, even noble, the way he was leading her— her face flushed as she thought, of male company, *I miss this.* She felt safe in his keep, as she'd felt safe in those first months with Crane. She turned away.

Across the street a high-rise residence towered above the surrounding line of one- and two-story shops and a *bustee* of thatch-roofed huts. Lights from apartments eight floors above them shone brighter than the kerosene lamps dotting the slum at ground level.

Naveen stopped in front of a short flight of stairs that led to an unmarked wooden door. Bijou stopped, too, and he casually placed his hand on her back, guiding her down the steps. Two young women burst through the door below at that point, startling her.

"Watch it," Naveen said as the women raced up past them. He pulled Bijou toward him, his hand on her waist and then off again as quickly. "Sorry."

She mumbled some thanks through her surprise at the unexpected touch.

Once inside, they maneuvered their way to a table near the back, where the light was brightest.

As Naveen spoke to the waiter, she set the album on the table. At the bottom of the red leather cover, the initials *A.M.* were embossed in yellow ink. Bijou opened it. The photos were held in place by black corner tabs, and the black pages were as thick and fibrous as construction paper, with crinkled overlays of opaque yellowing tissue. The first few pages contained snapshots of a young woman, caught in expressions ranging from serious to grave.

"Your mother?" She looked up at Naveen, whose eyes were on her. "Her hair was long then." He nodded. She turned another page, and there began a series of pictures so small she could have hid them in her palm. She bent closer to the album, studying. These were stills of young men in white dhotis, all of them wearing beards. Some with glasses, others enwrapped in shawls.

"I believe you missed your father," Naveen said as she was moving on. "Turn back."

"Where?" she said, returning to the former page. "They're microscopic. I can hardly distinguish their faces."

"You look so much like him," he muttered, leaning forward. He pointed to a photo in the middle of the page, in which two men were standing shoulder to shoulder next to bicycles, a shop sign with Bengali script on it in the background. "My father is on the left."

The young man on the right could have been anyone, so strange and like a stranger he was to Bijou. Not simply darker—an effect of the black-and-white, the exposure—but lankier than he would later be. Here was a boy, youthful, his ears too big for his head, his lips and jaw darkened by a closely trimmed mustache and beard.

"You think I look like this?" Bijou laughed. "How unfortunate.

He was far more handsome later, trust me. I'll show *you* some pictures someday."

"My great-uncle had given my mother a camera he'd gotten during a trip to Japan," Naveen said, smiling again. "She insisted on taking the pictures; most of them are hers. The next few pages, Bijou, those photos were taken near Malda, on the way to Darjeeling. It was not their first trip, or so the story goes. It was their last. I was with them, they say."

Bijou had a hard time picturing Naveen as an infant.

"There is so much I don't know," she said. "By the time I wanted to, it was too late to ask questions."

"It's very sad. Tragic," Naveen said.

"'Tragic' seems like the right word for it," she murmured. Then, more directly, she added, "When I finally asked, I got nowhere. My mother doesn't know anything about this. All this came before her, when she was still in Kashmir."

"Surely your father confided his story in her."

"What about your father? What about his story?"

Naveen raised an eyebrow, curiously. "His story begins right there." He indicated the photo album.

She returned her eyes to pictures on the pages, most of which were of her father now. They were all, thankfully, larger prints.

Her father, unshaved, a neatly folded shawl hanging over one shoulder. Caught in mid-step, he is looking over his shoulder at the camera from several yards away.

Next to it a close-up, in which she could see the reflection of slender, female hands and the camera lens in his eyes.

In another, he is sitting on the ground next to Naveen's mother, both of them leaning against a bale of straw. It is sunny, bright. Naveen's mother has her eyes closed, and her head is turned away from Bijou's father, whose hand has disappeared inside a rucksack. An empty soda bottle is between them.

After this, Naveen's parents eating food off a banana leaf for a plate.

Her father reading a gray book in the company of a villager, perhaps to him. The villager's head wrapped in a turban of thick cords.

Naveen's mother sitting with women who wore button-sized nose rings and no blouses under their tightly wrapped saris. Those women like Ketaki, perhaps Ketaki's foremothers among them.

Her father and Naveen's, standing with three other men, holding clay cups, only her father looking at the camera.

"It's so strange to think of him as an activist," Bijou said without raising her eyes, as though to herself. "Much less a Communist. Which seems so obsolete, like corsets or something."

"What do you mean?" Naveen said.

"They were really living it," she said. "They were really working alongside the people who needed help. They weren't afraid."

"Yet this is only one side of things, Bijou," he said quietly. "What they did in the cities was very different. The violence. Senseless deaths. Do you really know the history? What compelled them? It was a reactionary movement. The Naxalites took the ideals of Gandhiji and pacifism and twisted them; they abandoned everything without thinking to keep at least *some* of the old tactics, the ones that *had* worked, for God's sake. They turned to Mao, outside of their own people. Do you know how many men the cause cost us? Bright men. The kind that *should* have changed the world, would have eventually if they hadn't been so impulsive. Take it upon yourself to stir *revolutionary* spirit in the masses, and there will be dire consequences. Were they prepared for those consequences? They were carried away. It took us nowhere. You cannot slash and burn the past out of existence."

Policemen, he told her, were shot in broad daylight, as were informers. College professors were targeted, and businessmen, and all government officials. Anyone in a uniform, anyone *complicit,* anyone. When the police finally retaliated, their behavior was as inhumane as that of the felons they pursued. It was a nightmare.

"My father mentioned the violence," Bijou said. "But he wasn't a part of all that."

"*Wasn't?* Is that what he told you?" Naveen's brow shot up and down in a disappointed resignation. He interlaced his hands and brought them to his chin, his elbows sharp upon the table.

"If anything," she added, "he made it clear that he and his— that he and your father were actually victims of the violence."

A girl brought two glasses of cold coffee to the table. Bijou looked at Naveen apprehensively. "It's okay," he said. "Trust me. The water is filtered."

She wiped the sweat off her face with a napkin, notes of citronella from her mosquito repellant revisiting her for a moment while she looked around the room. The people sitting at other tables around them all seemed younger, caught up in lighter talk. The walls of the coffeehouse were bare, the furniture looked as if it came from parochial schools, and the floor was dusty. A young man was crossing the room, and then it became clear that he was approaching the table.

"Professor," he said to Naveen when he stood before them, "I thought that was you. Thought I would say hello. We're all sitting up there in front. Fantastic lecture last class; I'm really enjoying the essay by Chatterjee."

"Amit. How are you?" The two shook hands.

"First-class, sir."

Bijou smiled as Amit glanced at her curiously.

"This is a family friend," Naveen said. "She's visiting from Washington. Bijoya Roy."

"Hello," Amit said amicably. He turned back to Naveen, and they chatted.

Someone at a nearby table was arguing. *That idiot doesn't know a cricket wicket from his own arse. He threw the match, I'm telling you.* Bijou stared into her glass, stirring the drink with her straw. Her father, in those photographs, had known nothing of what was to come. Paris, a wife, America, sickness, death, and now his daughter older than he was at the time of these photographs, sitting with the son of his oldest friend, both of them like pirates with looted treasure. Was this a coincidence? She wondered if her father would think so. Perhaps there were no coincidences, only collisions, only physics and whatever copacetic philosophy could be sussed out in a place like this; if not this café, then one very much like it, somewhere halfway between home and the world, amid friends, cold glass, and smoke. Bijou rubbed her eyes, then took a sip of her coffee, which was sweet and thick with cream and shaved ice. It caught her off guard to enjoy it as much as she did; she savored it until she heard her name.

"It was nice to meet you." Amit, saying good-bye to her. "Enjoy your days off," he added to Naveen.

"Take care," Bijou replied. When Amit had returned to his table, she looked back at Naveen. "That must be nice—having a little fan club of students."

Naveen laughed loudly and drily. "I'm sorry for the interruption."

"Is there a holiday right now? Like spring break or something?"

"What's that?"

"He told you to enjoy your days off."

"Oh, that. You must have missed the rest," Naveen said. "I could tell you had tuned us out. Enjoying your cold coffee?"

She smiled. "It's so good."

"Excellent." He seemed to be swallowing a laugh. "Well now, are you through looking at the album?"

She shrugged, busying herself with her straw.

"Don't you have any questions?"

She looked at him directly then. "No."

"I'd be happy to lend you some books. We could discuss—"

"No. Thank you, really."

Amit, for the benefit of his friends, was drawing a large square in the air, as though a window. He said something, and the rest of them laughed. It seemed youthful and timeless, his presence. He glanced in Bijou's direction and held his smile, nodding at her before returning to his story.

"I'm sure you're a great teacher," Bijou said. "But I'd rather not pursue this."

"Why not? You should know these things. It's in the blood."

"I'm so tired of blood, and what's in it, what's not," she said quickly, "what makes us do what we do, live this way, die that way. Why can't blood just be blood? Why should everything be so *symbolic*? I'm tired of thinking that way."

"If you look that closely, you'll learn nothing. Seriously, you're not in the least bit curious?"

"Of course I am! But part of me can't stand it—can't stand hearing about this from anyone but my father. I want *him* to tell me."

Naveen's features began to cloud up before her. She hid her eyes behind her napkin. Suddenly the dregs of her iced coffee smelled like warm milk, like butter, and a mild wave of nausea swelled in her throat.

"It's still new," he said quietly. "Your mother told us you were having a hard time, with the rituals and all. I don't know why they put you through that. People get scared; they default to the old ways."

"It's not fair," she said. "And it really leaves me in no mood for these history lessons."

"You'll find out sooner or later. You have a right to the whole story." He ran his hands through his hair and sighed. "In time, Bijou. Your father would have told you eventually."

"But that's just it, that's the hardest thing," she said. "Knowing that."

He looked at his watch. "Let me take you home, you must be exhausted." He stood up then, left some money on the table, and added: "The album is yours for as long as you need. Choose some pictures to keep, if you like."

He reached for her elbow, and she let him guide her outside, let him keep his arm around her until they reached the car.

Six

CALCUTTA, 1967

Nitish, nineteen years old, is going through the motions of being a chemistry major at Presidency. He'd rather spend his time playing basketball, reading literary journals, and composing dramatic skits in his notebook. He is a decent student, but restless, never knows what to do with his hands when he's talking or reading. In certain lighting, his gesticulations stage their own quiet shadow plays on nearby walls. He smokes heavily. He has developed a very polite way of spitting off specks of tobacco from his lip.

He spends much of his time with his college mate Ashok, older than him by almost three years, a physics scholar. There is something compelling about Ashok—his acumen and confidence feed his charisma; he treads campus as though it is a theater for his perpetual soliloquy—and Nitish looks up to him, sees in Ashok a character he aspires not to become, for they are already similar enough, but a character he wishes to remain. After a few exchanges, the two young men are inseparable. They attract a following. During any group session of *adda*-style philosophizing, they emerge as the most eloquent debaters. Their *addas*, as essential to the culture as symposia were to the Greeks, are great forums for political debate (although, unlike Plato's circle, they forgo wine for tea and coffee, or occasional whiskies on the rocks).

Ashok is known for being the more reflective orator. He listens more than he speaks, and sits very still. Nitish, on the other hand, bounces his legs madly under the table, laughs like a boy still. When any newcomer wishes to join the group, he (or, less often, she) approaches Nitish first. Years of feeling lost and vexed among his own family have bestowed Nitish with a particularly well-primed personality for friendship. He needs his friends for the consensus they provide: that he has a place in the world.

One of their friends, Kamla, a classmate of Nitish's, has recently moved to Calcutta after her parents' deaths in a bus accident; now she lives with her paternal uncle's family. Kamla has a sharp tongue with men. She has no female friends. Her desire to become a doctor is driven by a desire to treat causes, not symptoms. But she will go to medical college only after she has finished a degree in economics; that is her way.

Ashok recognizes himself in what she says. He grows smitten with her. They marry.

Nitish is ever the self-sworn bachelor, but he is happy for his friends. Kamla is attractive, in a turbulent and unromantic way, a very *frank* girl. Nitish welcomes her into what had thus been a world occupied by only him and Ashok. They have shared interests now. Ashok is in the middle with arms outstretched, his closest friends on either side.

Among them, during breaks between classes and cricket, coffee-house conversation does not embrace banter about holiday plans in tourist hill stations, nor do they dissect the success of the latest crooner at the clubs on Park Street. This is not the gang who dresses to the teeth for a discotheque evening on Chowringhee, bubbly conversation with film stars or flatulent art and lit critics. They do not frequent Mocambo or Trincas, where the roster of entertainment is spiked with Continental dancers and clairvoyants, where the band continues to mindfully measure out a music that the Westerners had left in their wake two decades earlier.

Nitish, Ashok, and Kamla are uninterested in such bogus goings-on, as are their friends. Nothing can come between them. From a distant perspective, the picture is one of solidarity. It is only when one zooms in, to the very grain of the image, that things begin to appear fragmented. They appear this way because they *are* this way, but it is that particular strain of truth that can be brought to light only over time.

The way things are is this: Nehru is three years dead and his daughter has stepped out of grief and shadows and into power. East Pakistan is tearing at its seams, divisively sewn to begin with. Elections are jokes, rigged and stuffed, bloc votes bribed out of the villages in exchange for milk and clothing. Unemployment is getting worse—what is the use of university, these students wonder aloud, if on the other side of it you find yourself without a rich father's connections and consequently without a job? One cannot procure a degree in nepotism, now, can one?

Young men like Nitish and Ashok seethe to think that on top of everything else, their homeland will yet be sucked dry by foreign leeches. They think of Bhupendra Nath Datta, Abinash Bhattacharya, Khudiram Bose, Arabinda Ghosh—the list is impossible to dismiss. Bengal itself has a long line of martyrs. Historians cripple them by calling them *terrorists*. Weren't they essential? Brave men, the stuff of sovereigns. Where are they today in 1968?

Revolt brews in a series of rhetorical questions. Ashok and Nitish are not the only ones who rise.

Naxalbari is the district that connects the northern territories to the rest of the state of Bengal. There, toward the end of May, a policeman is killed in a peasant clash. Shortly thereafter, the police avenge themselves by sending forces into a Naxalbari village.

They open fire. They kill just under a dozen people, including women, including children.

This is it: the spark. When the news reaches Calcutta, it carries a message that runs like electricity through Nitish and Ashok, among others. Together, they perceive it as an omen. A green light.

The name "Naxalbari" shifts meaning and shape, finds itself rooted—from now on—in Naxalite.

Late in that year, sixty-eight, Ashok is arrested on the grounds of his connections with certain lawless people in Naxalbari. His apartment is raided; myriad copies of *Commune, Bidroha,* and other underground party journals are seized as evidence of his ongoing conspiracy. The police drag Ashok from his home, and Kamla is in no state to manage affairs with her characteristic grit. That night, Nitish has to take her to the hospital. She gives birth at dawn to a boy. Nitish suggests a name for the child: Naveen. He brings her a book of poems by Kazi Nazrul Islam to read while she rests. They read it together. She puts notes in the margins.

In *The Statesman* only days later, there is a photograph of Nitish protesting at the prison gate, his arms raised, his fists a blur of movement. He is cited in the caption below the picture as a proponent of violent revolution, a "sycophant" of the Naxalite leader Charu Mazumdar. For months, Nitish has been proving himself to be just that: he has been more than willing to integrate himself with the workers and the peasants, carrying on work in the country. He hardly lives in Calcutta anymore. With Ashok and Kamla, he has dwelled in villages and rural areas, educating even the reticent and skeptical workers, convincing them with his zeal that his zeal is only appropriate in the context of the revolution— achievable, at last—under way.

In early 1969, along with scores of men who had been incarcerated for two years now, Ashok is released. His son is hardly three months old, but Kamla goes. The baby goes. The cohort treks out of the city toward Darjeeling for what will be the last time.

It becomes apparent, during this trip, on a stop near Malda, that Ashok's imprisonment has changed him. He tells Nitish that they will be better off if they just leave village mobilizing to the others. Instead, let them take their skills back to Calcutta for good. He has been discussing these plans with others in their group, and they agree. He convinces Nitish that this is how they will best forward the agrarian struggle: from the city.

The rest of the week is a blur; Nitish will wonder why Ashok had not asked him his opinion on the matter. And why had he been so swift to agree?

On their way back to Calcutta, Ashok confides in his friend his hopes that, if nothing else, returning to the city will keep Kamla and the baby out of the way. She will stay home with the child happily, he suspects. Maybe she would even go stay long-term with her distant relatives in Punjab.

Again, Ashok applauds Nitish for not marrying. Having a woman compromises a man, he tells him; he feels obligated to live less impulsively, and resents it full-scale. Granted, Kamla is not any woman. She is his wife. At the same time, in the dark quiet after midnight, she has been asking him what will happen to their son if they continue to live this way. He knows they are not hypothetical questions. She has softened since the birth of that child, too content now to hide behind her camera or ask for their journeys away from home to be cut short.

Nitish is the wise one, Ashok contends, for remaining unfettered.

By the end of April, Lenin's birthday, the official formation of a new Communist party, the CPI (Marxist-Leninist), is announced.

On the first day of May, the party stages a rally by the Ochterlony Monument. Nitish and Ashok are there among the masses; Kamla is not. So she does not hear what the men hear, which is the call to carry forward the budding Indian revolution, to continue spreading the fire of the people's war against the hoax of parliamentary democracy.

"By the year 2000," a leader proclaims, "that is, only thirty-one years from now, the people of the whole world will be liberated from all kinds of exploitation of man by man and will celebrate the worldwide victory of Marxism, Leninism, Mao Tse-Tung's thought."

Old notions of ahimsa and peaceful demonstrations no longer serve. The revolution will require tremendous discipline.

Within a year, activities in the city have turned ruthless at best, far from the public burning of mortgage deeds and promissory notes in village squares, or the looting of rice and paddy. Portraits of Richard Nixon and Indira Gandhi are set afire in the streets. Ornaments of those streets, statues of the old heroes, are disfigured or hammered to dust.

Seven cinema halls in the city are mined with bombs that simultaneously detonate.

And there is terrorism more methodical, achieved by shooting, stabbing, blows of fists.

Nitish and Ashok are involved; if they do not actually deliver death to their targets, they are still complicit, toeing the party line. Like most, the two are part of a greater ring. The ring takes orders trickling down from elsewhere. In the idle periods between defined orders, the boys improvise activity, as though expanding the range of their hazing—their ragging, as they called it—of woebegone first-year students at the college to include virtually everyone.

Curfew is imposed by the Calcutta police. The city dreads nightfall, what these gangs of vigilante-type boys will design next. See how they carry posters of Mao in the streets, the walls of which already scream in graffiti CHINA'S CHAIRMAN IS OUR CHAIRMAN. See them on street corners, watching, even in broad daylight. As if immune to fear. Their weapons are not always concealed.

They are easily provoked. It is as if they are possessed by demons, ghosts.

One night, a university professor is murdered. His charred body is found in his own automobile, the windshield shattered. Molten to the seats like blisters are the scorched remains of books and flesh, a pair of deformed eyeglasses, exams that will never be graded. Ashok had once been the professor's protégé.

The police are tipped off; they go hunting for more. When they come to Ashok's house, they find only Nitish. They arrest him immediately; he goes. He is interrogated, in jail, by a commissioner notorious for his ability to extract information from his prisoners. But Nitish lies, gives information that will buy him time.

The Statesman runs Nitish's photo again—this one shot with the prison gate behind him, his face bruised—along with the shot of him protesting a year earlier; the two grainy images, side by side, make a good story.

He is released after less than a week in jail. Someone, anonymously, has posted his bail.

"Do you know who it was?" Nitish asks Ashok, when they meet again.

"Why would I know?" Ashok says. "How would I know more than you? We get our information from the same place, you and I."

Nitish reflects on this, then asks if Ashok had raised the bail.

Ashok shakes his head. "Where would I get it? Forget all this now. You're out of there, that's the best news of all."

"True," says Nitish. He is exhausted and in considerable pain from his prison stay. But he is equally restless and twitchy. He asks Ashok what their plans are, what is scheduled next.

"Absolutely nothing," Ashok says. "You will keep a low profile."

"That I won't be able to do," Nitish says. "Be serious."

Ashok insists that they focus on organizing their party rather than fostering what is increasingly arbitrary mayhem in the streets. He doesn't want the death toll on his shoulders. The camps on the battleground are becoming harder and harder to control—even certain Naxalite factions are turning on their own.

"I do not want an idle job," Nitish argues. "My work is with the people."

Kamla wants nothing to do with any of it. She, too, pleads with Nitish to restrain himself. She is sitting on the floor next to her son, patting his back gently. The boy sleeps on a thick blanket.

"What sort of example are you men setting?" Kamla asks.

Nitish knows that he has been asked to answer her with an action, not an explanation.

He yields.

But come July, floods are ravaging East Bengal, and refugees are pouring into the city from there. With the flooding arrives famine, and typhoid, and cholera.

Nitish runs out of patience. They are needed now more than ever.

Ashok agrees. Kamla still does not. Husband and wife argue, and once the fighting starts, it spirals until they are no longer laughing or sleeping or parenting or eating together, just living in attrition.

"Why should you care if I'm home or not?" Ashok says to her one evening, in Nitish's presence. "I'll do what I do—or am I your prisoner?"

"You've gone crazy," Kamla says. "Nitish, talk sense into him.

He has no shame. All I ask him is to think of his son, and he acts like he doesn't know what I'm talking about. Ask him. Does he remember who he married? How he begged her to marry him? Wasn't I better off before I ever met you people? I've sacrificed enough."

"Kamla, don't worry," Nitish says to her quietly. "It won't be like this always."

When he appeals to Ashok to be more considerate, however, he is met with obstinate resistance.

"You don't know what this is like," Ashok says.

Nitish lets the matter drop. It unstrings Nitish, spending time with them. He does not pride himself on being a mediator at such a domestic level. He cuts his visits back by half.

By September, when others in the city are planning for Durga Puja, Ashok and Nitish have been working every night with their comrades, sometimes all night, debating their movement, recrafting their plans. Kamla has washed her hands of all of it by now: the politics for certain; her husband, by extension. Ashok spends most nights on a makeshift berth in Nitish's flat. He says it's because the flat is in a more convenient location than his. The small, run-down flat is inhabited by two other men from their school, brothers named Sanjoy and Debashish Sen.

Ashok disappears some afternoons to go home. But he never stays long.

One day, he returns to Nitish's flat looking exceptionally crushed. Nitish assumes the worst: that Kamla has thrown him out for good.

"Now what? You married her; stop acting like a fool," he tells Ashok.

"You don't understand," Ashok says bitterly.

"Then make me understand."

"It's not about her. That's all I can say."

Nitish shrugs.

For days, they do not speak to each other of personal matters. When they are apart, Nitish assumes his friend has gone home, and perhaps things with Kamla are being patched up. Perhaps not. Why should he care, really?

Other than this, it is business as usual. The agenda now is largely devoted to the subject of guerrilla training. Despite difficulties in South India—seizure and confiscation of weapons, untimely deaths of leaders among their Andhra comrades—the agrarian revolution is still spreading. Peasant and youth activists keep the struggle alive yet, dodging police captivity by living in forests and among villagers. Gold and property mortgaged to despotic landlords is returned to its so-called rightful owners.

And then, things begin to fracture. Nitish is on his way home after a meeting one evening when he decides to stop by Ashok's house, to solicit his opinion on a few questions of travel. Inside the house, it is eerily quiet, and his first thought is that the couple must be in the bedroom, reconciled. But he hears low talking in the kitchen and finds them there: Kamla bandaging Ashok's wrist with gauze, a bowl on the counter soaking towels in a pinkish bath. From the two of them, he hears the story of an explosion, four of their friends, a bomb Ashok had seen them assembling. They'd had an argument because he'd called them novices, and the most insolent of them, the son of that wealthy bastard, had suggested that Ashok make himself useful by checking outside to make sure there were no potential witnesses. He'd gone outside; he'd had enough of their attitude.

"It could have easily been me," he tells Nitish.

"But it wasn't."

"One of these days, it will be both of you," Kamla says. Her voice is dry and heavy; she has clearly been crying. "Impossible. You men with your impulses and idiot temperaments. Nothing good will come of this, ever. You act like you are playing some game. You've all lost sight of the goal. You lack all discipline."

"It's a warning," Ashok says. "Someone may have seen me. I was thrown, and I couldn't move. The whole shop fell apart in blue flames, caved in, burned like a pyre, but the roof flew up like a grotesque kite, then came raining down in the middle of the street. All ashes. All four of them. I would have been the fifth."

"But I saw them all this morning," Nitish manages to say.

"You'll stay with us for a few days, do you understand? I won't let you out of my sight. There is bound to be an investigation, retaliation. We must disappear."

"What makes you think they won't come here?"

"This is what I said," Kamla mutters. She lifts the bowl and empties the water into the sink, then wrings the towels. A moment later, having snapped a towel open and seen its stains, she throws them all into the rubbish container. "I have to feed Naveen." She leaves.

Nitish stays with them for a week. He watches the two of them avoid each other, and marvels at the skill of one being at once totally aware of yet seemingly unaware of the other in the room. He watches them tend to the baby. At first, they ask him for help with the boy; after a few days, he offers it—he likes the way the boy tugs at his ears and sleeps in his arms.

"Your father says we're fighting for you," he tells the boy. "Remind him that if he ever bothers you. Tell him you have my backing."

Early in the last morning he will awake in their home, he walks from the sitting room, where he has been sleeping, past the bedroom. There, he sees Kamla sitting on the bed, the boy at her breast.

She is gazing at Ashok, who is standing at the window with one elbow propped against it, his arm bent, hand gripping the crown of his head. The light through the window is filtered by the orange curtain that Ashok is half-hiding from the world behind. For a moment, the scene seems almost painted, and almost peaceful.

Ashok turns around, greets Nitish gruffly, then leaves the room. Kamla watches him walk out, then looks at Nitish blankly as she puts the baby to her shoulder,

"Let me," he says, going to her and taking the boy. He pats his back.

"He hardly ate," Kamla says. "You can put him in the bassinet."

So he does. She comes over to make sure the boy is lying properly on his back, and they stand with their arms touching. When she leans over to adjust the baby's tiny *shameez* undershirt, Nitish puts his hand on her back without thinking, and he keeps it there as she turns back to him, as he pulls her to him, as she presses her cheek to his chest and clutches his shirt near the collar. Her body smells of roses and her hair like baby powder, and all Nitish knows is that he has yet to know a woman. She is soft in his arms, and he kisses the crown of her head once, then again, his hands feeling the curvature of her waist.

Suddenly, she tells him to go. So he does. In the other room, he throws his clothes into his knapsack. From the table, he picks up the Nazrul book. He flips through the pages, reading Kamla's notes in the margins. Then he picks up a pen, and leaves a trail of inky words for her, his own words.

Most are of love.

But he goes.

On the night of Bijoya Dashami—the tenth and final day of a Durga Puja that neither Ashok nor Nitish have been observing—

there is a mood of defeat and melancholy in the air; ponds and rivers swell with ornate idols of the city's patron goddess. It's over.

Ashok has had a severe argument, he tells Nitish, but not with Kamla.

They are sitting on the dug-out steps in front of Nitish's flat. It has been two weeks since they've last seen each other, and the separation was characterized by the strange sensation that it would be endless. It hadn't been like that even when Ashok was in jail.

Nitish kicks away a container for *sindhoor* that has been discarded in the street, and a bit of remaining vermilion powder dusts his toes. No one is out in this part of the neighborhood tonight, and he enjoys the fresher air. It is oddly cool, and he keeps a narrowly folded shawl over one of his shoulders.

Ashok is in a sour mood. He has been going on about Kamla, but Nitish is only half-listening. He can hear a steady buzzing in the distance, and wonders what it is until the conversation turns to his father. Apparently Ashok has seen him.

"Where?" Nitish asks. He has not seen his father in two years.

"He came to see me. At my home." He goes on to confess it hasn't been the first time. In fact, Ashok had met him once before, not long after the occasion of Nitish's arrest. "It is your father who posted your bail."

Nitish doesn't believe him. "He would rather ensure I was beaten to death in that prison."

Perhaps that's true, Ashok concedes. He'd been clear about his motives: not to protect his bastard son so much as the good name of his family. He'd burned the newspapers in which Nitish had appeared. And now he had a proposition for Ashok. Did Nitish want to hear it? Did he want to know? It was bribery. A large sum of money for Ashok if he put an end to Nitish's transgressions.

Nitish rises to his feet and is about to put several words to his anger when he hears the buzzing noise grow closer and closer. Out of the darkness comes a jeep; one of its wheels thunks against a pothole as it passes, and Nitish is relieved to learn that the noise had come from an innocuous motor. He sits down again, and says bitterly, "I trust you told him his tactics were grossly irrelevant."

"You don't understand anything!" Ashok's voice is no longer frayed but suddenly ripped to shreds. "He means to harm my family. He will not stop with me. Can you live with that? He will spare you, so that you will always suffer the loss."

Nitish listens, speechless. *So it has come to this,* is all he can think.

"You must leave," Ashok says. He stands up, and Nitish wonders if he means for him to leave right now. "You must go far from here, where he cannot reach you."

"How dare you sink to his level? How dare you betray me?"

"There's a bag inside, under your bed. Enough money to assist you. *Chol.* Let's go." He grabs Nitish's shawl and throws it over his own shoulder. He holds out his hand, beckoning with curt motions of his fingers for Nitish to rise. "I'm taking them to Kamla's cousin's place in Ludhiana tomorrow. You could, if you wanted, come with us. But then move on."

Nitish does not move. He is vaguely aware of noise in the distance like the jeep returning, but he's too preoccupied to mention it.

"*You accepted money from him? Ashok, why?*"

"It's rightfully yours. I only reclaimed it for you. Get up now!"

"At what cost?" He shouts this, mainly because he is in the mood to shout, but also because the same jeep as before is charging down the street.

In the moment he begins to tell Ashok that they should go

inside, gunshots are fired. Ashok falls upon Nitish, who sees blood spreading through the back of his friend's kurta in spiderlike shapes.

The jeep has vanished. The door to the flat is yanked open. Sanjoy stands there.

By the time Kamla is notified that her husband has been shot, Nitish is hours away from Calcutta, on a night train that will take him to Delhi, and beyond. Under his seat is a bag, a dusty brown knapsack full of bricks: rupees bound together like ransom money or a bribe. He doesn't stop to ask himself, *Why? Why run away?* It overcomes him like rain: he must run away from it all, now or never. Now or never.

In later years, he will realize why, and tell no one. And he will know, too, deep in his fearful heart, that one day, he would most certainly die of the shame.

Paris.

Why has he come here? A friend of Sanjoy's has assured Nitish it is the best escape. He sends him with the address of a few contacts. Over the next few days, these nominally like-minded people help Nitish at every turn. Of these assistants, the one who helps primarily is an Algerian named Mehdi. It is Mehdi who finds a place for Nitish to rest in: a small boardinghouse in Montparnasse where a handful of international students have set up camp; Mehdi is pleased to report that there are other Indians already there.

As it happens, Nitish ends up sharing a room with one of those Indians, a young man from Kashmir named Padam, who is in Paris on a scholarship.

The next day, Sunday, Padam invites Nitish out for dinner with him and his sister Sheela, who has just arrived from Srinagar for a holiday.

"She's very smart," Padam tells him. "Very fickle and, you know, somewhat opinionated at times, but otherwise lovely. We are simple people."

Sheela has planned to stay with her brother for ten days. She talks endlessly. About leaving Paris with her brother, for Padam is to be married in Kashmir before moving to America. This was the last opportunity she had for visiting him in Paris, and she is excited to have finally left India. Though she has no complaints about life there, she finds herself habitually envisioning other places, especially since her elder brother left. Most of her girlfriends are married now, and soon it will be her turn, but she has been disappointed with the offers thus far: all Kashmiri boys who are too familiar, too short, too thin, too complacent, too none of the above, too all of the above. The boys whom she, her friends, even her younger sister have centered their schoolgirl crushes on—if only from afar, never in a way that *meant* anything—have all been Muslim, and therefore out of the question.

She is the first one to make Nitish laugh since he has left home. He immediately associates her with comfort. They take to wandering together through museums and bookstores during the day, while Padam works.

All Nitish talks about is how he must get back to Calcutta soon. He feels stranded. Moreover, he resents the amount of time he has available to reflect upon feeling stranded.

"You haven't been here very long, but you talk about going back so soon," Sheela says. "I find it strange."

He lies, using lack of money as his excuse. "I cannot afford the fare just now."

The next day, Sheela tells him she will help. She and Padam will give him money, if that's what he needs. It will be a loan, of course, it can only be a loan. Her family does not have enough to spare, and what she can lend him is what she has left from her own tuition wages, almost all of which she used to take this trip in the first place.

"Why are you being so generous?" Nitish asks. "You don't know me."

"I know enough," she replies. "Don't expect a better answer than that."

"I don't need the money, Sheela. Please, Sheela, I would never take your money!"

"Because I'm a woman?"

"Because I would never take anyone's money."

"Then you are lying. You must not want to go back to India. You'll be just another wonderful boy who runs away to America, London, or Canada."

The day before she leaves Paris, over white cups of hot tea at a café on boulevard Saint-Michel, he tells her everything. Why he left Calcutta, about his friendship with Ashok, his ties with the Naxalites, his alienation from his family, and a woman named Kamla for whom he has (he says upon query from Sheela) a fraternal regard. But he has blood on his hands. His friend has died because of him. Murdered by someone who most likely had designs to finish Nitish, he knows. His life should have ended that night, and in many ways it has. But it is Nitish who sits here, alive, and Ashok who has left behind a wife and son who can never recover from their loss. A wife, but his friend, too. A son whom Nitish should have stayed back to guard. Instead, he ran.

Rain has been drizzling from the sky all day, and the dampness in their bones has put each in a sort of stupor from which nothing can rescue them—very different from the days before, when they seemed virtually intoxicated by each other.

"Nitish," she says, "all that is behind you now, isn't it?"

"I don't know," he says.

"We can put it behind us, though?"

By this point, he and Sheela acknowledge themselves as a couple; the topics of love and marriage have been more than broached. Mostly by Sheela, who wants to marry before she turns twenty-one, which gives her less than a year. Though Nitish is not much older, and perhaps too young for marriage, she had decided that it is actually more sensible to marry someone closer in age. She has not told her family about it, not yet. Only Padam knows, and he approves. The rest, she believes, will fall into place when it comes time. Nitish has held her by the hand, in his arms, and she has found an ability to believe in their future together, there. They want each other, and nothing else will do.

She looks away from Nitish. She sees a woman in a navy blue blouse, with hair as white as diamonds, sitting alone at a nearby table. The woman has her eyebrows raised and is nodding a little as she stares into her coffee cup, as though someone is inside it, speaking to her.

"You have to make choices in life," Sheela says.

"And I'm telling you," Nitish says, "I feel suddenly as though I am incapable of making decisions. It is as if part of me has died."

The old woman is sipping from her cup now, and her eyes are closed.

"We are too young," Sheela says, turning back to Nitish for a moment, "to be stopped now."

"Listen to me." He frowns. "Ashok left something with me. About his wife. I don't know what to do about it."

He draws out an envelope from his brown knapsack, the one he carries with him constantly. "It's in Bengali," he says, "or else I would let you read it."

"So explain it to me," she says flippantly, gazing at the woman at the other table with more scrutiny now. She tells Nitish in a sidebar that were that woman in different attire, she easily could be mistaken for Kashmiri. She already looks remarkably familiar. "Translate it, if you must, but I'd rather hear a summary."

"It was taken for granted," Nitish says after a while, "that I would marry Kamla if anything ever happened to Ashok. And take care of their son—"

"What nonsense," Sheela interjects. "This is the insanity with men, never asking the woman's opinion. Would she want you? Especially knowing if we—if your heart was elsewhere? Never."

"I don't know," he says. "I've lost my senses. I don't sleep; I can't think."

"You said it was dangerous for you there," she says. "The decision has been made for you, it seems."

He doesn't say anything. She feels they are talking in circles.

"Nothing is accidental, Nitish," she says. "What we do next is already written for us: whether or not I can convince you is written, whether or not you agree is written. Do what you feel is best."

Nitish stares out the window. He finishes his tea.

"I will never want anyone else," she cries out abruptly.

He won't go.

Later, as they rise from their chairs, he looks to the other table, and the woman there, her eyes a blue lighter than her blouse, her lips puckered at the edges from age, smiles.

"We understand each other," Sheela tells him on their way out, "don't we?"

She slips her arm around one of his, leaves it there as they half-run, half-walk to a restaurant around the corner.

They devour dinner, wiping up the last drops of béarnaise sauce with torn bread. Between them, they drink a carafe of wine.

When dinner is done, Sheela insists they have sherry. She

drinks it with appreciative sips, finishes it, and says, "I've been thinking, Nitish. About Kamla. You shouldn't lose touch with her. For the baby's sake. If I were in her place, I think I would be crazy by now. Why don't you write to her? You can explain. She must be in a terrible state. Haven't you imagined it? It makes me feel so sick, actually."

"I will write," he says. "Soon."

But two weeks later, they are still living in the same Montparnasse boardinghouse, and he has yet to post any mail.

"Look at it this way," Sheela says. "You escaped just in time."

"I have to go back there." He is turning a record around in his hands, something a housemate has left on a couch. Through the wall of his bedroom, he's heard the housemate play the record, and the woman singing—Billie Holiday, such a beautiful name, soft—seems to empathize with Nitish. He wants to hear her clearly, to listen to the words, to see if what he suspects is true. "I could never live anywhere else."

"You *will* go back. We'll go together."

Padam is on his way to the States now. He has written to them. An invitation. It will be easy to find a job for Nitish, things are taken care of in terms of immigration—it's a good time for them to come to America; the doors are open, they're begging. So, together, they go.

SEVEN

The morning following dinner at the Mazumdars, after a quick shower—witnessed by two little lizards who stuck to the ceiling of the bathroom and made her uneasy at best—Bijou rummaged through her suitcase for ibuprofen. Her head was aching again, and here was a fine excuse for spending the day in her bedroom, locked out of Calcutta. Why not, she thought, get used to this? Lethargy was not such a terrible companion; what it lacked in glamour and wit, it made up for with a total lack of demands.

Her mother called around lunchtime to inform her that she and Pari would be returning on the following Saturday. They were having a peaceful time, she reported. When Bijou asked to speak with Pari, her mother told her that Pari had found some friends—German girls who were visiting the ashram with their grandmother—and they were all out shopping.

"And what are you doing?" Bijou asked.

"I'm meditating, *beta*. I'm taking long walks, and I am praying. There is a guru here whom you would like. She's very modern, not one of those, you know, hard types."

"You're not joining some cult, are you?"

"People have come here from all over the world, Bijoya."

"Germany is not all over the world. Be careful."

"A little spirituality would do you a lot of good. Science is not a faith."

"Who said I had faith in science?"

"Don't be so headstrong, just like your father. What is the harm in prayer? You must be more humble. I wish I had known this at your age. It's too late for me, but you can still change your destiny."

"Oh, I changed my ticket! I'm leaving the Monday after next."

"You're sure it's what you want to do?"

"I couldn't get anything else. I'll come home next month, I promise. If you want, I'll even drive us to Chicago."

"Whatever's convenient."

In response to this, Bijou fished for a new topic. "We went to Kamla Auntie's house last night."

"Oh?"

"*Oh* what?"

"They came by the house last week. You could have met them then if you hadn't been so moody."

"Well, I met them anyway. Why do you make it sound like I do everything wrong? Naveen showed me some photographs from when Dad was doing that Naxalite work. They're interesting. I found them very interesting. Is that okay?"

"You don't have to talk about all that. Someone might hear you."

Bijou paused. "And then what?"

"Bijoya, those people are controversial. Don't play with fire. Since when are you interested in politics?"

"I'm talking about *photographs.*"

"You have no way of understanding; those Naxals were danger—" The phone was muffled as her mother seemed to bury it in her neck. Then she was back, saying, "We have to go. Pari wants to go to a temple. Okay, so don't be difficult for your *massi;* she may have other plans than taking you to dinners and things with your friends."

"*My* friends?" Bijou said, but her mother had hung up already.

In the bedroom, the curtain fluttered at the window. She picked up her Walkman from the bureau, slipped on her headphones, and went to the window, her clothes (Pari's gray dress, left behind; jeans; a white chiffon scarf of her aunt's because there had been some awkward discussion about modesty and breasts) billowing out around her under the ceiling fan. It was like moving through water. At least her skin was clearing, however, she noted, and though she perpetually smelled of mosquito repellant, she no longer felt like such a leper. She stood by the window, holding the curtain to the side. Billie sang, *He's sweeter than chocolate candy to me / He's confectionary.*

Before going to bed the night before, she'd looked again through the photo album Naveen had lent her and chosen three photographs of her father to keep. She'd tucked them in her backpack and planned to show them to Pari later, alone. While her mother found most material souvenirs of Bijou's father too painful to cope with, Bijou was drawn to them like a moth to flame. For a substantial part of her life, she'd kept his studio in the basement neat and organized, his ceramics tools and power tools on the proper shelves, his nails, paint buckets, socket wrenches, and saws in order, his golf clubs dust-free. More curator than daughter, perhaps, but it had kept her going, that basement; it had taught her a lot about her father's habits, which she was quick to acquire herself, and measure against the softer profile of her mother's kitchen gardens and hand-sewn linens.

"It is lucky you are like him," her mother had said time and time again at the hospital. Once she began to relish Bijou as a mature listener, she elaborated: "What I have with him, it's between husbands and wives. It is love, but isn't that mostly physical? Which is not everything, and you find ways to work out the rest so you don't kill each other. But you girls are lucky; you have the bond of blood. It is hard to be the wife. And be outside of that bond."

Since his death, that tune had changed. At Christmas, when Bijou had gone home for a few days, they'd had one of their signature moments of dim friction. The mix of sadness and bitterness that marked them during the holidays lent to those moments so easily. How had it even started? Her mother going on and on about something Bijou didn't want to hear. She remembered asking her mother, then, why she insisted on speaking in Bengali all the time.

For a moment, she had looked at Bijou as if she wondered who this girl was, and why she was speaking to her with such intimacy.

"I mean, it's not your first language," Bijou had continued. "It's not even your second."

"How could I speak to you in Kashmiri? You don't know a word of it."

"You never taught us."

"I don't know, Bijou, if you would understand me in any language."

"It's just odd, that's all. You're not Bengali."

"Neither are you."

Bijou had laughed. "I think I am! It's in my blood."

From her mother came a shake of the head and sighs. "One day, you will have a daughter, and when she asks you why you speak English, don't come apologize to me."

Bijou sighed now, to think of her mother with Pari and the German girls. Was this how they were going to live? As though fasting? Like ascetics. *Sanyasinis.* Sandra Dees. This was the long road ahead of them. Those years spent at the hospital, as caretakers, company, had held a sense of purpose. Now it felt as if they had been forced into retirement. There was no way back, and perhaps there was only one way forward; they just had to call their way by a name like happiness, and maybe it would be. Perhaps Crane had been right. Perhaps the thing to do was, in his words, get over it.

But what had Naveen said about people getting scared? She tried to recall it. Something about old ways. She pictured him sitting across from her at the coffeehouse, next to her in his car. He was not unattractive, in his towering, stubbled way, she conceded.

Bijou's aunt had been dropping insinuations, light though by no means subtle remarks about how things would be pleasant at last once the girls got married, wondering aloud what the family might do to facilitate such an occasion for Bijou, who would—naturally—have to go first. Just this morning at breakfast, her aunt had abruptly said to her, with the sort of breathless excitement a child would express over Halloween, "Let us find you a good Indian boy, Bijou. It's no good marrying late."

"Girls don't have to get married just because they're in their twenties. We're coming up on the twenty-first century, Anuja Massi."

"But grandchildren would give us reason to live. Is there *no one* you've met already, who you have liked? You're smart, you're so nice; surely boys have been interested?"

"My mother wants me to focus on my career first."

"Your mother? Who ran away with your father when she was all but a teenager still?"

Bijou smiled. "I think that's kind of the point."

Her aunt scowled. "Well, I think you can have both. Have your career-fareer, fine, and let us help you with the rest. What about Naveen?"

"Naveen?" she repeated in astonishment.

"Why not? He's available. Smart. Indian. Good-looking. We know the family. Why not?"

"I think I'd better have my bath. I have a bit of a headache," she replied, and insinuated that it was That Time of the Month, even though it wasn't. Her aunt let her go, sympathetically.

Now, turning away from the window, Bijou saw Ketaki peering out into the room from the doorway. She pulled off her headphones.

"Oh, *tumi ekhane?*" Ketaki called out. *You're here?*

Ketaki held out her hand as though stopping traffic, nodded her head, then disappeared. Frowning, Bijou began to walk to the door, thinking perhaps Ketaki was going to bring her a cup of tea, in which case she would save her the trip. She heard Ketaki from the stairwell saying, "Didi is in her room, she likes it there very much," and smiled to hear in the girl's voice a sense of possessiveness. *I know Bijoya Roy,* she might have been saying, *better than anyone else in the world knows her.*

Bijou heard a man respond in Bengali, and she stopped moving. Her aunt hadn't said anything about visitors, much less about the Mazumdars coming over; it was Naveen speaking. She felt her body responding with uncalled-for energy, a surge she recognized as that which accompanied the unexpected appearance of certain men, wherein her senses were at once supernaturally heightened and useless.

Naveen came into view, and he greeted her. "I hope I'm not disturbing you by stopping by."

"I'm not doing anything." She shifted her Walkman from one hand to the other.

"Are you feeling better? My mother wanted to come," he said, "but she was called on an emergency earlier. I'm glad, in a way, that she had to work. I think seeing you last night—I think it brought up things she hadn't thought of for a long time. You weren't well either, and I feel responsible, in some way."

"Oh, I'm fine," she said. "Thank you. Really, that's very thoughtful. Just a headache. Is your mother okay, though?"

"She says she's fine, too," he said. "But I know her." He looked around the room. He didn't seem at all uncomfortable. "I suspect you're similar, though. Independent. Efficient. Strong."

She felt suddenly self-conscious. "I can't tell if you're comparing us to men or to machines."

"Only to each other." He smiled and asked what she was listening to, and she told him. "Really? Billie Holiday? I have a good friend who's a big fan of her work. I don't understand it very well, but jazz was all he let us listen to in his flat. Perhaps you should meet him."

She looked at him in a way that must have conveyed her misgivings about any such rendezvous, for he proceeded to tell her that his friend lived in Glasgow these days, at any rate.

"Have you thought of anything you'd like to see yet? I'll be collecting my mother from the hospital in a little while, but I would be happy to take you for a drive."

She didn't say anything, trying to think of a polite way to decline his offer.

"The Maidan," he said. "We could go for a walk. Have you been?"

"I'm sure we drove past it."

"Well, it's essentially your backyard."

"Don't you have to work?"

"Do you ever just agree?"

As they walked along Shakespeare Sarani Road (formerly named and better known as Theatre Road, Naveen informed her), Bijou wondered if her father had ever missed Calcutta. She'd taken it for granted that he had, but she couldn't recall his ever explicitly saying so, now that she thought about it.

"Is there anything you'd like to see before you go?" Naveen was again offering. "The Birla is just there. Birla Planetarium. Haven't been there in years, myself. But I have a light week. My afternoons are yours for the asking. We could even catch a play. A movie?"

"I should stay with my *massi*."

"You aren't here for very long," he said, gesturing for her to cross Chowringhee. "Still, it would be a pity if you left feeling shortchanged."

"Aren't you on vacation right now? Shouldn't you go somewhere where it's cooler? I probably should have gone to Darjeeling."

"I have saved up some time for research," he replied. "And what I need to research is here."

They entered the expansive lawns of the Maidan, and in the distance she saw the Victoria Memorial, enough like the Capitol that if she squinted her eyes—and she did—she felt as if she was on the Mall.

"You should let me know if you're ever in Washington," she said. "It's really nice of you to keep me company like this."

He smiled, then gestured toward a large weeping willow and asked if she'd like to sit for a while.

"Is it getting cooler?" she asked. "The air doesn't feel as heavy."

"Not really," he said. "You might be acclimating."

They sat in the shade of the tree, and she wrapped her arms around her knees, leaning against the trunk, its thick roots bared to the eye and hard as bones underneath her. The Maidan was alive: people walking and conversing in large groups, children playing impromptu games of ubiquitous cricket or running with kites.

"Down there," Naveen said, waving a hand before him, "is the

Esplanade. And the old Ochterlony Monument, around which your father and mine were part of a historical rally."

Bijou looked into the distance. "I just can't see him here, Naveen," she confided. "All this feels like another planet."

"Because you're visiting; it's your first time," he said. "You should try living here. No, really, I mean it. You belong here. What? Why not?"

"Wouldn't they be shocked?" she said. "If they knew that you and I were sitting here now? How people come together . . . It's the strangest thing."

"Is it?" Naveen involved himself in examining a leaf he held by the stem and slowly spun between two fingers. His skin pulled taut and dark over his knuckles and the delicate bones of his wrists. Hands that would probably be best fit to perform surgery. Bijou remembered the feel of his hand on her waist the evening before, firm. It seemed Naveen had left the neutral territory of being a stranger so quickly. She drew back and looked down to better regard her ring, the little gardenia she had come to regard almost as a pet.

"I used to have a friend named Sally," she said. "She lived across the street from me growing up. Once—we were just girls—we pricked our fingers with the jagged lid of this, like, metal can. Well, Sally pricked her finger. I slit myself right open. The cut looked like a gill, like a fish gill, honestly, and I almost threw up at the sight of my own blood. Who knew how much damage you could do with a tuna fish container?

But we pressed our fingers together, Sally and I, to seal a pact as blood sisters. When my father saw the bandage on my finger, he asked what had happened. So I told him. The truth." She laughed. "He was so upset that I had cut myself, especially on my hand. I told him over and over again how we just wanted to be sisters, more than just best friends. But he said that friends, above all, would make life bearable, often besting family."

"Pari wasn't born, I take it?"

"No, definitely not," Bijou said. "But that wouldn't have mattered. I was defenseless against information circulating on the playground. Everybody wanted to be somebody's blood sister. Or brother, I guess. No one said you might end up in the emergency room with an infected slash on your finger, and get stitches, and that your mother would make you feel like a complete fool for at least the next five years. *Bijoya, let me cut that apple. You'll just end up in the hospital.*" Bijou held up her forefinger. He was looking at her oddly. She wondered if he'd been listening. "Still have the scar."

"So you do."

"Funny," she said, looking away. "I haven't thought of that moment in forever. Maybe never since! Isn't it weird how we remember things?"

"Very weird."

Perhaps he was listening, Bijou thought, and wondered if she should go on. Not long after their courageous show of friendship, things changed. Sally's father lost his job and moved the family back to Korea. Miraculously, Bijou and Sally had kept their friendship alive with letters for years (Sally with much cooler stationery and signing her name Hyun Sil now). By high school, those letters thinned down to birthday cards, and by college, a note one December describing the windy winter in Seoul for four of four paragraphs, with a postscript explaining she was going to get married the following spring, and then no correspondence again. Would Sally remember her? Surely she would. And she would be heartbroken, too, to hear about Bijou's father, wouldn't she?

"Anyway, she grew up and got married and I haven't heard from her in ten years. So much for blood sisters."

"And you?"

"And me?"

"You're at a very marriageable age."

Bijou winced. "I don't know about that. I still feel twelve." She raised her eyebrows. "Really!"

"You have such unusual eyes—no, they're pretty," Naveen said. "The color is just like your mother's. Very nice. The Persian in you. I can appreciate that." He dropped the leaf to his side, then slapped his hand against his shin and held it there.

Bijou thought she'd heard a heavier note surfacing in his voice, not unlike a lover's tone, but pushed the thought aside. Without looking at him, she replied, "I've always thought hers were prettier," she replied. "Mine don't seem to fit me the way hers fit her, if that makes any sense."

The sun had begun its initial descent. She tried not to think of where it would be rising next. She would be there soon enough.

"Your mother has been through a lot," Naveen said. "It must have been so difficult with Nitish Uncle in the hospital."

"She was like a warrior."

"You helped her. She couldn't have done it without you."

"She would have, believe me, no one knows her like I do. And for how hard she fought, to have lost him, still—he was her life. My grief will never match hers."

Naveen sat up much straighter. "Why would you measure these things? Why should my grief for my father, for instance, be lesser than my mother's? Different, yes, but why not equal?"

"Why not? I don't know. Maybe it's like that for you. It's not like that for daughters, maybe."

"You think that matters? We aren't in the dark ages about that anymore; you're speaking of such old beliefs."

"They linger, though, don't they? Maybe I'm sensitive, but I have felt like Plan B in all of this. Like a *son* would have done things better."

"People get scared—"

"'They default to the old ways.' You've mentioned it before. Well, it doesn't really help me to know that, is the problem. It justifies their actions. But it doesn't help me clarify my role. Even my mother, she's got rules. There are rules for widows."

"But does she follow them?"

"Yes and no. Some. Not all. She gets to choose to wear white, and sometimes she does. I think she's not eating meat right now, either. Again, her choice. Me and Pari, what are the rules? What's okay for us to do and say now?"

"You do whatever you like, Bijou. You wouldn't do anything inappropriate. What's the fear?"

"I think I would do something very," she said, "inappropriate. I think all the time about throwing things. All the time. Dinner plates and things. Mugs, books, hammers."

"That's reasonable. You don't actually follow through, do you? You're fine."

"Or I'm not fine," she said, "and one day I will completely lose my mind, and somehow, don't doubt it, on that day fate will have a baseball—no, a *cricket* bat in my hand by noon. Or a golf club. It will be a mess."

Naveen grinned, slumping again into comfort with his elbows perched on his knees, hands loosely tangled.

She looked away, then covered her face with her hands, then rubbed at her temples. As she opened her eyes and drew her hands away, she told Naveen that even now, this stab at humor felt inappropriate. "Any kind of laughter, in fact," she said, "has seemed almost inhumane."

He conceded with a quick raise of his eyebrows, and said, "But that gets easier in time. Trust me. You're caught up in it—in all those things that have to happen when a tradition doesn't fit its people anymore. You're not proof that the tradition still exists, right?"

"How?"

"You're proof that it's dying. On its way out."

"No," she said. "It's not dying. It's changing into something else."

"Even better! How can you be upset about being a part of that?"

She was conscious of not having a couth response. Was he picturing caterpillars and butterflies? Extra childishly then, she could do nothing but shrug, thinking of how many things often changed into worse things—lethal things—especially in the very blood of those who messed with old ways.

"Naveen, no one talks about it like that at all. I am left constantly feeling like I have no choice, and maybe that's because everyone knows that if I was presented with a choice, I would pick the wrong thing. I should probably move back to Michigan and be close to my mother now, but I won't."

"And you'll feel guilty."

"Always."

"Look, you won't. You can't."

Again, she shrugged, and mostly felt like going home and crawling into bed.

"It's a strange thing, Bijou," Naveen said. "Your father used to send us letters once in a while, you know. I don't remember him, of course, any more than I remember my own father. When Nitish Uncle stopped writing to us from the States, I think it hurt my mother. To have lost this last real connection to my father. We didn't even know what had happened—the illness, I mean—until I met your uncle here. As you said, the ways people meet often seem fated. I agree. But what I mean to say is that I feel I knew Nitish Uncle, as much as I can know any of them. He was like family to my mother in their youth." He looked at Bijou directly then. "I envied you and your mother. That you had him."

She didn't know what to say. She hadn't known about any correspondence, though of course it was perfectly possible. Her father at the kitchen table with felt-tip pens and sky-blue aerograms. Bijou never asked where they were being posted. It wasn't her business, was it?

"When you're still a schoolboy, see, envy—or call it anger—is like a drug," Naveen said. "It can rewire you. Maybe I did things knowing my father wouldn't have approved, maybe I was stupid enough to think it *risky*. When he wasn't even there to scold me . . ."

"Is that why you went to England? Oxford reformed you?"

He laughed, and said it probably was, and it certainly did. "My father would have insisted on a homespun education, I'm sure." Ashok, he elaborated, had dropped out of university (despite genius-rank promise) for the sake of Calcutta. Naveen had spent his youth longing to drop out of Calcutta for the sake of university. It was only now, as an adult, that he appreciated this place as his home.

"I know I'm not half the scholar my father would have been," he said. "I've been foolish, of course—in stupid juvenile ways—although I never designed that behavior to affect anyone but myself."

"In what ways? What did you do?"

"It would be sheer humiliation to tell you. Let's say I was up to no good, and in this city, that is a very lucrative occupation. I was in the wrong company. An arrant knave, if you will. My own Prince of Denmark."

She smiled. "I wonder sometimes," she said tentatively, "if Hamlet killed Ophelia's father just so she would know—like, really know—his pain. Understand why he was so crazy."

"But it was an accident."

"Was it? Well, she gets his pain either way. And drowns in a stream."

Naveen clapped his hands together once, and said in a low, confident tone, "There you have it, then. You do have choices. You chose not to drown in a stream."

"Ha-ha," she mumbled. "Very funny."

He smiled. "So you've read Shakespeare."

She nodded. "It was required."

They sat a while longer before he suggested they head back, take a look around (*There's the statue of Gandhi—you do recognize him, don't you?*) on the way out. He stood up and extended his hand, and she took it, rising. He didn't let her go once they started walking, but kept her hand loosely entangled in his as he continued to discourse on this and that. When he gestured for her to look at something, she looked. When he asked if she was interested in hearing more about whatever—*You're sure? You're curious?*—she said, "Yes."

And when he left her at her aunt's threshold, she thanked him, invited him in for tea. He declined, told her amiably that he did actually have work to do.

"But why not tomorrow?" he said. "There's so much more I will show you—not just photographs. Bijou, that's only one part—"

"I agree."

"Forget your work, you're here now," he said.

"I said okay." To her own surprise, if not embarrassment, she heard herself giggle.

He nodded, grinning. "Right. Good. See you then." He walked away, adding over his shoulder, "I'll collect you around eleven, okay? We'll go for lunch."

Anuja Massi greeted her loudly from the kitchen, where she and Ketaki were cooking. "Perfect timing! You have a phone call. Go, go, get it! I think your uncle is still taking the message!"

"Who would call me?"

Her aunt waved her hands rapidly. "I don't know! You can find out!"

"I was just out with Naveen. We went for a walk."

"Good, good! The fresh air has obviously helped, eh? You have some glow in your pretty face again. But really, Bijou, the phone. Go!"

While Bijou would have been perfectly content to wait for the message, she recognized that receiving a call on someone else's dime, rather than returning a call on her uncle's, was the right thing to do. She ran upstairs.

Her uncle had the phone clamped between his ear and his shoulder. He was writing on a pad of paper and saying, very slowly, "Okay. Okay. Okay." When he saw Bijou, he interrupted whoever was on the other line abruptly: "Oh, wait, here she is, you can talk to her direct" and put the phone on the table. "Ah, Bijou, good you are here—he is speaking so fast, saying he works with you." He tore the paper from the pad, crumpled it, and held out the receiver while calling out to her aunt.

Bijou thanked him and took the receiver, puzzled. "Hello?"

"Bee, is that you? Can you hear me?"

For what seemed the most accurate approximation of an eternity she had ever experienced, she stood inert.

"Say something, Bee."

Though she was alone in the room now, she instinctively cupped her hand to her mouth. "How do you know this number?"

"I want to see you."

"I can't talk to you here. I'll call you when I'm back home."

"No, you can't hang up," Crane said. "I have to talk to you now."

"I promise I'll call," she said. "This will cost you a fortune. Are you crazy? I'll be back next week, anyway."

"No! I'm not calling from home," Crane said. "That's the thing. We have to talk now because, like, I'm here. I came to see you."

Bijou whispered, "What? You're in Calcutta?"

"At the Taj Bengal. Do you know it? Are you nearby? I wasn't sure exactly where you were staying, and that guy, Alok, at work, he suggested I stay here. I guess his uncle owns—"

"You're here?"

He laughed.

"This is funny?"

"Come on. Are you really that surprised?"

"Oh my God," she said hoarsely. "But you *know* there's no way I can *see* you here. What would I tell my family? I just don't understand—we discussed this six months ago, and we decided then: you would not come here. Oh, Crane. Crane! What the hell?"

"Bee, I haven't flown thousands of miles to be hung up on. I'll come to the house. Don't think I won't."

"You and I agreed you wouldn't come with me." She squinted. "We were in my kitchen. You said you wouldn't come with me."

"Well, I came *after* you. That's how this works. I chase you, if I have to. Maybe now's a good time for your mom to find out about us."

"No. That's not how it works." She shook her head. "I can't believe you're here."

There was a long pause before he replied. When he did, his tone was almost solemn, "Funny, I was hoping you would say that."

"Don't start down that path, Crane, please. Give me your number or something, and I'll call you tomorrow, all right? Wait. How long are you planning to stay?"

"You'll call me tomorrow? You can't say no. I *will* come to the house, if I have to. And don't act like I'm stalking you."

"You take advantage of me, Crane, you really do. You can't call here, you can't *come* here; things don't *work* like that here. I'll call you; I will. Because I know I owe it to you, so don't act like I don't. I'll call as soon as I can. Tomorrow." She hung up, and stared at the phone as if it had just been invented.

So. He had come all this way. In truth, she *was* surprised. And to think she had spent all day with Naveen—what would Crane think of it? She herself didn't even know what to think, except that it was not going to be easy. How was she going to handle *this*? She didn't feel twelve now; she felt six, and wondered where, oh, where was that girl who gravitated toward her mother's body every evening around nine o'clock, fatigued and in need of pre-bedtime coddling, mother's fingers raking through her tangled wisps of hair while afloat in conversation with Bijou's father. Her parents having the conversations adults had to keep them close, day in, day out.

Her parents had made domestic life seem *so easy*. What she remembered was how she begged her father to cross his legs at the ankle, so she could slide down them, or to let her ride piggyback while he danced with her mother, a record spinning a woman's scratched voice, peppered with clarinet and piano. *Ooh, ooh, ooh / What a little moonlight can do*, the voice sang, and Bijou deduced from listening carefully that just a little moonlight was enough to inspire stuttering and kissing—equally unappealing actions. What she remembered was being a small thing with simple if stubborn ways, a girl who laughed with her whole body, her mouth hanging open to her knees, her hands clenched and her shoulders hunched. Where was that girl?

Crane, listening to her try to explain this once, had pushed pharmaceuticals and therapy. But the women in her family did not do that, she'd retorted. There had to be alternatives. What would psychologists do for her now? They might listen, they might agree that things were complex, and they could talk about her childhood, too, about the hospital, about dreams, and then what? Would they take Bijou's inertia and store it in their offices, where they could sort through the whole mess of her existence, make a bonfire of the things she didn't want to keep? She didn't want explanations; she wanted active changes in the human condition. First rule: no one would die young, ever.

"Don't forget, Crane," she had said once. "All of it, all of it has made me who I am. I don't want to *forget* any of it. What I want is probably entirely the opposite of that."

If her mother believed in reincarnation, as she now claimed to, in the certainty that one's life was spent doing and undoing vestigial tasks from a previous existence, then what Bijou would have to embrace was starting over in the midst of things. You could start over. By her age, after all, her father had changed his name and left two continents for greener pastures. By her age, her mother had married, learned an entirely new language, and given birth to her first child.

"I can tell you this much," her mother had often said, "you must do something for others. There was a reason you were born to this family. Your father once took me to a place in Paris one night, I can't tell you where exactly, some bistro-type restaurant—it was near the street with all the crepe shops, I think. We liked this bistro, in particular, because they had a lamb dish, very nice. It was there your father told me about why he'd left Calcutta, his involvement in those politics and whatnot. He spoke of trips he and his comrade-*wallahs* had taken to the villages, how the very sight of living conditions there had filled him with what he called rage. How he had felt obligated to help.

"I was young, and in Kashmir my parents never had the money, you know, to have the kind of household your father had been raised in. We were very simple people, Bijou, though not *less* for it. One thing my parents taught me was compassion. *They* were not the ones who turned me away when I decided to marry your father, it was those others, extended family, casting stones. That's what extended family is good for: gossips and scandal. They feed on it like rats in sewers. Your father and I have never missed that in America. Here we see the other extreme. Either way, we are treated like aliens. I don't feel at home anywhere.

"What I will never forget about that night is the woman. She must have been French. Quite elderly, probably in her seventies. At the time, she seemed in her hundreds. Frail. She was sitting by herself, very fair, her very white hair cut rather short, sitting alone at the little table just near ours, with only an umbrella on the seat beside her to keep her company. Isn't that a shame? What happens to women? I'll tell you this: when you see a woman dining alone, and she seems lost, you know immediately that she was beautiful once, the sort of girl who never would have guessed she'd end up like this.

"While your father is telling me about walking fifteen miles a day from one village to the next, and his friends, and his plans, I cannot stop looking at this woman. You know how sometimes you think you know someone, but you don't? It was like that. When your father and I got up to leave, the woman and I smiled at each other. She was so wise! I'll *never* forget it. I'm telling you, Bijou, that smile is your smile. You saw me in Paris, you knew what I was getting into, and you vowed to return to this earth as my daughter. You came after me."

EIGHT

She was at Naveen's house now, seated across from him in the living room. He was telling her about his current project, a book he was writing, encouraged by professors he'd met in Europe. He spoke about how much he had read about the Naxalites—newspapers, training manuals, autobiographical accounts, fiction—long before he'd decided to construct an academic career around it.

As he spoke, he maintained eye contact. Bijou feared looking away and appearing disinterested, but the more he spoke, the more confused she grew about what she was doing here. Her aunt had seemed almost relieved to let her go this morning—she was planning a small dinner party for when Bijou's mother and Pari returned from their trip, and she wanted to take care of some of the arrangements over the weekend.

"This way," she'd said, "you won't get bored running errands with me and Ketaki. But don't stay away too long, okay?"

She'd tried calling Crane, but no one had answered; she left the message that she would call again. After saying good-bye to her aunt and uncle, she went down to meet Naveen outside. He was talking to Ramesh—with whom she had hardly spoken since the night of the immersion ceremony—in his cheery didactic manner. She had paused on the stairs and overheard the two

men, through the windows, exchange news about the construction of flyover bridges and the state of affairs at the cotton mill
where Ramesh's cousin worked. On the drive to Alipur, she'd
asked what they had been talking about. But where she'd hoped
to garner details of Ramesh's village, life, his family—where were
they? how often did he see them?—Naveen provided instead
broad lectures on Calcutta, its industry of indigo, its export of
jute, its dependence on migrant labor. It seemed to Bijou that he
was the sort who would have a hard time drawing the fine line
between focus and psychosis, as the doctor she worked with at
the NIH had described once in a colloquium about research
practice. Some people practiced tunnel vision, and it hurt them.

Now, as she blinked and tried to concentrate, she noticed that
Naveen must have shaved this morning. She didn't prefer this
clean-cut look to his other, which was sexier for its scrappiness, she
decided; and then she frowned, ashamed for thinking such things.

"I know, it's repulsive, isn't it?" Naveen said, evidently assuming her discomfort was in response to whatever he'd been saying.
"Every generation buys into rebellion. A pattern since the beginning of recorded time. Sons against fathers—was that what history came down to? Sometimes I think so. Political movements
could begin with noble desires, but they germinate at the very
personal level. People wish they could change themselves, change
their families, but since they can't—or won't—they take on the
world. It is rather paradoxical.

"And some did it for love. Or what got away being labeled as
such. It was not above men to sink into the depths of a movement
just to bide time. Once they got jobs, wives, children, what use did
they have for revolution? By and large, not much."

Bijou cleared her throat. "That seems unfair to say," she said
cautiously.

"Your own father? Didn't he put it all behind him?"

She lowered her head a bit, and slowly tucked her hair behind her ears with both hands. "So," she said, huddling slightly with her arms crossed and forearms resting on her legs, "what's your book's title?"

"I'm not sure, actually. I suppose I'll know when I'm done." He explained that for the moment, all he had was an array of propaganda materials—newspaper clippings, books, a few memoirs and the like—and ideas. He had so many ideas, which in due time would form and inform a collection of essays, profiles, and interviews tracing the lives of Bengali intelligentsia involved in the Naxalite movement. Most of the people he was studying were in their fifties now, the age of Independent India itself, and many of them had long since left behind their radicalism. Just as many had left India behind, as well, in the brain drain of the seventies. He told her that all he wanted was for these voices to have their place in history.

"Naxalbari is in Darjeeling, right?" she asked. "That's where it all started."

"The Darjeeling District. The concentration of tribal peoples living in Naxalbari was several times the number of tribals living throughout West Bengal in sum—and of course you know their staple crops. Many tea gardeners up there. Those who owned the lands—*jotedars*—versus those who tilled it."

"Have you been?"

"Not yet," he said. "There hasn't been time."

"My mom and sister are there now," she said. "Maybe I should have gone with them. Seen the place for myself."

"No doubt they're staying in the tourist areas, however."

"Yes," she said. "They've met up with Germans." But for the whir of the air-conditioning unit in the window, it was rather quiet. "My mother said something—I don't know—it's like she thinks the Naxalites were criminals. Controversial."

"Yes, well, at the risk of oversimplifying the matter, Bijou, I remind you it was not a politics of warm humor. They used violence and intimidation. Cold-blooded murder."

"But my father never hurt anyone, I know that. He couldn't have."

"How do you know for sure?"

"Maybe they didn't understand what they were getting involved with," she said. "He felt strongly about how wrong the system was—about the terrific gaps among the classes here. I've always been rather proud that he would dare to change the system. It's easy to be apathetic. You never met him, Naveen. He was all good."

"Perhaps he was. But their actions weren't always good. You could argue that they were, in fact, very, very bad. You have to imagine what it was like. To live in a city under curfew, paralyzed with fear of the next act of violence," Naveen said. "The Naxalite strategy had been to mobilize in the rural areas, then encircle the cities and destroy them. Typical. The destruction of property—statues decapitated, cinema halls bombed, all the literature at the Gandhi Center burned—was one thing. But they didn't stop there."

He told her then about the strategy of *gherao,* in which large assemblies of protestors surrounded their victims—landlords, factory bosses, anyone they suspected was out to exploit the working classes. Whether they chose to target one person or an entire office building's worth of people, it was impossible for captives to escape. The protest could last for hours. It could last all day and into the night—people staging the *gherao* appointed shifts so that when one team departed the scene, another arrived to take its place. Yet even this kind of confinement, he concluded—however suffocating or immobilizing it was—was a pleasant event when compared with the litany of Naxalite butchery: disemboweled landlords found in fields, lorries full of axe-murdered corpses. In the mayhem of the time, the police force overwhelmed, most perpetrators of these crimes were never indicted. Crime in general was at a new high; in any case of violence, the Naxalites were blamed—convenient for the usual thugs and thieves who had nothing but opportunistic associations with the Communist cause.

"There are some letters here," he said finally, gesturing to the shirt box from where he remained standing, his father's portrait on the bookshelf behind him. "What do you know of your parents' time in France?"

She leaned back on the couch. Sighing, eyes fixed on a hairline fissure in the ceiling, she said, "Only that they met there. My mother wanted to go to America because her older brother was there. So they left Paris for the States . . ." She stopped and squinted at Naveen. "Is this what you want to hear? Because I'm not a very reliable source of information, so if this is some kind of . . . one of your interviews . . . I mean, I am not qualified for any sort of academic reference—"

"I know that," Naveen interjected. He returned to his seat, and rested his elbows on the arms of the chair, holding his hands like a steeple under his chin. "There's no need to get rattled. Okay, so let me tell you what I know. It may fill some of the gaps."

"But I'm telling you," she said, "I don't think I can be of any use. Everything I know is vignettes. Secondhand."

He shrugged. "Don't you wonder why your father chose to leave Calcutta, why he never returned?"

"I've heard it differently. He couldn't have stayed if he'd wanted to. After your father was killed, he didn't want anything else to do with the Naxalites. He was in agony. So he left. He didn't run away like a coward. He had no choice."

Naveen looked directly at her for the first time since they'd begun speaking. "You know he was imprisoned, right?"

"What? My dad? In jail?"

"As was mine. My father was in jail when I was born; for the first few weeks of my life, in fact."

"He never talked about jail."

"My father was murdered, you realize." (She frowned, and nodded.) He continued: "But we have an idea of who did it. Another friend of his—of his and your father's—had died, you see. And my father was held responsible for that death."

This deceased friend, he told her, was the son of a very wealthy Bengali businessman. The friend's death had been an accident, one of many bitterly ironic casualties. A cadre of Naxalites, all young men, had been assembling their trademark bombs in the back room of a tobacco shop. It was the middle of the night. Naveen's father had left the shop at the sound of a suspicious noise. He had been outside hardly five minutes when he was thrown across the street by the force of an explosion. One of the bomb-builders made a blunder, to say the least; the detonation immediately subtracted four lives from the scene. Four bodies blown to pieces and impossible to identify in the smoldering ruins. For the sake of their families' peace, Naveen's mother had, in the end, been the one to notify the police of the boys' names. She did so anonymously, though with her husband's approval.

"And my father was there?" Bijou asked. "Are you implying that he walked away from this?"

"Not to my knowledge. He disappeared. Just as my own father did."

"What do you mean, *disappeared*?"

"Your father left Calcutta. He was called away somewhere near Naxalbari. No one knows exactly what he did there, only that it left him no choice but to leave the country. Much later, he wrote to my mother, from Paris, about my father's death. Of course, by that point, Nitish Uncle was only affirming what everyone else had deduced. My father had been assassinated. A body like his was actually found in the river, tangled up in fishnet. It may have been my father."

"I thought he was killed by the enemy. A stranger, I mean."

"No, that's very unlikely. Whoever did it knew him, and your father. Probably knew one or both of them quite well."

"You think it was this other guy's father? The businessman?"

"I've always thought so. As a revenge killing. It makes sense."

After a few minutes, Bijou looked back up at him and asked, "Did my father ever explain his disappearance? He must have, if he'd been writing to your mother. She must have wondered."

"It was taken for granted," Naveen said, "that he had fled for his life. And that's all anyone knows about it."

He moved to the edge of his chair and took an envelope from his shirt pocket. He tossed it to the edge of the table closer to her.

"I just have a feeling," he said, "that it was all an accident. That Nitish Uncle was actually the target. I just don't know who would have put the contract out. I haven't been able to connect the dots in that regard."

She was horrified. "You mean—you mean your father died for mine? And my father would walk away from that?"

"I don't know. Sometimes I think they were all just looking for a way to kill themselves." His tone was grim. "They didn't seem to value life the way most of us do. But it's what made them, well, so fearless, I suppose."

Bijou leaned over the table and looked at the letter. It was addressed to Mrs. Ashok Mazumdar in the familiar script of her father and bore an American postage stamp, canceled. It had been cleanly opened, as if with a knife.

Naveen left his seat to turn on one of the lamps in the room.

"Read what's inside," he said.

Bijou took the envelope in her hands now, frowning, and extracted two sheets of paper.

"I can't read this, Naveen," she said helplessly after unfolding one of them. "It's all in Bengali."

He returned to his seat, and folding his arms behind his head, leaned back into the chair.

"I can tell you what they say—verbatim, if I wanted to. My father wrote one. It is an ostensible will. You see, my father knew the gravity of his political actions, that they could be a matter of life or death. And in the event of his death, he'd asked your father to take care of the wife and son he'd leave behind. He actually goes as far as asking your father to marry my mother." Naveen dropped his hands to the arms of his chair. "But your father disappeared. And then he was married. To your mother."

Bijou didn't blink.

"Here," he said, putting on his glasses. He took back the letters. "I'll translate the one your father wrote. 'Dear Kamla—I return Ashok's letter to you so that it might help settle matters of Ashok's property, as you wrote last that there had been problems. Perhaps this will help. Read it and see. In the end, my returning to India would not have been Ashok's true desire. He had not known, upon fashioning this trust, what the future would hold—details of circumstances that would make his request simply impossible. I have explained to my wife what has come to pass—as much as I could, in confidence. Though it may appear otherwise, I always did anything Ashok requested. I wish of you one favor, Kamla. Do not doubt my character. Perhaps someday I will be free to evidence it with words that matter. Meanwhile, contact me with any needs. Consider me always a brother.'"

Naveen handed the letter back to Bijou.

"It's dated January 1972," he added.

"My parents were living in Detroit then," she mumbled. "I wasn't even born yet." She folded the letter along its original creases and sat motionless, eyes lowered. "I'm sure it—you and your mother, I mean, were important to him. But my parents must not have seen any reason to tell me."

After a while Naveen said, "I'm not saying your father broke any promises, Bijou. Nor that we suffered at great length because of what he did or did not do."

She continued staring at the letter in her hands.

"Why are you telling me this?" she said. "You think I can explain this to you? When I never knew—"

"That's why I'm telling you. So you can know now."

"I just thought we were going to have lunch. Chat about things that people chat about. The weather, movies, I don't know." She sighed again. "I should go. I have something I need to do. I wanted to thank you most of all for sharing this," she said, withdrawing the photo album he'd lent her from her shoulder bag. "I kept a few of the photographs. I hope you don't mind."

"You won't show the album to your sister?" he asked. "There's no hurry in returning it."

"It's okay, it belongs to you," she said. "You've been very kind to spend this time with me. Pari and my mom will be back from Darjeeling this weekend."

"I know. We're all looking forward to the get-together then."

He checked his watch, said he had to grab a couple of things from his room before heading out, and told her he'd be right back.

Several minutes later, Naveen had still not returned downstairs. She decided to check on him.

Much like her aunt's house, the top floor of the Mazumdar

home was reserved for bedrooms and bath, and the stairwell continued to the roof. Two of the three doors she encountered were shut; the third was not. She peered in, but Naveen was not there. She stepped inside the room, and looked around at the sparse furnishings: a jute mat on the hardwood floor, an antiquated map of the world above a desk, a black-and-white plaid bedspread. On a bedside table, a tower of journals. The air was warm, and smelled familiar, like Naveen—one part sandalwood, another part soap.

The head of the bed rested almost flush with the sill of the room's only window. Light came through the window like the colors on the inside of a conch shell, and outside a bird—or birds, more likely; maybe blue jays, maybe sparrows—twittered in waltz-like phrases. The walls were painted a rich brown mustard color, but for one that was papered in raw pearly silk, in a style that the royal would call rustic.

A long bookshelf was bracketed to one wall above the length of the bed. The books were arranged in a neat row, but to read their spines would have required a certain intimacy with the mattress that Bijou felt would be inappropriate. The only titles she could make out from where she stood were those of four volumes belonging to two different sets of English dictionaries.

She turned from the bed to the wardrobe, a hulking piece of furniture with a cabinet and several brass-latched drawers. It rose up almost as high as her chin. Upon looking here, she smiled to see an old *Archie Digest*.

Resting next to the comic was a black plastic comb and a small silver picture frame that seemed to have toppled over. The back side of the frame was tarnished with rust-colored streaks. She lifted the frame up, and drew her breath so sharply in reaction to what she saw that she began to cough.

With the frame in hand, Bijou turned to walk out of the room. She ran into Naveen near the threshold.

"What are you doing upstairs?" he said. "Everything okay?"

"Why do you have this in here?" she asked, thrusting the photograph toward him. She was still choking a bit. "Where did you get it?"

Naveen frowned. He took the framed picture and placed it inside one of the wardrobe's drawers.

Bijou followed at his heels. "How did it get here, Naveen?"

"Do you often go through people's things?" he said, unruffled. "It's nothing. I told you. Your father used to write to us. He sent it with one of the letters."

"But you *framed* it."

"Oohf, stop scowling," he said, taking off his glasses and putting them in his pocket. "There's no reason to be this upset. If anything, I should be angry that you came in here without permission. I came up here looking for a draft of my book I might lend you."

"I remember when that photo was taken. I was twelve years old; it's one of the last pictures of my father and me together. You made it sound as though he'd only written in the beginning, that he'd only written once or twice—"

"He wrote us up until the day he was hospitalized, Bijou."

"Why? What went on between him and your mother? What aren't you telling me? Just tell me. Did they have an affair?"

"Calm down, Bijou." Naveen took a step closer to her. "They were friends. I told you. I don't know—I liked the photograph. The snow. Your house in the background. It's a souvenir."

"Do you have others? Are there more?"

He shook his head, almost guiltily.

In the photograph, it was virtually impossible to discern Bijou's face from within the tightly cinched hood of her winter parka. Her father, however, who stood just behind her, was clearly laughing. Next to them stood a half-melted snowman wearing an old trucker's hat of her dad's, with barbecue briquettes for eyes, a spattering of weathered red golf tees for a mouth, and—because her mother had needed all the carrots for dinner—a large cactus-like piece of gingerroot representing its nose. Bijou had extended both her arms toward her grotesque Frosty, as if he were a coveted game-show prize. Her father had extended his arms toward her.

"My mom took that picture to finish off a roll of photos from Florida. I remember that day," she said, semimesmerized. Then she looked up.

Naveen had come to stand hardly an inch in front of her now, and she grew dizzy, as though standing at a great height above him.

"Why would you call it a souvenir, if you'd never been there?"

"I felt like I was there," he said quietly. Then he startled her by laying his hands on her shoulders, stooping toward her, and adding, "Now you're here. By some stroke of fate, you are here before me, and it feels like a gift." His eyes darted between hers in an attempt to keep her gaze. "What are you thinking?"

She was thinking that it would be inappropriate of him to kiss her; that it was probably inappropriate to be thinking that he might. She was thinking, too, of all the little things the photograph had triggered in her memory: the smell of Michigan winter air, the warmth of a heat register under her feet in her father's study as she huddled near his collection of indecipherable books about engineering and Bengal. She was thinking that last night she'd had a dream about this, or something like this, or nothing like this. In short, she was not thinking clearly, and indicated as much.

He stepped back.

"Are you, at home," he said slowly, "with someone? I'm just curious. Your aunt thinks no, but I've learned to double-check these things."

"Then I doubly wish I could say I wasn't," she said. "But it would be a lie."

"I see." He stepped back, pursing his lips, then rubbing a clenched fist across them. "Well. I won't get in your way."

"You're not in the way," she responded at once. "I am. I'm in everyone's way. Just ask my mother, she'll tell you."

"Not necessary."

"I should probably go. Can I take a taxi, maybe? I think I'd be fine in a taxi."

"Am I scaring you off? Because I'd rather you didn't go alone."

She let him drive her, but they exchanged few words on the way, listening—or at least she pretended to be listening—to a program on the radio about Sonia Gandhi's presidency instead. Mostly she was looking out her window at sidewalks and road. When they reached her aunt and uncle's house, Bijou made an awkward attempt at addressing the awkwardness in the air. "I am actually very glad to know you now. I don't take these connections lightly. I'm sure there's a reason we've met here. We needed to meet, I suppose."

He did not seem to want to discuss this, dismissing her with a perfunctory farewell, saying, "And we'll meet again."

"Okay. Good," she said, hesitating for a moment before shutting the door. He drove off, and she went inside to find Ketaki in the foyer setting coasters and a small vase of flowers back on the table. They greeted each other, and Ketaki said she would make Bijou some tea. As she crossed the threshold out of the foyer, she turned to Bijou and asked if she was going to go upstairs.

Bijou pointed to the phone and said no.

* * *

The phone in Crane's room rang six or seven times, and then the hotel operator took the call back and apologized.

"Would you please try again?" she replied. Crane never answered the phone quickly enough; it had been a point of conflict in their relationship, with him claiming that she had trained him too well to ignore all rings. Even at his own apartment, he had grown to believe that Bijou's mother or some other relative would be on the other end of the line. "He may be asleep."

But there was still no answer. She tried a few more times throughout the course of the afternoon, without success. Worried that something had happened to him—maybe he was lying sick in his room, or maybe he'd switched hotels, or maybe he'd gone back home—she finally asked to speak with someone at the reception desk. They informed her that Crane was indeed still a guest, but that he had gone on an excursion with a group from the hotel.

"An excursion?" she repeated. "Do you know when he's going to return?"

"They'll be back tomorrow."

Bijou frowned, said her thanks, and hung up. If Crane had gone ahead and gotten out of her way, as she'd essentially told him to, then she had no reason to be irate. Had he been there, however, and had she gone to see him, as she suddenly wanted to more than anything—well, perhaps it wasn't meant to be; perhaps fate was taking her cue. She shook her head, and she had to snicker at herself. This is why they said to be careful what you wished for.

She decided a walk would clear her head.

Ketaki, however, didn't think it was wise when Bijou asked to drink her tea later.

"It's okay," Bijou said. "I will stay just near here."

So, with the caution of Gretel, no desire to lose her way, she walked as straight a path as possible away from the house so that the return would be easy. She had changed into the *salwaar kameez* her aunt had brought home for her the evening before as a gift—moss green cotton, with a matching *dhupatta* shot through with silver embroidery.

"I'm so glad it fits you," her aunt had said. "Now you have something to wear. I'll get you another one for the dinner on Saturday." She was careful to say "dinner" without "party," knowing Bijou's mother would not be pleased with any event that suggested they were here for pleasure. *Just a few people over, and we might as well eat dinner, it's only polite*, her aunt kept telling her lightly. *Just a few people who have heard many things about you all over the years. They care.*

Twenty minutes into her stroll, Bijou thought of turning back. While the *salwaar kameez* afforded her a certain level of camouflage, she was aware of others regarding her oddly. The heat was thick and getting smokier with the onset of evening. Her lack of destination made her antsy, and she felt as if everyone could tell she was trying to mask her discomfort. At street corners and alley entranceways, young men congregated in small circles, some still straddling bikes or scooters. They shared cigarettes, and conversation, perhaps; most of them looked not at one another, however, but at those who passed them by. Bijou felt their presence, their gaze as palpable and stifling as the very heat; at times, they were silent and motionless, staring obliquely, all simulated coolness as she approached. Then they muttered at her back just low enough that she couldn't really hear what they were saying, tempting her to turn around, if only to make sure they weren't following. The part of her that felt confident enough to deflect this behavior on American streets was now telling her she was probably asking for trouble. But these were just neighborhood guys, she reasoned. She was a safe distance from the commercial areas, where hawkers and beggars would be upon her without fail. So she continued, striding forth as she imagined her mother would, taking longer looks at her watch than necessary, then adjusting her *dhupatta* and sighing as if she was almost late for an important appointment. She didn't want to go back to the house and just sit there idly. It would only compound the sense of claustrophobia with which she had awoken.

She'd slept poorly, dreamed of nothing good. Not for the first time, she'd had a nightmare, in most of its usual details: left alone in a cell-like room, the antechamber to a bedroom, she sits in a red Banarsi sari with henna designs on her hands. A bride. Happy at first, then finding it difficult to recall whom she is marrying, and finally realizing it is no one she's met. Panic ensues. *But how will I get out of this?* she asks herself. Sometimes, she thinks Crane will rescue her; he never does. The unidentified groom will certainly reject her on the basis that she is far from virginal. In the dream, this seems the best thing, that everyone who feels they own her will disown her. She reminds herself that she has been careful with money; she has just enough to relocate. She will move to Spain, she decides, because no one will look for her there. She will masquerade as a descendent of Moors. Yes, this design of escape seems entirely rational. In the dream, she studies her hands and notices that the henna is not set right—where there should be a lace embossing of flora and vineyards, instead there are words. What she reads there is usually indecipherable.

Last night, however, she remembered all at once, the *mehndi* had spelled Naveen's name in distinct cider-colored chains gloving both her hands to well below the wrists. Her palms were coated with a thick layer of gray ash, which transferred muddily to her face as she wiped away tears.

She'd woken up with her heart racing. While it was a dream

she'd learned to brush off as some asinine subconscious terror of a thing she really knew better than to fear, Naveen's name appearing there this time gave her pause. Did she want him? Maybe she did. But what did she want him for? Wasn't it opportunistic of him to act as if he held some claim on her because their fathers had been friends thirty years ago? But maybe he had no agenda at all. Maybe he was altogether empathic, a man who could deeply understand her because they were prepared to connect like this. Not even because he was Indian. And not because their fathers had been friends those thirty years ago, but simply because both those men were now forever gone.

Waiting for an opportune moment to cross a street that intersected her path, Bijou noted a lack of traffic in the way of sidewalk vendors and shops down the street. There was no sign naming it, and she couldn't see to the end; it seemed to wind through another jammed assembly of cement houses. Painted on the side wall of the shop that stood on the corner were graffiti, advertisements, and what might have been a slogan for the CPI—it was marked by a stenciled sickle and star and a line of Bengali script written underneath the three letters of the party. Bijou ran a hand over the sickle, then traced the characters with her finger.

What had her father really done here? He had not been like these young men she passed on the street, part of an indolent clique with no pressing business elsewhere. He had, with his squad, his book of Mao in a kit bag, gone with Naveen's parents to the villages. He had tried to educate them, to better their lives, hadn't he? But nothing he'd ever told her even implicated guerrilla units and violence; whenever he'd said "revolutionary" she'd never heard what Naveen seemed to hear: "terrorist."

She decided to walk a little ways down the street, just to see what was there. Half a block or so later, the street was sliced by an alley, and she noticed on the opposite corner a man kneeling in front of a wall of black iron bars. The bars fenced in the ground floor of a narrow two-story building. The man appeared to be praying. For an instant, she thought it might be Naveen, and her pulse quickened—but it wouldn't be him, couldn't be. The man stood up and moved on.

She crossed the street, noting that her sandals and feet had been coated in a layer of dust.

From the sidewalk, just where the man had knelt to pray moments before, Bijou stood to survey the barred-in room. It was closetlike, its three walls painted light green, and sparsely furnished: nothing but a table covered in orange satin, upon which rested a ceramic idol of Durga. Above the goddess, on the wall, hung a plastic clock. Incense had been lit, and its smoke shimmied toward the ceiling. A thick garland of pink carnations hung around Durga's neck. Her face was glazed to a dewy shine, and she wore a crown of gold with large gold earrings. There was a locked collection box affixed to another wall of the shrine. Bijou could just reach its slot.

At another time in her life, she might have made a donation and asked for the goddess's *ashirvad.* Blessings for the asking. She did neither—in any case, she had no money on her—but continued to stare at the clay idol's elongated eyes and red lips, gold hoop affixed to the small, straight nose parting the fair, round face. Durga was enveloped in a light blue satin skirt embroidered with gold thread and mirror work. A lion's head, cast in a ferocious growl, pushed out from under the plaits of the goddess's skirt (the skirt concealing the rest of the feline body and who knew what else).

Bijou withdrew her hands from the iron bars, clapping away bits of rust and paint that had stuck there. The image of Naveen's name inscribed on her fingers and wrists came to her again, yet more vividly than in the dream. *No,* she thought suddenly. *Not for you.* She would never betray her father. If he had carried with him to his death some secret regarding his friendship with Ashok Mazumdar, then he had done so with good reason. It had taken courage for him to leave this city and all that was familiar, natural, to leave *home.* Then to start anew in America, where it never had been easy for him. Far from it. Nothing in a photograph of his daughter and a snowman could tell the entire truth, and she decided it was too strange of Naveen to have kept it as he had.

Then she thought of Crane, trying to imagine what it would be like seeing him here. This, too, seemed very strange, as if lines connecting all the male figures in her life were being drawn before her eyes on a chalkboard. If she loved one, perhaps she loved them all. If she removed herself from one, perhaps she removed herself from them all.

She wiped her hands with the end of her *dhupatta,* then blotted the sweat on her forehead and above her lips. There was a brass cup of water across the room, sitting at Durga's feet on the altar, and Bijou wished she'd had the wherewithal to bring along a bottle of water. She decided to head back home. Night was blackening the sky overhead, but there were still wide ribbons of orange, pink, red, and blue on the horizon.

Approaching her aunt's house, she saw Ketaki out front, leaning against the gate with her hands behind her back. Hovering over her was a young man with two fat and shaggy dogs lying at his feet, their leashes slack. As Bijou was about to cross the street, Ketaki saw her; Bijou waved. The young man turned to look at her, then fumbled with the leashes, pulling up the dogs and dragging them down the street as quickly as he could such reluctant animals. By the time Bijou was at the gate, Ketaki had slipped up to the porch. She stood in the doorway as Bijou greeted her.

"*Aie ma!*" Ketaki said, going on to exclaim that Bijou looked very bad. She asked if she was feeling ill. "Dinner is made, are you hungry?"

"Everybody's home?"

"Yes. They sent me to look for you."

Bijou raised her eyebrows, and looked in the direction of where the young man had dragged off the dogs.

"But," Ketaki said quickly, ushering Bijou inside, "just as I came outside, there you were."

In her room that night, Bijou looked again at the pictures she'd taken from the red album, lingering on the photo of her father standing next to Ashok, along with other men their age. The eyes of the other men were upon Ashok, caught in mid-sentence; his lips were parted. Bijou tried to imagine what he might have been saying. Was he issuing instructions for tackling the next round of villages? Slandering the local *jotedar*? Couldn't he simply be re-marking on the taste of the tea in these rural areas?

Only her father appeared to be distracted from the conversation. He must have noticed Kamla approaching with the camera. He was smiling—or perhaps it was a trick of light, a crease in the photograph. Bijou brought the photo closer to her eyes, half-hating that she could not slip into the photograph, and back in time. Now it was clear that while Ashok spoke, he was also watching her father. And perhaps on the brink of looking at Kamla. His wife.

Three friends, Bijou thought, two married. Her father would never have betrayed Ashok. She thought again of the letters, the promises—broken and otherwise. Her father might have married Kamla after Ashok's death. He'd had the chance. Perhaps he had betrayed her, ultimately. Perhaps there had been a bond there worth preserving in marriage.

And then? The Roy family would have been a very different

entity. Her father might still be alive. Bijou would not exist. If she didn't exist now, she would neither mourn nor—more if perversely agonizing—catch herself not mourning.

Bijou placed the pictures in between pages of her laboratory notebook, then flipped through it, then through a few articles she had brought along from the institute with the intentions of organizing some data, compiling notes for the next phase of the project. There was her handwriting, her indelible annotations and arrows and underlining. She had once loved such laboring and analysis to the point of addiction, happy to pass late nights with lab rats and vending machines, long after her preceptor had left for a warm dinner with his family. Work was safe. A place Bijou could use everything she knew and where others could know nothing about her.

Glycolipids, GT3, progenitors, loss, pathology, adhesion, signaling. She stared at her notes, terms she'd used with fluency just weeks earlier. Nothing there to hold her now. Nothing she felt she understood anymore, all of it just part of some grandiose, hopeless, endless *idea*. A cure that would come too late, if ever.

Since her father's death in September until the end of February, she'd worked relentlessly. Knowing, at her core, that this—this apathy for her work now, for Washington, for the life she was calling her own—would be the end result of breaking her stride. Even as it had seemed clear to her along the way that India would be nothing less than an interruption, now it appeared that "conclusion" would have been the more accurate term after all. What was the word for not wanting to leave? Was it "fear"? And the word for wanting to stay? Was that "hope"?

"We have a saying in India," her uncle said at breakfast the next morning, after grunting at length over what he had been reading in the newspaper. "You can be marching in a funeral procession and, in the distance, hear the *shenai* playing its wedding song. This is life." He sighed.

Bijou's aunt rolled her eyes, then quietly said, "We have many sayings in India. Not enough doings."

"How much better off I was as a child. The kind of simple life I had in Kashmir, it is hard to appreciate these days. With this television and Internet and frequent flying. Nuclear weapons!" He slapped the folded newspaper with the back of his hand. "We have made it too easy to destroy everything at once. Most menacing. Who knows what the rest of 1999 will bring? Apocalypse? They're predicting it."

"Bijou, sweetie," her aunt said, "have some more tea or juice. Should I get you more cereal?"

"I will retire," her uncle announced excitedly. "Soon. Let them have it, these juvenile know-it-all scholars. Such is the cycle, at any rate. No use fighting it."

Ketaki came into the room to clear the breakfast plates and cups, and Bijou's aunt and uncle rose from their seats, preparing to depart for the university.

"A few days, and then you leave," her aunt told her before kissing her forehead. "Like a dream, this visit. It will be as if you were never here. And that makes me very sad."

"I know," Bijou said. "Part of me wishes we could afford to come here every year. It would be good for Ma, too, in so many ways."

"Well, you are blessed to have so many homes," her aunt said. "Next time you come to this one, it must be for a happy occasion, hm? Maybe—I don't know—for your wedding? Don't you think Bjiou should get married here, Shankar?"

He shot Bijou a look as if to say, *What does your kind usually do?* Then he asked her how old she was, considered the number with some interest, and told her to give herself three more years before marriage. "Three," he said firmly, "is very reasonable."

"Medical school," Bijou replied, "is six."

"Then marry a surgeon."

Her aunt's eyes danced. "Yes, a surgeon. Rich and handsome."

Bijou laughed. "You guys are very cute."

As they turned to go downstairs, she took a light hold of her aunt's arm and inquired if it would be possible for Ramesh to drive her somewhere later.

"It should be no problem," her aunt said. "What do you need to do?"

"See some people I was told to meet, since I happen to be here, and they're here, too," Bijou said. She had invented a story about researchers the institute had recommended she meet with, specialists in her field. Her preceptor, she told her aunt, was holding his breath in Washington waiting for a report from Bijou. She was obligated to meet these people at least once to avoid disappointing her colleagues back home. "It won't take long."

"Do you know where you have to go?" her uncle asked.

"I know one of them is staying at the Taj Bengal." She withheld the details in hopes she wouldn't be pressed further. It made her feel physically ill, lying to them like this.

Her aunt nodded. "Oh, that's a very good hotel. I'll tell Ramesh to wait for you."

"It won't take long, I promise. I plan to keep the visit very short."

NINE

Ramesh informed her as they approached Belvedere Road that they were nearing the hotel. Bijou fidgeted with the things in her bag, fishing out a compact mirror from a strange beach of dead batteries, nickels, pennies, credit card receipts, lip gloss, and hair clips. Imagining Crane's first sight of her, here, unstrung her in a way she couldn't wrap her mind around: he was the man who'd seen her every way she could be. Why, then, the dull tremor in her hands, the dryness in her mouth? As if they had not seen each other just a matter of months ago. As if they were at the beginning again, acquaintances. Children.

She raked her fingers through her hair, a mess of waves the humidity had inspired. It was tangled, and not entirely clean. She tucked some behind one ear, repeating the motion unconsciously. Her hair was uneven as ever, and less than half the length it had been most her life. The result of one October morning's tedium while brushing her teeth before work, gazing emptily into the mirror, not quite seeing the sum of her features. She'd reached in the cabinet under the sink for a sponge to wipe the counter, and come up with scissors instead. Without forethought or fanfare, she'd clipped her hair just under the rubber band that had been holding it together at her nape. It wasn't as easy as she'd expected—she had to work the scissors through a few times. She threw the tail in the garbage, and bought some bobby pins on the way to work.

The next time Crane had seen her, he'd looked at her as though she'd cut out her heart.

"It's not *your* hair," she'd said.

"I liked it," he'd said with conviction, and she knew he was thinking of the way it had, just days earlier, fallen down her back. How, months ago, it had hung over her breasts in a fashion that had unfailingly aroused him: *Bee, my Indian Eve.*

"It's just *hair,* Crane. I wanted to feel lighter."

"It'll grow back. It'll be the same again."

"I can assure you that it won't." She stared at him hard. "It's the twenty-first century, right?"

"Technically, no. Let's not get ahead of ourselves!"

Later, he'd apologized. Later still, he'd said, grinning, "You're still pretty cute. You definitely get by on your cuteness. Survival skill."

She hadn't found it amusing. "You think you're not like other men, but you are."

"What do you know about men?" He half-smiled. "I'm getting used to this new look of yours, I guess. But it helps if I close my eyes and remember what it was like before."

That strategy, Bijou thought now, *might be the one thing we still share.*

The lobby of the Taj, for all its amenities—a look best described as East meeting West and yielding to it—felt awfully sterile: potted fronds, pink marble, octagonal Persian rugs under smart plush furniture arranged for conversational ease, dwarfed by the story-high ceilings. Everything tastefully placed, uncluttered, in a controlled climate that only the tiniest fraction of Calcuttans could themselves afford. Chandeliers blazing, floor lamps glowing in spite of the ample sunlight pouring through the entrance's glass walls and revolving doors.

Her father would have had something to say about it. What she would tell him now, however, was that it said more about the futility of his twenty-something political stance than anything else—things had definitely not changed in the way he'd once hoped. That would be a disappointment. *And where else would your daughter meet Crane but here?* She suddenly wondered if her father would have approved of Crane. The more she thought about it, sitting there, the more perverse grew her thoughts. Maybe the reason she hadn't let go of Crane sooner was because he was the only guy she'd ever date who had met her father.

Did that matter?

She had someone at the desk ring Crane's room, then sat in the atrium between two of the symmetrically placed potted coconut palm trees under the skylights—could the trees possibly be real? what about roots?—waiting, watching others as they entered this refuge from everything the city outside had to offer or inflict upon them. A mix of tourists and business travelers, couples heading to one of the restaurants or the bar, perhaps, hushed and well-heeled, nearly waltzing across the polished tile. Bijou realized that the absence of noise and bustle, from which this place was sheltered, felt absolutely unnatural to her now. *Or, just American.* She wanted to get back into the clamor, even if just into its fringes. She wanted, as her father would have said, hullabaloo. She hardly noticed when a hand placed itself on her back, then nestled into the curve between her neck and her shoulder.

It was him, of course; she knew the smell of his skin better than her own name. She let her cheek touch his hand for an instant, because it seemed the only thing to do.

"Hey," he said. "Let me look at you."

She rose, turning to him. He was wearing linen pants and a thin henna-colored T-shirt that set off the gold in his beard, a new feature. He was very tanned and seemed taller than she remembered. "Bee," he murmured, his hands on her elbows. "You look starving." He leaned forward a little, as if he might kiss her. "Come on. Aren't you a little happy to see me?"

With him standing in front of her, the issue forced, her impulse was to say yes. She thought how easy it would be to retrace her way back to what they once were. She could ask him to take her from here and all its madness, to keep her from looking back as they fled from this country. He would say yes. They would go back to their city and resume their ways of reading the paper in bed and walking through streets and parks with their hands loosely laced together. He would make her laugh again; they would sit in narrow bars and feed dollars into the jukebox; there would be noise. This man had loved her, seen her in the dead of sleep and the surly blur of waking up, held pieces of her that no one else could accumulate. She did belong to him, perhaps more than she was willing to admit to either of them. Had it been rash of her to think, as she had thought last fall, that she had lost two years of her life, denied herself all the things she might have done had she not been with him?

Maybe she hadn't lost anything, had just given it to someone who didn't know better than to hold it so close it seemed hidden from her.

Maybe now they would work through the impasse, and be stronger for it. It was possible, Bijou concluded, that enough time had passed, that he could indeed share—and therefore lighten—her sorrow.

She put her arms around him, her lips to his cheek. She said, "It feels like I haven't seen you in years," and felt some of the comfort it had once given her to rest against him.

He pushed her away, squeezed her arms in return; his smile ran up to his eyes. It had often made her believe her work on earth was done if she could spark such happiness in another person. "I love it here," he said.

She had expected him to say he loved *her*. To cover her surprise, she said, "Well, it is a five-star hotel."

He laughed. "I mean Calcutta."

"*Cal*cutta."

"Kolkata, actually, if they can manage it. All the big cities are going pre-Raj. It's so modern."

"You're something else."

"I wasn't about to sit in my room all day. I met some people, and we went around. What? Don't look so surprised. You know I love this stuff."

He confessed that it had always been his plan. That he had, back in the fall, carefully listened to her talking to her mother on the phone whenever they discussed the dates of their trip. He'd bought his ticket then; in fact, the last time they'd seen each other, he'd wanted to tell her. Then—the parting, well, it hadn't been too good, had it? He was sure he would cancel the trip. But he never did.

"Where did your," she said slowly, "little excursion take you?"

"I'll tell you later. One place was Tagore's," he said. He put his hands at either side of her hips. "You're not mad? Let's go upstairs."

"You went to Santiniketan? How did you even know about it?"

"Let's go upstairs and I'll tell you!"

She shook her head.

"You wanna see the digs, don't you? Come on."

They could have been anywhere, she thought. Alipur or Adams

Morgan, what was the difference? She pointed behind him. "Let's see if they have iced coffee in the restaurant."

"Come on. We'll have some privacy. I doubt you want people to hear us."

She hesitated, he didn't blink, and then she agreed.

His room had a view of the swimming pool. He'd explained on the way up that his dad had helped book arrangements, knew people who knew people, and voilà. Bijou stood by the window, watching Crane's reflection as he emptied his pockets onto the console table, next to a tall empty bottle of Kingfisher, glancing at her once, then twice. He rubbed the back of his neck, then stared at the ceiling, rolling his head from shoulder to shoulder.

Out of old habit, she kneaded his neck gently in passing before she sat on the edge of the bed. "What did you tell your mother about this visit?" He half-smiled and sat down next to her.

"My mother took my sister to Darjeeling," she murmured. "But they're coming back this weekend."

"Why didn't you go with them?" He put his hand at her nape, now, and lightly scratched.

She sighed, slowly rolled her head over the slatted cradle of his palm. "If I had, I wouldn't be here." She closed her eyes, and Crane's hands ran down her back; he pressed his thumbs down the trench of her spine, sliding them sideways under her shoulder blades, then back.

"Relax," he said quietly.

"I really want to, you know? But it's like I never knew how."

"You knew," he said, his hands dropping away. She pulled him back, asked him not to stop, and soon she was undressed and underneath him. He hovered over her like a canopy, a shelter, saying all the things he used to say to her but hadn't in so long, beginning to manipulate her body in ways he'd practiced before. And she responded much as she always had in the beginning. His eyes were closed, hers were open, watching him escape to whatever place he went when they did this. The angle his neck formed at his shoulder could dovetail with the tip of an arrow; for a moment she didn't see Crane so much as the space around him. Then he disappeared, and there was only the ceiling in view, a bit of the wall and the beveled trim above the door. He was lying on his back with his arms behind his head, under the pillow. When she turned to him, totally, he released one arm and wrapped it around her. He drew her in. She rested her head on his chest, her lips just grazing his breastbone, and they lay like this for minutes. When she blinked, her eyelashes skipped against his skin. He ran his fingers along her spine. The trail of his touch flared out from her back to every nerve ending, pulsing, keen to be controlled.

But it wasn't Crane she wanted, not in particular, and he seemed to realize that.

"You don't want to do this," he said.

"This?" She waited. "I don't know."

For a while, he refused to look at her. "Don't apologize, I guess. I swore I wouldn't beg, Bee. But I saw you, and I forgot."

His lips were parted a fraction of an inch, warm salty breath scratching out of his dry throat. It had once seemed so fated, the way they'd met, fantastic and divinely touched. She'd made no effort to find him in D.C., nor had he to find her; therefore, it must have been some greater power behind their coming together. Only now she was wondering if that power was not the entirely benevolent force she'd imagined. Worse, it was probably no power at all, just chaos and ecology, in a sequence you could only ever read backward. Perhaps it would be the same with Naveen—again, the lines on the chalkboard loomed before her—and perhaps to prevent any further damage, the right thing to do now was to bury the hatchet.

"I forgot, too," she said.

Crane suddenly hovered over her again, hands under her back, arms braced to her sides. The sheets had wound up around them; the bedspread was on the floor. "I miss you so much."

"It's my fault." He seemed almost too pleased to hear her say this, but she continued: "I've been an awful friend. I thought it would be better, not seeing you at all. And you've come all the way here, and I want to show you I recognize that. I think it's crazy, and I know why you think it isn't, but this is not the way . . ."

She left the bed, collected her clothes, and disappeared behind the bathroom door. He was saying something; it sounded sad and angry. She turned on the lights after she'd wrapped herself in towels. She ran water in the tub, sat on the edge, put her face in her hands, and broke into tears. Her thoughts turned again to Naveen; part of her wanted to call him, have him rescue her from here.

A knock on the door, and it came ajar. Crane cleared his throat, staying out of her view. "You okay? Can I come in?"

"Hang on." She turned around and slid into the tub, pulling the curtain. She splashed water on her face and slid down into the water. "I'll be out in five minutes."

Now he peeked around the door. "You're sure you're okay?"

She splashed some water on her face, pulled the curtain back a bit, and smiled at him weakly. "Five minutes."

"Take your time," he said. "But you're going to eat with me before you leave."

Crane led her through the atrium lounge to a place they could get a bite. Following him, she noted he had new leather *chapals,* much like the ones Naveen always wore.

"Where'd you get those sandals? And those, uh, breezy pants?" she said.

"I went to one of the markets. Why?"

"I never pictured you dressed like this."

"I dress like this every summer, Bee."

"But here," she said, "it looks so colonial."

"You're still cute, Bee." He gave her a look of mild disdain.

They settled at a table near the bottom of the stairs that had led down to an informal dining area. A beautiful arrangement of twigs and fire-red blossoms drooped over the top of the wall adjacent to the steps. Crane ordered food and she asked for iced coffee.

"Are you really leaving next week?" he asked. "Because I'm planning on going up to Nepal after this. I want you to come with me."

She stared at him for a bit. "How long," she finally thought to ask, "are you going to be here?"

"I've already made all the arrangements."

"What kind of arrangements?"

"Tickets, lodging, some hiking stuff. I thought it would be nice."

"To go hiking? Are you serious? I don't—did you quit your job or something?"

"We always talked about doing that kind of thing for a honeymoon."

"Right, which *this* is not." She drew back slightly, then said, "I'm going back to D.C. on Monday, Crane. That's not changing."

"You were supposed to stay a month."

"I don't think you get what it's been like for me—"

"Did you miss me? Is that why you decided to go back early?"

"Do you remember why I came here?"

"I just thought," he said, "that some time together, in a new place, might be good for us. I don't understand: you always wanted to go to Nepal. I am offering to take you there. Where's the problem?"

The waiter brought their food to the table: fish kebabs, *paneer pakora,* a skewer of grilled shrimp with charred peppers, and naan. Crane thanked him, and informed Bijou that he was living on these four items, plus bottled water, plus iced coffee, which he thought was even better than Thai iced coffee, plus pale ale.

"I'm not very hungry," she mumbled.

The waiter had set down two plates and the silverware when another man—the manager or the maitre d'—approached the table to ask if they needed anything else.

"We're fine," Bijou said.

The man smiled, nodded, said he was happy to see them here. "Is this your first trip to India together?"

"Yes, it is," Crane said, grinning. "Our first trip. But not our last."

"Oh, I see," the man said, with a glance toward Bijou. "Will you return for a wedding, perhaps?"

"We're not even engaged," Bijou interjected. "Why is everyone so obsessed with marriage?"

The man chuckled, bowed slightly, and left them to their food, which Crane was quick to begin eating. He filled his plate, urging Bijou to do the same.

"You don't have to be rude, Bee."

"I don't have a lot of time."

"Anyway," he said, exasperated, "Nepal should be amazing. I don't think it can be better, exactly, than India, but it could be cool. I wish we could go to Bombay, but Nepal seemed more, you know, just good for us. So I do *get* what you're going through, at least a little."

She watched him. The square hands, the wristwatch she'd given him for his birthday, the brown pins of stubble on his neck and face, the faint scar above his eyebrow that she used to love to kiss.

He stopped eating and looked at her. "Would you please eat something?"

"Why couldn't you wait until it was over? Until I was back?"

"Nothing is ever over with you. You're always going to have some excuse." He stuck his fork into a piece of fish, then rested it on the plate. Looking up at her, he went on: "I always figured I would come here for you, you know. It's a part of you I wanted to see. I want to meet your family. So I'm here, doing what I want to do, and I'm with you. It's not as I'd planned, but I'll take my lumps."

"Are you saying it's like *I'd* planned?"

He tore at a piece of naan and stuffed it in his mouth, chewed rapidly, swallowed, looked around, took a drink of water. She had seen him go through this routine countless times. She knew he was organizing his anger, lining up the words that would give some structure of reason to his grievances. He was thinking, *Why the hell can't you meet me halfway? Why do I do this to myself, for you?* The wrinkles in his forehead seemed deeper, Bijou noticed, than before. He actually looked quite tired, and she felt sick for how she was provoking him, how he provoked her. Had they ever behaved like adults? How did adults behave? Not like this.

"All we ever do together is eat." Her voice was low and breakable. She busied herself in stirring her drink.

"That's not true. Come on, be positive. Tell me something that will make me feel I haven't totally wasted the last two years of my life pursuing a future with someone who won't even meet me halfway, after I come halfway around the world to see her."

"I didn't know two years ago that this is where I'd end up."

"*We'd* end up. Why don't you ever say 'we'? And it was inevitable, wasn't it?" He lowered his voice. "You knew your dad wasn't going to live like that forever. You wouldn't have wanted him to."

For a moment, Bijou's voice failed her. When she found it, it had taken on the quality of ice. "You don't even know," she said. "But would it kill you to ask? To ask me as soon as you saw me, how it went? How I'm doing? Aren't you even the least bit curious about what I've been doing here, the people I've met, what I've learned? Or is it just about you, getting sunburned while you hang out at Tagore's house? And your appetite for—for all this?" She frowned at the food on the table, waving her hand over it. "Maybe you should just stay here, marry a *real* Indian girl. Maybe I was just your stepping-stone. Sometimes, people are just stepping-stones."

"Have you met someone?" he said, horrified.

"For fuck's sake . . ."

"Is he Indian?"

"Why do we do this? We're both such children; my younger sister is maturing faster than I am! She's, like, half our age. All we do is go in circles, Crane. It's just not working anymore. I don't think we'll ever forgive each other."

"Well, then I guess you won't forgive me for thinking that marriage was a step toward adulthood."

"That's just it. I don't want to take on the big, huge, vast responsibility that marriage is just so I can escape a bunch of other ones. Can you tell me, honestly, that you are truly ready for marriage? For the rest of our lives? Me in the hell that is medical school, children, mortgages, Christmases in Detroit, my mother all but moving in with us because she's going to visit *all the time*? Have you thought this through at all?"

He took a long time with his response. "Not like that."

It wasn't in an instant, or as if a series of images from the preceding days went flashing before her eyes; but in trying to imagine a way to begin telling Crane about her father's questionable past or how Ketaki seemed to hate her, and ask if *he* had seen the Howrah Bridge yet, because she wasn't sure if that was the bridge she'd seen the night she'd placed her father's ashes in the river, and could she just tell him how she had cried that night, like a banshee, and sometimes it felt as if she would never be functional again—in trying to piece together a beginning and an end, she failed to produce anything but a messy middle.

"I don't know what else to say," she said, leaning forward almost desperately. "Maybe it's just time. Maybe in *another* two years, I could be yours again. Who knows?"

"It doesn't work that way. You'll never come back."

"How do you *know*? Why can't you even entertain the *idea*? It's just an idea—" She stopped short. He had relaxed his stance and was now rubbing his eyes with his hands, elbows on the table, plate empty. Suddenly, it struck her that there might be more to his ultimatum than she had assumed. She had been clear, and he didn't appear defeated. "You're not telling me everything, are you?"

He shook his head and told her no before he looked her in the eye again.

She drew back a little and frowned. "You're kidding."

"I met someone. I met someone, and I liked her. I missed you, but then I met her. And she's serious."

"She's *serious*?" Bijou said with disbelief. "Are you kidding me?"

"I couldn't joke about this. I came here for you, Bee. I came here for us. I couldn't be with anyone until I knew for sure about us."

"When were you going to tell me about her?" She shook her head. "I can't believe this is happening. I can't believe I almost slept with you up there. Who is she? When were you going to tell me?"

"I didn't think I'd have to. She's—"

"How do you treat people like this?"

"What's unreasonable here? I haven't done anything but try to keep you."

"I don't know." She stood up. "I have to go."

"You can't go." He followed her out of the lounge, abandoning the table. "Just come with me!"

In the foyer, she stopped and faced him. "I thought I was impatient," she said. "But you—you are. I go through a rough patch, and your response is to give me an ultimatum?" Her voice was unsteady, and she felt weak, as if she could collapse. "No more pressure. It's coming from everywhere; I can't handle it from you, too. If you can't wait for me, then what's the point, Crane? Really?"

Was that all? She was going to leave him like this? After he'd come all this way to have her?

"You had me," she said. "Maybe that's all there was to your share."

In the living room sat her aunt, her uncle, and Kamla Auntie, drinking tea and watching a variety show on television. She greeted them.

"How was your meeting? Everything work out?" said her aunt.

"Oh, yeah, it was really good," she said, sitting on the rug by her chair. "Thanks for letting Ramesh drive me."

Her aunt leaned forward and ran her hand gently over Bijou's head. "I brought home some sweets. Would you like some?"

"Oh, I ate."

"Lovely," her uncle said, glancing away from the television. "It's a fine hotel, isn't it?"

"Pretty posh."

Her aunt said, "You can stay there for your honeymoon! Don't you think, Kamla Di? Don't you think it's time to marry this one off, to a prince?"

"But I don't want to get married right now. Really, let's not talk about this anymore."

Kamla laughed. "Let her finish medical school first! Let her become something."

Bijou's aunt considered this. "But she said six years. Why wait that long? No good boys will be left then."

"That's absolutely true," Kamla said. "But by then, they might be good men."

"No, no," Bijou's aunt murmured. "She shouldn't be alone. And the sooner my sister gets a wonderful son-in-law, the happier she can be. Whatever you say, it's nice to have men about. Right? Come now, I know how you feel about Naveen. It's about balance, yin and yang. Plain and simple."

Bijou's uncle threw a quick puzzled look at his wife.

Kamla took a sip of her tea, and nodded. "Don't listen to me, Bijou. Your aunt is much wiser in these matters. I'm sure your mother is, too."

Bijou gave Kamla a long look. She wondered how she really felt about the woman her old friend Nitish would marry instead of her. All those years, did she harbor any resentment? Did she receive those letters in hopes that one day, one of them would inform her of his return?

"Why don't you come to the clinic tomorrow, Bijou?" Kamla was asking her. "I know I can at least offer you expertise in one respect. And I really am interested in your research. Some of the other doctors would be, too."

"I'd love that," Bijou said. "There's so much I already want to ask you."

"Kamla Di," her aunt said, "isn't it true that you did the *mehndi* for Piya Das's wedding? You could do Bijou's *mehndi*. When it's time."

"Anuja Massi," Bijou said, "please don't think of these things, please, please." She looked at her hands then, and emitted a faint gasp: her ring was gone. She must have left it in the hotel. Yes, she had, stupidly, forgotten it in Crane's room.

"What is it?" her aunt said.

"What happened?" Kamla said.

"I seem to have lost my ring," Bijou replied, cheerlessly. "I'm so sorry, Anuja Massi. After I made you buy it for me!" She wondered if it would ever be found: had Crane slipped it into his pocket? Would he keep it for the rest of his life? Or had a stranger done the same? Were the two scenarios that different? Perhaps it had simply fallen down the sink drainpipe. What happened to things?

She heard her aunt laughing it off. "It's easily replaceable. Don't be so sad."

Bijou kissed her aunt good night, then Kamla, and her uncle, too. "It's been a long day. Thanks again for everything. I'll see you in the morning."

The only dream she remembered having that night was of being driven to a hospital, where Crane sat up in bed, sipping purple juice from a clear plastic tumbler and reading the letters her father had sent to Kamla, years and years before, each one asking after Naveen.

If ever asked to provide the place most opposite to the Taj Bengal Hotel, Bijou decided she would, without reservation, say it was Bala Healthy House, the site where Kamla spent most of her waking hours. The small edifice, painted the cheery mustard color of a marigold, stood quietly on an unnamed street they had reached through a warren of narrow dirt paths. The clinic had a concrete fence around the perimeter of what little land it had staked out for itself on a dusty block of squatters' lots and a few residential tenements with wooden porches like scaffolding; they reminded Bijou, oddly, of the saloons one would see in old Westerns. There was a pleasant garden near the entry of the clinic, however, and inside the walls were blue as robins' eggs. A young woman was washing the linoleum floors, which reflected the steel of medical carts and IV-drip poles.

Kamla had taken Bijou on her rounds of the patients, all children, and introduced her to the nurses and two resident medical students who were about Bijou's age. There were six small beds—no vacancies—to each of the nine rooms. The rooms enclosed a paved courtyard that, by noon, was so full of sunshine it was as impossible to see to the other side as if it had been the middle of the night.

When the tour was over and Kamla had taken care of a few outpatient appointments, the two of them sat in her office with some tea and savory black cumin-flecked biscuits. Half the size of the other rooms, and further compressed by rows of light-green filing cabinets, the office dedicated whatever space it had left to an examination table, four rolling metal stools, and a small desk. The X-ray reader above it was yellowing from age.

"Those children are wonderful," Bijou said. "They're lucky to have you."

"In a city this populous, you never feel you're doing enough. Just when you think you've adequately stocked vaccinations, you must order a hundred more. When I'm not here, I try to spend as much time as I can at the family-planning centers. So much of this is just a result of lack of education."

"I couldn't imagine this," Bijou confessed. "I've seen the way things run in the cities back home, but this, this is on an entirely different scale. How do you do it? How do you persevere?"

"Oh, I don't see it like that. I can't be bothered to think what would happen if I quit. I won't even retire until I have three more doctors enlisted to replace me." She drank some tea, then added, "Like you. Could you do it?"

"Could I do it?" Bijou repeated. "Assuming I make it to medical school, much less through it. But, yes, I would love to practice at a place like this, if I could. It would contradict all the reasons I've gotten this far if I said otherwise. I just don't seem to have gotten very far as yet."

"But you will, you will. You must. I have every faith in you, *beta*. I know what sort of standards you were taught, after all. Your father held himself to the highest."

"Do you believe that, still?"

"Why wouldn't I? He was very dear to me."

"I know," Bijou said. She brushed a few crumbs of biscuit off her lap. "Naveen has been—" she said, then stopped to clear her throat and start again. "Naveen showed me some of the letters my father sent you. I was actually quite surprised by them. I never knew that you . . . that he was quite that involved with you."

"Yes, we kept in touch," Kamla said pleasantly. "It was very good of him."

"But," Bijou said, "what I mean to say is—"

As she interrupted, Kamla's tone became less flexible. "Bijou, I've learned it is wise not to trouble yourself with things that happened very long ago. Indians are too good at it, I'm afraid. Consumed not just with what happened in this lifetime but all the rest! What is good karma, Bijou, if not to live in the present, to take each moment and make the most of it? I would much rather think of what I can accomplish this week than what I ought to have done differently a hundred years ago. Perhaps if I had done anything differently, I wouldn't have the blessing of this clinic. Who's to say, hm?"

"Certainly not me. I don't have a clue."

Kamla smiled. "I have a special history with this clinic, you know? It wasn't always like what you see. When I started here, before we opened it to the children, it was the private surgery of Dr. Sen, whose sons had been friends of Ashok's and Nitish's. In fact, one of the sons is your aunt's physician, now. But back then, well, these rooms were filled with different stories. For instance, it was here that Naveen was born."

"Really?" Bijou said. "That's pretty cool."

Kamla glanced at the clock, and stood up. "I should probably be getting back to work soon." She walked toward the far corner of the office. "But now that I'm thinking of it . . ."

She pulled a slim book out from a stack on top of a cabinet, then returned to Bijou and handed it to her. The book was hardbound in orange cloth. "Nitish gave me this," she said, "when Naveen was born, so that I might have something to read in the hospital. It's a book of poems by Nazrul Islam. Famous poet."

Bijou turned the thin fibrous pages, the parchment the color of brown sugar. The poems were set in pristine lines of Bengali type, although here and there the print had faded. The margins of several pages in the middle brimmed with annotations in diluted indigo ink and pencil.

"You took a lot of notes," Bijou said. "I do that, too."

"The thing is that I never write them in ink. Those belong to Nitish. You might say it's the one letter he sent that Naveen doesn't know about—that silly boy, still hanging on to those things. The only reason I have this now is I'm too busy to buy a new one, and it's a very good book." She smiled a bit nervously, which invited Bijou's speculation that she was bluffing.

"And I can't read one word of it," Bijou said, sadly. "It's terrible being locked out by your own language. What did he write? To you?"

"Bijou, we were very close." Her voice dropped into a kind of tired casualness, honest. She straightened up then, and added, "Your father was the type of man who left a piece of himself behind with everyone he met. I used to wonder how he'd left so much with us, here, and still had more to spare."

"But what did he write?"

"In several places, he simply corrected my spelling." She laughed. "There's nothing but mischief in those notes, Bijou. It's like a code, but probably today I couldn't even decipher it. There was affection, too, and as I remember there was an apology. Which I accepted."

"Even after he left? Even after he never came back?"

"Yes." Her eyes fell to the book in Bijou's hands. "Although it would have been nice to see him again. He was forever a good friend." She sighed. "Do stay in touch with us, *beta*. If there's anything I can do to help, whatever you need, don't ever hesitate to ask."

"I promise. We'll stay connected."

"I hope so. And, actually, one more thing," Kamla said as she accompanied Bijou out of her office. "Perhaps you can spend some more time with Naveen before you leave. He's quite enjoyed your company. I know, it must sound peculiar coming from me—to you—but I think you might help him put some ghosts to rest, as they say. It's something I've failed to do."

Bijou nodded, gently clasping Kamla's hand. "I don't know if it's karma or what," she said, "but he's helped me in ways no one else ever has. I'd be happy to see him again."

"Of course it's karma, Bijou. We all come into and go out of each other's lives for some purpose. Now you think it's for one reason; in five years, you'll think it's for another one, and probably in ten, then you will see the *real* reason."

"Ten years? What am I supposed to do meanwhile?"

"The obvious. You make something of yourself. You have a big responsibility now, Bijou. You have to make the world better. Never let your compassion—and that's what you get from your father, from his loss—never let it go to waste."

TEN

The next morning, Naveen came again to ferry her away, this time with the promise of an afternoon in an air-conditioned cinema hall on Chowringhee Street.

"No," he had assured her on the phone, "it doesn't have to be the typical Hindi movie."

"I like the old ones," she had said. "If it's an old one, I don't mind."

"Bijoya has preferences. Discriminating tastes."

It still disconcerted her, this tone he took when he spoke of her character as if dropping nuggets of gold wisdom onto her plate. What was this habit of talking to her by talking about her? Was she supposed to applaud him for making obvious statements sound like declarations of discovery? Suppose she asked him about it. Perhaps he would think she was crazy. Perhaps he was only trying to be good company, and the problem was that she no longer understood what was natural about anything, much less building a friendship.

"I just like the old ones better," she'd said, sounding to herself entirely like a child.

Now, as she mounted the scooter and settled into the seat behind Naveen, a similar awkwardness crept through her skin; she noticed Ketaki watching them from the veranda upstairs, dragging her straw whisk broom along the railing. Though she'd told herself Ketaki was simply indifferent to her—and why not, why shouldn't she be?—it was difficult to ignore the likelihood that, in truth, Ketaki disliked her, and was counting the seconds until Bijoya Roy would return to America, where she could *do her work alone.*

Then they started moving, and within minutes all suspicious musings were replaced by survival instincts; she clutched Naveen's shoulders for her life as they motored through streets and alleys. It was the first time she thought of Calcutta as a windy place, and she understood better why her uncle had referred to this scooter as a death trap. The road underneath them was gravelly at best, spelling out the ride in a series of bumps and lurches. Bijou sat up as straight as possible, narrowing herself into what seemed an ever decreasing margin for the scooter. If she could have, she would have folded herself like a dollar bill and hid in Naveen's wallet. In the small circular rearview mirror that stuck out from the scooter handles like an antler, she saw very quickly the back sides of things that would have, at a reasonable clip, still loomed before them.

Naveen jerked the handles, swerving around a pothole the size of a sewer lid. They came to a full stop at a traffic light. Bijou slumped, took off her sunglasses, and rubbed the dust from her eyes. Near the corner of the street where they idled, a few men and a woman cowered over a small brick oven. They were working with their hands, kneading and pinching away at some matter. At first, Bijou assumed they were cooking. The woman laughed at something one of the men said, leaned back and held one hand against her taut belly. She wore a yellow sari, frayed along the borders, brightened by the sun. Bijou watched as the woman knelt to the ground, then placed the object she had been working on inside the oven with a pair of rusted tongs. Arranged on the sidewalk next to the oven were rows upon rows of cups, small, handleless, the one identical to the next. Just as her father had told her, Bijou reflected. The potters and their wares were not myth.

Over his shoulder, Naveen asked her how she'd enjoyed her visit to the clinic.

She gathered herself, still shaken by the ride. "Honestly, I don't know how to thank either of you for spending all this time with me. I hate to think I've disrupted your lives."

"Rubbish. Our first-year students will be sitting for exams in a matter of weeks, you see. Other than that, it's not *terribly* busy."

"My aunt and uncle are very busy."

"Yes, well . . . Perhaps they're more committed to their students than I am."

He was being modest. At dinner just the evening before, Bijou's uncle had described Naveen as quite favored by senior officials at the college. Envious as the others might have been, they didn't begrudge the young scholar his exalted standing. Even the invitations for a post abroad—there was no resentment in the department over those; on the contrary, weren't they all being very supportive? Bijou's uncle thought so.

He'd also mentioned how Naveen had never taken any leave before now. His peers weren't surprised that his request for some time off had been granted; they were simply puzzled as to why he'd taken leave *only* to stay in town. Bijou's uncle, too, was at a total loss for explanations.

"I hope Naveen isn't suffering from *tension*," he'd said. "It would be a shame if he felt overworked so soon into his career."

In Bijou's view, there was no apparent sign that Naveen was suffering from tension, now or ever. The light changed, he gunned the engine, and they were off again. By the time they reached

Chowringhee, she had left her forehead to rest against Naveen's back. Surrender.

He guided her to the theater with his hand hovering behind her elbow until they turned a corner, and he expressed surprise upon seeing how long the line was for tickets. He questioned whether or not it would be worth waiting, and she shrugged. There were indeed many people milling about, and it felt strange to be out in the daylight among those who were seeking entertainment, a leisurely break. She hadn't, after all, come to Calcutta to go to the movies, had she? That's what her mother would have said.

"We tried," Bijou said, and shrugged again. Naveen was looking around and pursing his lips.

"Let me look," he said, "up at the—let me go ask someone something. Okay? You can stay right here yourself?"

She blinked. "I guess so. I can't come with you?"

A few young men were suddenly behind her, asking if she was in line or not.

"We are," Naveen said to them, then to her: "We'll wait here and see."

Over his shoulder, Bijou caught smirks on two of the guys' faces. They were looking at her. She kept her expression blank, and looked away slowly, as if she had always been planning to do just this, to just take in the panorama of Chowringhee Street. Then she stared at the ground.

As they waited, the guys behind them bantered about the last movie they had seen here, and snickered, and feigned shock, and trafficked heavily in sarcasm. In front of them, a group of five or six schoolgirls stood around like bonded molecules, speaking in sensible tones about what role a parent really ought to play in a teenager's social life. As the line inched forward, it was the girls to whom

Bijou paid more attention, especially as Naveen was not speaking to her. After about ten minutes, however, he said, "Let's go."

"Why?"

"I don't want a scene," he said, somewhat loudly. Bijou frowned, but she followed him as they turned in the direction of the scooter.

"What was that about?"

"They were being idiots."

"Who?"

Naveen stopped and turned to face her, but he avoided eye contact. He seemed at once angry and a bit nervous. "They were saying things, those *chokras* behind us, those guys. You know. Suggestive things?"

"Are you sure? I tuned them out."

He shook his head. "You have to stay alert, Bijoya."

"They wouldn't have done anything. Come on. Broad daylight."

"You're just," he said, "somewhat conspicuous. It's not your fault, of course."

She thought back to when she had gone to New Market, and her aunt had said much the same thing. "Is it so obvious I'm not from here?"

"Listen, Bijoya, there is simply something about fair-skinned women that will always be problematic in this culture."

Bijou felt her anger rise. Why should she be judged like this? If she could have walked away from him, she would have, but of course she was entirely dependent on him to get her home. "No one ever calls me Bijoya if they know me as Bijou," she said. "Let's just go."

"I'm sorry."

"So am I," she said quickly, though she wasn't sure why.

As they made their way back to Naveen's scooter, his cell phone rang.

"It's your aunt," he said, and as he listened, Bijou could hear her aunt chattering. After a minute, the call was over, and Naveen's sullen visage had morphed entirely. He reported with a grin: "See how things work out? She's made it clear she wanted you home immediately. There's a surprise waiting for you."

"What?"

"I can't tell you. Okay, I'll give you a hint: it's not a question of *what* but of *who*." He took his scooter key from his pocket and gestured for her to get on.

"Who is it?"

"Let's go, Bijoya. Not another word."

"Did she tell you not to tell me?"

"It's a surprise, *yaar*. But why are you so nervous? Have you done something wrong? Expecting the police?"

She was nervous, she did not say aloud, because left to his own devices, Crane may have decided to ambush her on Park Street. For all she knew, he was packing her bags for her right now, with her aunt standing by in utter shock. Her fear of Crane eclipsed all fears of the ride back.

But Ramesh was carrying two familiar suitcases into the house when they arrived. Ketaki was there, as well. Bijou did a double take when she saw the luggage.

"They've come back?" she said. "Ramesh?"

He nodded. "I picked them up from the station just a while ago."

Ketaki told her that they were upstairs, and commanded her to join them *quick quick,* for they had all been waiting *kobe theke,* making it sound like *since the beginning of time.*

"I'll see you later," Naveen said.

"Why? You can come, too, if you want. Do you want to come inside?"

"I'm sure they'll want you to themselves. Give them my regards, and I'll see you at the get-together, okay?"

They hugged each other good-bye on the porch. Bijou waved at him as he scootered away. When she turned back to go inside, Ketaki was looking at her queerly again.

She ran upstairs to find her mother and sister in her aunt's bedroom. Pari and her aunt were lounging on the bed. Her mother stood unzipping a duffel bag.

"Surprise, Bijou," her aunt said when she saw her enter. "They're early!"

"This is awesome," she replied, embracing her sister. "What happened?"

"I missed you," Pari whispered loudly into Bijou's ear. "One week was enough."

"Tell me about it."

They held each other tightly. Then Bijou went to their mother and kissed her cheek. "I missed you, too."

Her mother gave her a look that suggested she needed more convincing, but she said, "It's good to see you, *beta*. You seem rested, finally."

Pari plopped down on the bed again to lie down, and Bijou perched on the foot of it, playfully tweaking her sister's toes.

"Tell me, who was this doctor you went to see?" her mother inquired. "At the Taj? Rather fancy."

"There's a research team here. I just needed to learn some more about their project."

"And you've been at Kamla's house again today?"

"No, Naveen was just taking me out, like, for lunch," Bijou said. "I didn't know you'd be home early."

"I didn't think you would be anywhere else but here." Her mother went about withdrawing toiletries and cotton nightgowns from her bag. After a minute, she said, "Aren't you going to ask about Darjeeling?"

Bijou looked up from her sister's feet. "Didn't I?" she said. "I want to hear everything. But, first, I should wash up. That scooter of Naveen's is more like a dirt bike."

Pari whined, "You got to ride on a scooter? I want to!"

Ketaki came into the room with a small steel tray holding a glass of water, which she handed to Bijou's mother. Accepting the water with words of thanks, her mother then asked the girl to assure her that Bijou had been a pleasant guest.

Ketaki laughed in what came off as a backhanded affirmation. "Don't forget to show them your new ring," she said to Bijou.

"You didn't buy her jewelry, did you?" her mother said, turning to Bijou's aunt. "I told you this was not the time. A few new suits was quite enough."

"No, no. She just got something artificial. Small thing. If it made her happy, don't give her a hard time!"

"Let me see it then," her mother said.

"It looked like a gardenia," Bijou said.

"Did you get one for me?" Pari said.

"Gardenias smell wonderful," her aunt said. "Like jasmine."

Bijou agreed. "Make me think of Billie Holiday."

"But she wore them in her hair, no?" her mother said. She took a long sip from her glass of water. "That woman had such a sad life. Always sang like she was weeping. She reminded Nitish of the old Bengali film actresses."

"Oh, remember *Sahib Bibi Aur Ghulam*?" Bijou's aunt said. "Meena Kumari's husband was hateful, running to see Waheeda

Rehman dancing—hateful! Drinking, drunkard, womanizer. Kashmiri men are not so cuckoo like that, are they?"

"I haven't seen that film in so long," Bijou's mother said. "I never liked Meena Kumari. She was *too* unhappy. Her films always left me in a desperate mood. Likewise, I never cared for Bette Davis."

"How can anyone not like Bette Davis?" Bijou said.

"You just have to see those old movies, girls, to understand what your father meant by his comparison," her mother said. "Very tragic women. But they were strong. I don't think I could have handled what women of that generation put up with; I give them credit."

"So where's the ring, Didi?" Pari asked. "You aren't wearing any rings."

"I lost it," Bijou said with a frown.

"You *lost* it?" her mother said.

"By accident!"

Her aunt ran interference: "It's okay! It's okay! So easy to replace. Bijou is a very generous girl, so sweet. She keeps giving Ketaki chocolates."

"Why?" Bijou's mother said.

"I only did it once," Bijou said. "I don't think she was pleased."

"Did you get any chocolate for me? No, why would you?" Pari said. "No one gets me anything."

"Maybe I should have given her *more*," Bijou said. "I could have easily brought her more, but I just didn't think to do that."

"Do you remember that maidservant who worked next door to us?" Bijou's mother asked her aunt, waving a toothbrush case in the air. "Ketaki reminds me . . . Laxmi. That was her name."

"*Nahi, nahi,*" Bijou's aunt objected. "Leela. I remember. She rhymed with you!" She went on to describe Leela as the ayah for a young Kashmiri couple who lived not next door but across the street from them in Srinagar.

"Leela had taken quite a fancy to the wife, who had been raised in Australia," her aunt said. "Rumor had it that the wife had worked with aboriginal tribes after completing a convent-school education. She returned to India after marriage because her husband insisted.

"The neighbors referred to most of the wife's clothes as safari outfits, khaki trousers and funny-button blouses with so many pockets! But for evening affairs, she would wear decadent saris and the highest heels, her hair twisted and piled in a beehive style. Men were crazy for it, clearly, because the other wives in the community all hated her.

"Leela was brought in immediately after the birth of her first child, and the wife treated her very well. She took Leela on picnics and trips, gave her nice clothes, paid her handsomely, even taught her how to read and write.

"Well, we all noticed—how could we not?—that this ayah was behaving more and more like the wife, nose in the air, walking on the wind." She stopped speaking momentarily, and managed quite well to portray the ayah's *insolence* through a series of herky-jerky arm and neck movements. "Then one day," her aunt continued, "the wife comes home and do you know what she finds?"

Bijou shook her head. "The husband . . . ?"

"She found this ayah sitting at the wife's dressing table and putting on the wife's lipstick!"

"Oh my *God*," Pari said, throwing her arms in the air. "I thought you were going to say that she—"

"That she'd run off with the husband," Bijou interjected, gripping Pari's ankles. "Right?"

Pari raised her head slightly from her pillow and looked at her askance. "That she had kidnapped the baby."

"Well, it wasn't long before Leela was replaced," her aunt said. "Of course, she'll probably run for PM one day. Prime Minister Leelaji. Why not? She wouldn't be the first Kashmiri to hold office, now would she?"

Bijou's mother laughed. "Nitish used to love that story," she said over her shoulder. "He called Leela a champion. *Blue ribbon.*" Her back was turned to the rest of them as she unlocked the door of the *almirah* cabinet.

"Really?" Bijou said. "But why haven't you ever told us this before?"

Her mother placed a folded set of nighties in the closet before turning back toward Bijou. "Why? I don't know. It never came up."

"I would have liked hearing it earlier," Bijou said.

Her mother zipped the empty duffel bag shut in one quick gesture. "Better late than never, isn't it?" she said. "It was so long ago."

"You say that about everything. You create all these mysteries."

"Mysteries? My God, you blow things out of proportion."

"It's not the greatest story, anyway," Pari said glibly, rising from the bed. "I'm going to watch some television."

Bijou followed her, mumbling that she would clean up and join them at lunch. As she left the room, she heard her aunt and mother reminiscing again about the time in their lives when Leela was a star, when they went to the banks of the Jhelum River and climbed the apple trees, taking the vista of blue sky and snowcapped mountains for granted, when their valley knew only peace.

After her bath, Bijou went up to the roof to let her hair dry. Through a window of the house next door, she could make out a woman sitting on the kitchen floor, her head downturned, her hair sugar-white at the roots. Someone else in the kitchen was chopping something. Bijou slowly pulled her towel down from her shoulders as she looked closer. The woman was busy cutting a large fish into steaks, running the body through a hooked blade affixed to a baseboard. She cut off the fish's head and handed it to a young maidservant, who stood before the woman, wiping her eyes with the back of her hand, still holding a knife. Another woman, unseen, said something in a shrill voice about the cost of chicken.

Bijou leaned over the edge of the roof, where, days before, she'd watched the boy slip out of his shorts. The stall where the man came to iron was empty. Where were they now? Where into the world had they disappeared to?

She would leave India. Of course she would leave India; that had always been the plan. She would leave soon. She pictured Crane in his hotel room, and wondered how she'd see him again now that her mother had returned. Coincidental with the thought, her mother came out onto the roof and told her that lunch was almost ready.

"You're looking feverish. Is everything okay?"

"I was just thinking." Bijou buried her face in her towel for a moment, then looked up at her mother and smiled. "Everything's okay." Her voice sounded girlish and taut to her.

Her mother leaned her back against the ledge of the roof. One end of her *dhupatta* hung over the side. After a while, she said, "Your *massi* tells me you've been spending a great deal of time with the Mazumdars. Not just today, but ever since we left."

"Not every day," Bijou said. "Everyone here is busy with their own lives."

Her mother ran one of her hands through Bijou's hair, untangling the damp strands. "But Naveen made time," she said. "You saw *him* every day?"

"He insisted."

"How did he insist?" her mother responded quickly.

"Everyone else was at work," Bijou said. "Shankar Uncle, Anuja Massi—they were busy. It was sweet of Naveen to keep me company. Even Anuja Massi said so."

"What does your aunt know?" her mother said. She turned around and leaned over the ledge, crossing her arms upon it. "No children of her own to test her."

Bijou fixed her mother's *dhupatta* so it hung evenly. "Have we been that difficult?" she said, then sat down in the wicker chair. She drew her knees up to her chest, feet balanced over the seat's edge. The scars around her ankles from the mosquito bites looked like something written in Braille. She twisted a thread dangling from the hem of her jeans.

"Why are you acting like I've done something wrong?" She looked up at her mother. "Naveen and I have something in common, that's all."

"I didn't say anything of the sort. You're an adult; you should know what's appropriate."

Bijou stretched her neck back. A flock of small birds flew by overhead and disappeared into the sun.

"You're the one who said I should take up Kamla Auntie's offer to see the clinic," she said. "I didn't ask to have dinner with them or anything, remember?"

"People make offers like that just to be polite. You can't say yes to everything," her mother said. She had straightened up and moved away from the ledge, though her arms remained crossed. Her *dhupatta* hung asymmetrically again. "This is not the time to be running around with perfect strangers, to have dinner parties," she continued. "Is that why you came to India? And after all your talk about leaving early. You couldn't spare yourself for a few days with your own sister."

"Don't use Pari as an excuse," Bijou said. She stood up. "I know her better than anyone. I worry about her in ways you are blind to."

"You should talk," her mother said. "You weren't very worried last week when you refused to accompany us."

"I should talk? Why don't *you* talk?" Bijou held out her arms, palms up, toward her mother. "Here's an idea: you could start by telling me how you could marry a man you hardly knew, and leave all this behind?"

"How? Because his life was at risk, Bijou. And I thought I was saving him. That's been my only work in this life. I had no idea. I wanted to be with him, and I didn't care where. Maybe he only loved me because I was one of those girls—not from a family like his, nearer to the people he fought for. I didn't care *why* he loved me. He took care of me. Of us. Always."

"But you ran off with him. My God, if I did such a thing—you would kill me."

"I was *twenty* years old. And my brother liked him."

"Still, you hardly knew him! I mean, how could you make such a huge decision without thinking about it for longer? It's not like choosing a pair of shoes or whatever—it's *marriage*. It's irreversible!"

"Don't I know that?" She shook her head. "What crime have your father and I committed, that you should be so hurt? Yes, we might have found a way to live here, and maybe he would still be alive. Don't I wonder? But did we raise you any the worse because we didn't raise you here? You have the opportunity to be successful there. No one will stand in your way. Have we stood in your way? No."

"You've always told me to keep medical school my first priority."

Her mother gave her a long look. "What is this about? Is something going wrong at work?"

"No." Over the next few minutes, Bijou gathered her courage, running hastily through different ways she could preface saying to her mother, *Crane is here.* There was a breeze on the roof, a welcome note of coolness in the air. Bijou stood leaning over the roof's edge a while longer, studying the dance of some dried leaves on the street below as they darted up from the gully where they'd congregated. "I just wonder, that's all. If we'll ever be happy again, I guess."

"Of course you will. I'm still here, right? We'll find a way." Her mother was not looking at her while she spoke now. "It's a strange thing, what a woman will do for a man. If I knew that it would end so soon, that he would put us through all this . . ."

"What?" Bijou pleaded. "What would you do?"

"I would do it all just the same." Her mother seemed to sing just then. "Again and again, if I had to."

They both looked down into the street now. A dog was relieving himself on the wall, as was his owner. They gasped, then giggled.

"She's having people over on Saturday," her mother said, averting her eyes. "She means well. At least these people know— knew—your father. I won't have to explain."

"It's just a few people." Bijou put her hand on her mother's arm. "I'll be there, this time, with you."

"I don't know what I've done to deserve this. I see him everywhere; I feel like he is still with us. As though, when we go home, things will resume the same as before."

"We did everything we could, didn't we?"

"We did. This is what was meant to be. This is what I am paying for, for whatever terrible things I did in my last life."

Bijou frowned. "I know what you're trying to say, Mummie. But can we focus on *this* life for a minute?"

Her mother sighed, and drummed her fingers against the ledge. "What is there to focus on?" she said, flicking a crumb of cement into the street. "After lunch, I want to spend some time alone with my sister. You should do the same. How that girl has missed you!"

So Bijou spent the afternoon in the bedroom playing gin rummy with her sister, who was full of things to say about Darjeeling. As Pari described it, she and her girlfriends (*From Düsseldorf. They invited me to visit this summer. How many people do* you *know in Düsseldorf?*) had taken long walks along mountain paths every day after morning yoga, waiting for the sight of Mount Kanchenjunga's peak. The girls had bonded over similar tastes in music and distastes in food. Pari liked the ashram atmosphere of vegetarianism, unspoiled nature, and understated appearances. Darjeeling itself reminded her of "a weird watercolor painting, with lots of pastel wooden shacks and super-rural people, such a simple life, and these gorgeous flowers and temples, and rusty old blue trucks, and these hilarious Nepalese kids running around wearing the funkiest sweaters and beanies. You know, like those farmy parts of Michigan, but really, really pretty, with huge valleys and tea gardens."

"You love Darjeeling!" Bijou said, laughing. "You're going to marry it."

"It was like the rest of the world didn't matter anymore. And Sheela was busy doing her own thing, too, which was really nice for a change. Not worrying about her, you know?" She traded one of her cards for one from the pile and chewed her lip. "There was this really old temple in the middle of the woods. It was totally falling apart, you know? Like, monkeys were living there, and the noses had been chipped off all the statue carvings. It might have been a

Buddhist temple; it wasn't far from one of the monasteries. Anyway, we hung out there a lot. Sometimes we'd sit there for hours without talking, or we'd talk about how *cool* it would be if we could live there forever."

"Sounds good to me," Bijou said. "Let's run away and live like super-rural monkeys."

"But you could," Pari said. "And then, when I finish school, I could come, too."

Bijou raised an eyebrow. "You're serious! You want to live in India? What has our mother been filling *your* head with?"

"You weren't there, Didi; it was so awesome. Even yoga was fun." Pari laid her cards facedown on the bed and stood up. She moved her feet apart slowly, lifted her arms, and said gravely, "*Virabhadhrasana*. That's Sanskrit for 'proud warrior.' "

"Cool. You'll have to teach me that one."

"What were you really doing while we were gone?" Pari said, resettling on the bed. "I overheard Anuja Massi and Sheela talking about that professor-wallah."

"Naveen?" Bijou said. She drew a card from the pile.

"He was the one coming by the house, you know, even before you got here. Man, he was asking so many questions about you."

Bijou stopped fiddling with her cards and looked up at Pari. "What sort of questions?"

Pari grinned. "Like, *When is she coming? When will she be here? I could pick her up from the airport.* Very . . . what's the word? When a guy is, like, trying to be helpful but not so much that it's creepy?"

Bijou squinted. "Chivalrous?" she said, her inflection swinging up to a squeal.

"*Yeah*, like that. He was the only person who treated me like I wasn't invisible." She frowned at her cards, then rearranged them. "So?"

"So?"

Pari sighed dramatically and threw her cards on the bed. She'd won the game.

"You didn't cheat, did you? You dealt me such a heinous hand," Bijou said, laying her cards on the bed. "Is this why you never let us keep score?"

"Okay, I'll give you a choice," Pari said. "Tell me about that guy, Crane, or tell me about Novocain. Choose one. Come *on*. You *used* to *tell* me *funny* things."

"Quit your whining, child."

"Why are you being so boring?" Pari fell back, shouting.

Because, Bijou wanted to say, *I have been reckless in ways I would not want you to learn. Because I may have no long-term hope, only short-term impulses. Because I don't want to end up like our parents, except I do. Because something is gnawing at my heart. Because I have to leave soon.*

"Here," she said instead. "I have some pictures of Daddy I want to show you."

"I don't believe you," Pari said. "There's something going on with you and the professor. You're not as mysterious as you think you are."

"Yes, I am, actually."

"Are you going to marry him?"

"If you marry Darjeeling."

"You should run away with him. It would be scandalous!"

"Not for everyone, it wouldn't." She extracted the photographs from her backpack and handed them to Pari, who leafed through the short stack and asked where they'd been found.

"Naveen had them. His mother took them."

Pari looked through them more carefully. "They're on vacation?"

"You remember that stuff I told you about Daddy, how when

he was younger he was an activist, a Naxalite? They used to go into these villages and, basically, they were trying to defend workers' rights. Because the landowners were really corrupt. It was a Communist movement . . . That one was actually taken near Darjeeling. Does it look familiar?"

"Yes! That's so cool. This is what I want to do," Pari said, fixated on the photographs. "Help people. I'm totally going to join the Peace Corps. Or Doctors Without Borders. Look at him in this one. He's such a badass with that beard. How old is he?"

"About twenty."

"If you grew a beard—and I hope you never do—you'd look just like this, Didi. But I have his eyes, don't I?" She stared at the photograph. It was the one of their father looking over his shoulder in mid-step away from the camera.

Bijou smiled. "You do. And sometimes you even stand the way he used to, with your hip all jutted out."

"I miss him, too, Didi," Pari said after a while. The slight muscles around her lips trembled as she looked up to the ceiling; when Pari was in kindergarten, Bijou had taught her to throw her head back at the onset of tears so as to swallow them before they fell out. "You guys aren't the only ones who miss him."

"You're so right," Bijou said, enfolding Pari in her arms, clasping her with sisterly power. "Okay, I'll tell you one secret at a time."

Pari drew back slightly and stared at Bijou. She held the back of her hand to her nose and sniffled. "Okay."

"The first is that Crane actually did ask me to marry him."

"Did you say yes?"

Bijou shook her head. "He asked me in November. I said no."

"That's a dumb secret. I'm not surprised."

"And he came to Calcutta to see me."

"Shut up. He *flew* here?" Now Pari seemed if not surprised, then exponentially more interested.

"I didn't know he was planning that. But I went to see him here while you were in Darjeeling."

"Are you going to see him again? Oh my God. You should invite Crane to come over for dinner tomorrow."

"Are you insane? I can't put all those people in the same room!"

"He came all this way! Shouldn't that be, like, romantic? Why haven't you said yes? You love Naveen!"

"Pari, no. I'm too young for any of this. I'm just not ready."

"Are you, like, going to be a nun?"

"Absolutely not," Bijou said. "Oh my God, absolutely not."

"Okay, good. Just checking. But you really aren't a mystery."

That night, Pari fell asleep in front of the television, a Radiohead cassette still playing through headphones beside her, her untouched dessert of *kulfi* a pool of beige cream flecked with neon green and purplish pistachio bits. The rest of them had polished off their servings in a matter of minutes. It was the only confection Bijou's aunt loved to make as much as she enjoyed feeding it to others on a humid evening.

Bijou went to the couch and put a pillow underneath Pari's head. Ketaki came to clear Pari's bowl from the coffee table. After assessing its contents, she covered the bowl with her hand and looked baffled.

"Pari doesn't like Indian sweets," Bijou explained.

Ketaki shook her head and responded that based on what she had seen, Pari didn't like anything homemade.

Bijou gently lifted one of her sister's braids away from her face and moved it out of the way. Pari shifted, curling in her legs. She pulled the pillow from under her head and hugged it to her chest.

Her mouth was slightly open, and she was almost smiling, the way she used to when Bijou could still carry her in her arms. How blessed she was to have her, she thought. How blessed they both were.

Their aunt and uncle came into the living room and settled into the other sofa, while her mother sat down in one of the armchairs. Ketaki had returned downstairs; Bijou could just barely hear her yammering with the cook.

"Shouldn't we go see a movie?" Bijou's aunt said. "Do you know what's playing, Shankar? Something with nice songs?"

"Do you really want to put up with the queues?" He took the television remote control from the table and flipped through the channels.

Her mother had picked up a newspaper from the table and was reading it now.

"Any interesting news?" Bijou asked.

Her mother shrugged. "Local events," she said. "I'm out of touch."

Bijou's aunt turned her attention from the television, and said, "Oh, did I tell you, Didi—no, I think I forgot—about our plans for holiday?"

"Hmm?"

"Kerala. We'll go in May, and come back after the rains. I have always wanted to see the Backwaters."

Bijou's mother agreed, then said, "You could also use your break to come visit us, Anuja. We have no plans."

Her aunt appeared to be thinking such a trip over. After a while she said, "Bijou, why don't you take your mother and sister to Chicago for a break?"

"Are we refugees?" her mother answered before Bijou could. "He can come to Detroit if he wants."

Bijou's aunt sighed. "Shankar," she said, nudging him, "maybe we should get out of India for a change."

"Good idea!"

"Bijou, if you would just get married. What a perfect excuse that would be for us to come!"

No one said anything for a while.

To break the silence, Bijou said, "How long do the rains last, Anuja Massi? Is it terrible?"

"Sometimes it seems it will never end. The streets are like rivers," her aunt said. "I'm used to it, now. The first few years, of course, were the hardest. I usually went to Srinagar at that time."

Bijou's uncle looked away from the television. Commercial break. "What are you discussing?" he said.

"Oh, now you have time for us," Bijou's aunt said.

"Don't be stubborn. I was listening. Monsoons."

Bijou's mother folded the newspaper neatly and placed it on the shelf under the coffee table. There was a glitter in her eyes. She smiled coyly and said, "Anuja wasn't so stubborn before marriage, Shankar. She was the most tame of us all, so shy. Such a shy girl before."

He tried to shrug off the sexual innuendo, but he was visibly flushing. Both her aunt and mother burst into laughter, harmonic, and Bijou couldn't help but smile. Here was a woman, Bijou considered, who once delighted in matching wits with men, and of course drew pleasure from it still. Surely, it must be painful as well, to sit here and watch her sister and brother-in-law engage in their rapport. She wouldn't envy them, not her own family, but how did the reminder of all she'd lost not kill her? Days like this, exchanges like this—she'd had them once; Bijou had born witness to them—they were all behind her. There would not be another kiss, another embrace, from the man she loved. The idea wrenched Bijou's heart now, perhaps more than ever.

"The role of the monsoons in romance, Bijou," her uncle said, leaning forward, "is quite the Bengali motif. You should know this—it's part of your heritage—so let me tell you. The rains separate lovers because often the chaps are off working somewhere, right? How can they travel? Outside it is *torrential*. The roads are rivers and mud to the neck. The women weep. Their tears collude with the raindrops; it's all *very* poetic. Very *Bengali*. Passions are strengthened for the lack of—how shall I say it in English?— the lack of consummation." He settled back into the couch.

Pari stirred from beside Bijou. She sat up and yawned. "That's a very depressing story, guys," she said. "I don't see why they couldn't stay home and work." She rested her head in Bijou's lap. "I mean, did all the men from one place go to some other place to work and the men from *that* place went somewhere else, like a vicious circle? People should just chill where they are."

"Oh, Pari, go back to sleep," Bijou said. "My little innocent. My proud warrior."

Pari lifted a hand and waved as if to swat Bijou's words away. Then she rose and said she was going upstairs.

"Why couldn't you define some Kashmiri themes for the girls?" her aunt said, facetious. "They're half ours, too."

Bijou's mother emitted a sigh, then gave a tired smile and stared into the corner of the room, at a chair there.

"I told your aunt we would all go out together tomorrow. Pari wants to see a movie and do some shopping."

"Fine," Bijou said.

"Fine?"

"Yep."

She went upstairs thinking she might talk her sister out of at least part of the shopping-cinema plan. But Pari wasn't in their room. Bijou returned to the hallway, imagining her sister had gone up to the roof. As she moved to ascend the stairs, however, she noticed the doors to the *puja* alcove were ajar.

Pari sat cross-legged in front of the altar, her back upright; she was softly chanting. She bowed her head for a moment, then shifted to her knees and lifted a brass *diya* from the table. She led the *diya* in circles, from idol to idol. Black smoke rose like ribbons from the flame and twirled toward the ceiling. When she sat back, she continued to hold the *diya* with both her hands.

It seemed a long while that Bijou stood there watching silently. She thought at length about Crane, in circles, remembering the words he said in an order she could not put together straight. *You're rude. Time together in a new place. Arrangements. Met someone. Serious. She's serious.* Was this what people did to each other, was this what she was going to do? She knew she had gotten herself into it, and assumed she had to be the one to get herself out. But what on earth were her options? Beyond that, how would she know what to choose? If this was what people did to each other, then she didn't want anything to do with it.

Pari blew out the candle, but she continued to sit there until finally Bijou walked softly down the hallway to the bedroom. She felt it was hours before Pari joined her, and then hours more while they curled up on opposite ends of the bed, both of them feigning sleep.

ELEVEN

The next morning: shopping on Rash Behari Avenue, surveying goods laid out on white sheets along the sidewalk, poking in and out of sari shops and dime stores. Bijou's mother purchased ayurvedic face cream made from carrots; her aunt picked up blouses from her tailor; and, Pari, who had grown infatuated with tiffin boxes, was purchasing the steel lunch containers with the eye of a professional collector. She especially liked the ones with interlocking tiers and dishes, but other, smaller ones had more interesting latches. She filled one bag strictly with sandwich-sized cases.

"What are you going to *do* with all these?" Bijou asked.

Pari looked at her in wonder. "Isn't it obvious?"

"Open your own tiffin store?"

Around noon, their aunt took them to a shopping plaza in Gariahat—two levels of shops surrounding an open courtyard, a modern building, Bijou thought, totally lacking the character of New Market. They shared a lunch of *kachori*, salt *lassis, bhel poori, aloo chat*. Pari ate it all, and then asked for a prepackaged chocolate ice cream cone.

All morning, Bijou had felt slightly exhausted. She'd tried to contact Crane again, but he hadn't taken her calls. Now her fatigue was deepened by a heavy lunch consumed in the heat; she felt somewhat disoriented by the sight of her sister consuming so much food, and with such relish.

"You two go on," her mother said. "Anuja Massi and I will rest here."

Bijou let Pari take her by the hand. She had had her fill of tiffin shopping, she informed her, and now wanted to look for clothes. She loved this market. It was air-conditioned.

She stopped them in front of a clothing boutique, attracted to a lavender *lengha-choli* that hung loosely on a mannequin. For a while, she involved Bijou in a debate as to whether or not the color would suit them. She decided it would not, but that they should go inside anyway, and see if they could find something basic that she could wear on Saturday. She wanted to buy a sari.

Inside the boutique, the woman behind the counter pulled one sari after another from the shelves. Even if Pari didn't seem to like one, the sari was pulled out of its bag and briskly fanned out, billowing up, then slowly falling to the counter like a flag or a sail. With alarming speed, the woman unleashed a dozen saris, on automatic pilot, her eyes rarely on Pari and Bijou, but more often staring at the door, or at her nails. Perhaps this bored her, Bijou thought. Perhaps nothing could bore her more, except the chore of refolding all these saris when they left.

"Um," Pari was saying, "do you have any simple *salwaar ka-meezes*?"

As Bijou stood back, watching, and offering her opinions when her sister asked her for them, she contemplated what they'd be doing if her father were here with them. Perhaps one day, he'd have relented. They would have come here as a family. How she missed him. How she missed talking to him. What would she say, now? *Is this how you remember Calcutta? They tell me it's changed, and I believe them. Think of how much Detroit has changed since you ar-*

rived there. She wondered if places have their own memory, if buildings and streets could torture themselves with what they witnessed; she would ask her father what he thought. *In my next life, can I come back as a city? If not Paris, then how about a tree offering some shade at the intersection of two small, brick-paved streets in Montparnasse? Maybe those two streets don't even have names; that, too, would be fine by me.* What would he say?

Her mother and aunt found them in the store. Pari had changed her mind about buying anything, but felt miserable that the shopgirl had gone to so much trouble to show her options.

"I just started thinking, like, where would I wear this stuff, anyway?" she asked Bijou as they exited. "When you come home next time, will you take me shopping?"

"Of course."

"And you'll come home for the summer?"

"Unless you're in Germany."

Too exhausted to deal with any cinema outings, they all agreed to go home. Bijou's aunt, in particular, wanted to rest up before tomorrow, before hosting what she continued to not refer to as a dinner party.

An hour before the guests were due to arrive, chaos descended upon the household. Ketaki had gone out first thing in the morning and had not yet returned home. Confusion over her absence had turned into concern by afternoon, and now they were alarmed: Bijou's aunt had just discovered, in the midst of dressing for company, that two of her gold bangles and a matching necklace were missing from her jewelry chest, the lock of which had clearly been broken.

Bijou's uncle suggested they phone the police. They were all sitting at the kitchen table.

"Could they find her? What if she's hurt?" Bijou's mother said.

"Would they *look* for her?" Bijou's aunt shoved her jewelry box away. It made a little ringing noise from inside. "Shankar, go with Ramesh to the station. Go in person and file a report." She sighed. "It's no use. She's not coming back after taking the bangles. Foolish girl."

Bijou's uncle went downstairs.

"Maybe she lost track of time," Bijou said, hopeful. No one seemed willing to buy this hypothesis. "It happens."

"This is why I have two locks on my suitcase," Pari said.

"I doubt she'd want your tiffin boxes," Bijou replied.

Her aunt and mother wondered what had precipitated Ketaki's running away, if that's what it was. Had her aunt noticed anything unusual? No, she'd hardly seen her. It was Bijou who had been at the house most.

"Did you notice anything, Bijou?"

"How would I," she replied weakly, "know if she was behaving like usual or not?"

"Let's wait until the morning," her mother said. "Perhaps she'll change her mind."

"No," Bijou's aunt said. She sounded exhausted. "She wouldn't dare come back. She doesn't understand."

The rest of them sat quietly until Pari suggested there was nothing to do now but pray that Ketaki was safe. She said she was going upstairs to change, and urged everyone to do the same.

But their uncle returned with news: it had been confirmed by Ramesh that Ketaki had run off; she was in no harm, as it were. She was not alone. She'd gone with the boy, that *chokra* who took care of the Maliks' dogs. Apparently, the boy had been boasting to Ramesh of his and Ketaki's plans last night. Now it seemed she'd been truthful: she was going to marry the boy; they were headed for their village to get their familys' blessings. She wasn't coming back.

"Those Maliks have never hired anyone reliable, never. Remember, Anuja, that opium-addicted driver? It's a miracle they didn't all die in that automobile accident. Can they not look after their dogs on their own? I've seen those pathetic things. They're slow. Why have dogs, tell me, if they cannot even guard the house?"

"What a *tamasha*! I cannot believe the nerve of that girl," Bijou's aunt said, but she looked very much relieved to hear Ketaki was not in harm's way. "I would have given her new bangles, better ones. I don't understand. Why did the girl have to go behind our backs, tell me? I would have paid for the wedding with pleasure!"

"No one knows what their future holds." Bijou's mother looked wearily at her hands, playing with her wedding ring. "Such a young girl, so bold. God bless her—let her have happiness with him."

"She's so young! You don't think it's kind of impulsive?" Bijou said, but her mother and aunt were already on to discussing the untimeliness, really, of Ketaki's departure. There would be so much work now, the trouble of finding another girl, et cetera, et cetera.

Pari stopped Bijou on the stairs as they went up to their room. "I thought Ketaki was, like, fifteen."

Bijou nodded.

"I guess I would run away, too," Pari said. "Do you think she'll still be a maidservant after she's married?"

"Good question." Bijou didn't know; all she knew was that girls like Ketaki and her mother fled for their happiness, and with every fiber of her being she envied them their fearlessness, spirit, and precocity to choose a man who chose them over everyone and everything else.

* * *

Two professors from the Hindi department were the first to arrive for dinner. They came with their wives, and one couple had two small children. Then came a very attractive woman named Zenia, who was evidently finishing her dissertation on the topic of eighteenth-century nawabs; she was a former student of Bijou's uncle.

Bijou stood making small talk with Zenia, rooted by the stairs in the same place they'd been introduced moments before.

"Isn't it true your father's side is from East Bengal originally?" Zenia asked. "I'm sure your uncle mentioned it once. Was it your grandmother, perhaps?"

Bijou lifted her gaze from the stairwell. "I don't know," she said. She was debating, inwardly, whether or not Naveen would come tonight—had been fearing all day that he wouldn't, hoping that he would, and then wondering why she was debating any of this at all. "My grandmother passed away when my father was fairly young."

Zenia murmured sympathetically. Her grandparents had all passed on as well, she told Bijou. They had died not long after Bangladesh won its independence, when Zenia was still a girl.

"My parents have moved back to Dhaka now," she said. "But I could never leave Calcutta. It's my home."

"Don't you miss your parents?" Bijou said. "Or do you see them often? I don't know how far away Dhaka is, to be honest."

"I'm married," Zenia said, as if that was the best reply to any question. "My husband and I live here together. He's a doctor, like you. I wish he'd been able to come tonight." She slid her hand along the banister of the stairs, looked down to where Bijou had just been looking herself. Zenia's hair draped over her face for a moment—her hair hung to her waist, just as Bijou's once had—and she seemed in such a state of yearning, Bijou supposed the husband was on an endless trip in a remote village, healing the destitute. She asked where he was.

Zenia tucked her hair behind her ear languidly. "He was in surgery all day. I won't be staying here very long, actually. But he was sleeping, and it was so sweet of you all to invite us. I wanted to come. I wanted to come before, but we have been so busy."

At last, Kamla and Naveen made their entrance. Another man came with them, but he was ushered directly into the living room by Bijou's uncle.

"Bijou, you're looking so nice," Kamla said.

"I think I'm finally over my jet lag, that's all," she replied. She asked if Kamla knew Zenia, then introduced them. Kamla smiled graciously, then excused herself to join the others.

"*We've* actually met before, however," Naveen said, extending his hand to Zenia, who had visibly brightened upon seeing him.

"Don't be so formal, Naveen. How are things, hm? I hear you're the star professor this year."

He smiled. "We should join the others." He gestured for the women to proceed, and Zenia fluttered off. Bijou could feel Naveen's hand hovering over the small of her back, and she stopped abruptly. He said, "Let's get a minute alone, later. Just to chat."

She nodded.

In the living room, the men and women had gravitated to polar opposite ends, with the two small children running as go-betweens. Zenia scooped one of the children into her arms. Those who spoke were speaking in polite modulations, neither excited nor grim.

Bijou sat near Kamla as Naveen joined the men. She fidgeted with her hands, missing her little gardenia ring most of all now for the physical distraction it provided.

"We were just talking about you," Kamla said, but she did not elaborate. She had turned away from the two professors' wives next to her, who were engaged in some discussion about the proportions required of anise powder versus asafetida in, as they kept saying, *typical* Kashmiri cooking.

"Where's Mummie?" Bijou said. "And Anuja Massi?"

"I thought they were in the kitchen. I was just going to go there myself." Kamla smiled. "I heard the news."

"News?"

"It sounds like a love story to me. True love. The first time your *massi* told me of the rumors, I sensed that this would happen. It was inevitable. Poor Anuja. She treated Ketaki like her own child."

Of course. Ketaki. "Well, I hope it's true."

"What do you mean?"

"That she went of her own accord," Bijou said earnestly. Kamla looked at her with a cocked eyebrow, and Bijou laughed. It *was* flimsy, the notion of Ketaki's doing anything against her will. "No, you're right. It is a love story."

After a minute, Kamla pointed out to Bijou the man who had come in with her and Naveen. No, they hadn't come together; they'd shown up outside at the same time. Had Bijou met him before? Well, she might like to; she might like to talk to him later.

"His name is Debashish Sen," Kamla said. "Remember, I was telling you of him? He's your aunt's physician now. Not so politically active anymore."

Debashish Sen was awfully docile-looking compared to what Bijou'd imagined. He was rather short, gaunt, with wide, amphibian lips. He had lost all the hair at his crown, which was dappled with dark spots on the skin there, and stood talking to the others with both hands in his pockets. He seemed quite jolly, balancing on his heels, peering over the black plastic frames of his eyeglasses.

"Ah, look!" Kamla said, touching Bijou's elbow but looking out into the room. "That's so sweet."

Bijou agreed, as she saw one of the children attempting to climb up Naveen's legs; Naveen turned around to lift the girl in his arms. He held her quite naturally, as he continued his conversation with the girl's father.

In lifting up the little girl, Naveen had met Bijou's eye.

"His father was not so good with children," Kamla told her. "He was never fit for the domestic lifestyle. If we met again, I would recognize that. I would not expect him to change his nature; I would know that a man like that, his nature does not change."

"You wanted a big family?"

"Oh, I'd have settled for two. But Ashok was—well, we had our disagreements, too. Your father knew ... Your mother and I, when you think about it, we both lost our husbands long before they passed on. But there is love left in your mother's case; you can see that. Of course, I have Naveen. Until he gets married, and then, who knows?"

Bijou's aunt announced that it was time to dine.

People filled their plates from a variety of dishes—*yakhni, paneer,* greens with turnips—set out on the dining table, over which Bijou's aunt had thrown a new tablecloth. (*A simple dinner, nothing more. I won't even make dessert; we can have rusk with* kahvah. *They know it's not celebration.*)

As the men helped themselves to food, under her aunt's supervision—"Take more"—and assisted by Kamla, Bijou sat with her mother. Pari and Zenia sat with the two children, helping their mother feed them.

Bijou's mother patted her back. "God willing," she said, "I will return soon for another visit. And perhaps, eventually, for much longer." She alluded to her plans to sell the house once Pari went to college, how she'd felt more at home at the ashram than she'd felt anywhere in such a long time.

"I'll help you," Bijou said, "do whatever you want."

Even as they ate, the men conferred about work. Conversation had turned to the subject of Naveen's book, for which he had interviewed Debashish nearly a year earlier. For a while, they spoke of what shape Naveen hoped to give the project. (He wanted to wait until it was completely assembled, worry about contours and transitions later.) Bijou's uncle again broached the topic of Naveen's plans for his sabbatical in the fall.

"I don't know. I have many conditions—new ones every day, it feels—to consider," he replied, in such a way that the dialogue came to a full stop.

There was a momentary silence among the men as they tasted their food, then they complimented Bijou's aunt on a meal well done.

"But when I know," Naveen said to Bijou's uncle, "you'll be the first person I tell, how's that? Promise."

Her uncle seemed appeased by this, and commented on the high value he accorded to Naveen's word.

"I always wanted to write a book about the experience myself," Debashish said. "But it never went anywhere. I did write some short stories, but they were very bad."

"Well, actually, I think I might lead with your interview," Naveen said. "Yours is the most compelling by far."

"Why is that?" Bijou said.

The others turned to look at her—first Naveen, who gazed at her steadily, then Debashish and the other men, glancing her way as if to check whether or not she had meant to lend her voice to their discussion.

"What set it apart?" she said.

"I read that piece, didn't I, Naveen?" Zenia was collecting some of the cleaned plates. One of the children trailed her, holding on to the hem of her kurta. "As I recall, it was rather long."

"We met every day," Debashish said. "For how many weeks? Months, maybe."

"What sets this particular interview apart, Bijou," Naveen said, "is that Debashish spent a great deal of his time and energy in defending the human rights of those Naxalites who were imprisoned. So many of them were brutally tortured."

"I wasn't alone," Debashish said. He held up his hand, waving it stiffly in objection. "My brother was even more involved. And Kamla—you, too."

Kamla looked up from her dinner plate, then back at it.

"I only gathered signatures for some petitions," she said. "It was the last thing I did. Before that, I had withdrawn myself for almost two years. Maybe three . . . But yes. There were many wives, and mothers, campaigning. We were relatively well organized, I think."

"Will you be a part of the book?" Bijou asked her.

"I should hope not." She threw Naveen a sharp look and stood up. As she adjusted her *dhupatta*, the bracelets on her arm slid down, chiming. She told Zenia she would help clear the dishes, and followed her downstairs.

"What about your brother?" Bijou asked Debashish. He looked away from her immediately. Naveen flinched, then seemed on the brink of crossing the room to speak to her at closer range, but he took only one step before stopping.

"Sanjoy left Calcutta years ago," Debashish said.

"Oh," Bijou said quietly. A communal hush fell over the living room, wakeful but resigned, before the guests reverted to more intimate conversations. Bijou's aunt mumbled that she needed help bringing up the tea, and took her downstairs.

"*Beta,*" she told her in the kitchen, taking a tea cozy and linen napkins out of the cupboard, "I know you're curious about these things, but it's hard for some people to talk of all that happened. You understand. Sensitive topic. Let's just enjoy the tea, make your mother feel better, hm?"

"I'm sorry."

"Don't be sorry. You haven't done anything wrong." She glanced at Bijou, then stopped in the middle of her work. "*Arré,* don't cry!" She cupped Bijou's face in her soft hands. "You are beautiful. You don't worry."

Bijou looked to the ceiling and trapped the tears that had collected so quickly in her eyes. "It's like I woke up in someone else's body six months ago."

Her aunt took her in her arms. "How else could you be, tell me?" Now she was wiping her own eyes. "It will get better. Time heals all wounds."

Gold-rimmed saucers had been stacked neatly, but the fourteen cups—their delicate porcelain basins flecked with bits of shalelike leaves and crushed almonds from the *kahvah*—were spread out on the dining table like a psychic medium's final opus.

Nearly everyone had left—the children were sleepy, and Zenia's husband awaited her. No one went away without entreating Bijou's mother to visit them again soon.

Now it was nearing midnight, and only Naveen and Debashish remained in the living room. Bijou's uncle had gone to walk Zenia home. The women collected the teacups and took them to the kitchen for washing. They washed them in an assembly line of sorts.

"So it takes five of you to do what Ketaki had to do alone?" said Naveen from the kitchen door. "I'd have run off, too."

"But, Naveen, where's Debashish?"

"He left, Auntie. He's going to Ranchi tomorrow for a wedding or something."

Bijou turned to him. "He left? But I didn't have a chance to talk to him."

"That's really too bad," Kamla said, frowning. "If anyone has stories, it's Debashish. Sanjoy and I went to the same medical college. Their father was an *exemplary* physician. He helped, in those days, when the young boys were wounded—he even treated Ashok once, for burns."

"What happened to him?" Bijou said.

"There was an explosion," Kamla explained. "Ashok barely escaped with his life."

"I mean Sanjoy—what happened to him?"

Kamla raised her shoulders in doubt. "There are many of us," she said, "who do not enjoy discussing those days. When the movement was spent, it didn't mean that animosities disappeared. To this day . . . Sometimes it was safer to hide and stay quiet."

"This is what I tried to explain to her!" Bijou's mother said. "But Debashish seems like a nice man. His wife grew up in Kashmir, he told me. Though she is not originally from there. We had quite a nice talk about Nitish. Nitish would be pleased to be remembered that way." She thanked Bijou's aunt for inviting him.

"I'm just glad he could come," she replied. "They all wanted to see you."

Kamla added: "His wife—Chhaya is her name—she is lovely. I became better friends with them after Ashok died." It had been Debashish, she told them, who'd broken the news of Ashok's death to her, in fact.

Bijou's mother winced. She turned to face Kamla and said, "Do you feel, sometimes, as if they're still here?"

Kamla responded with a sorrowful, fervent yes. "The dreams I still have, after all these years, it's as if he comes to me in spirit, and we've made our peace."

"You never talk about these things with me, Ma," Naveen said gently.

"Well, she and I understand each other, Naveen. We have many things in common." Kamla turned back to Bijou's mother and added: "We'll have Debashish over when he's back, and with his wife, too. You can all come for dinner next week, and Bijou can hear more about Nitish, those days, if she wants."

"But Bijou leaves on Monday," her mother pointed out.

"So soon? Can't you change your ticket?"

"I already did."

"What did you say?" Kamla said.

Bijou cleared her throat, and repeated herself so she could be heard, adding, "I was in a rush to get back to D.C. I didn't realize how much that would change."

Kamla set the last teacup on the counter. "So this is our last meeting? That's terrible. I haven't even given you anything to re-member us by."

Bijou picked up the teacup, dried it slowly. A gold lattice design ran around the rim like a frieze. It reminded her of the trim in Naveen's bedroom.

"I'll come back," she said.

"Naturally," Kamla declared. She and the others, minus Naveen, trailed out of the kitchen.

"I'll miss Ketaki," Naveen said theatrically. "I'm hurt that I didn't get an invitation to the wedding."

"She didn't have to run away like that."

"Oh, but what harm are they doing? It's all for love, isn't it?"

She put the last teacup back in the china cabinet and followed Naveen to the foyer. The others were standing outside on the street below the porch, drawing out their good-byes with their arms crossed before them in the evening air.

"I suppose we should join them," Bijou said.

"Yes," Naveen replied. He crossed his arms and lowered his gaze to the floor, taking a few steps backward to stand next to her. "I'd hoped we would be able to talk some more."

"Maybe you could stay longer? No, I suppose it's getting late."

"They'll all be going to bed."

"Tomorrow, maybe? We could take Pari somewhere?"

"She's wonderful."

"Isn't she?" They lingered for a bit in silence. "Tomorrow, then?"

"Yes," Naveen said. "And there's no reason I can't see you off at the airport, as well, is there?"

Bijou's uncle had returned from Zenia's; they heard him ask for Naveen, then a hush.

"It's strange without Ketaki," Bijou said. "I got really used to having her around."

"Oh, they'll have her replaced by the middle of next week." He put his hand on her arm. "So? You're going home."

She covered his hand with her own. "I don't want to go home. This feels like home."

He ran his other hand along her arm. "Didn't I tell you?"

"Will you do me a favor? I want to go somewhere. Right now. Can your mother go without you? Is that terrible?"

"What is it, Bijou?"

She told him where she wanted to go, and he replied that there was no question about it. They would go together, at once.

They don't speak much during the rest of the ride, during a long walk, or as they make their way past Eden Gardens, down to and then alongside the Hooghly.

—Is this where . . . ?

—Probably not. It doesn't matter.

—Do you want to be alone?

—Would you mind staying with me? Let's sit here. Let's just sit together.

Now they sit here, on a jut of cement like a makeshift pier, the bottom edge of it craggy where it hangs into the water's edge, whisking river swells to a froth. So quiet now, right now, so quiet here, Bijou thinks she hears each bubble in the river's foam nestling in with its neighbor, *hiss Hello hiss It's been too long, hasn't it? hiss*, before popping. Then another lapping and purling, and another. She looks across at the wobbling skiffs, a few tired, faded, wooden shapes outlined by moonlight, tied to a dock on the opposite bank. A group of men and boys scuttles up the bank beyond; she has already watched them cross the river in their skiff, and now they disappear.

They sit here cross-legged as if at a temple performing *puja*, two together, far apart. Her back hurts, and it is hot despite the rustling of breezes in the mangroves. She thinks how she will have the longest summer ever this year. She is bound to return to a season of heat much like this. Washington will be pared down to the people who can't afford to get away. She likes the city in summer; one only had to ignore the tourists, and she would. *Every lovely summer's day.* She slips out of her sandals and dangles her feet over the water. Doesn't immerse them too deep, just so her soles are flush with the surface. *You've been here before.* Today the river feels precisely a part of Calcutta, and she feels a part of the river. There are feathery poplar seeds falling or floating in the water, and pine needles, and insects with wings like vellum, weightless things, everything silver against the dark waters.

Naveen shifts position, too, puts one of his knees up, rests his arm on it, leans back on the other hand. He seems relaxed but tired.

Farther south, in Shibpur on the opposite bank, he tells her, are the Botanical Gardens. He would have liked to have taken her there, if only to see the famed banyan tree, more than two centuries old.

"How do you get there?" she asks.

There is a ferry service from Metiabruz Ghat.

"Let's go now," she says. It is something she could say she has seen. There is a simple story to it. *When I was in India, I saw a tree older than America.*

But there's no way they can. Not today. It's too late; the grounds are closed until morning.

Later, as he leads her up the river, she assumes they are retracing their steps back to Eden Gardens. It is a little darker. Bijou hears Lady Day in her ears, crooning how much she hates to see the evening sun go down, 'cause her baby left town, and if she's feeling tomorrow like she feels today, she'll pack her trunk, make her getaway.

"Where are we going, Naveen?"

"The seven seas."

"The seventies? I've had quite enough of them."

He glances over his shoulder. He's amused, and he isn't.

He holds out his hand, then clutches hers. "Come down this way."

They reach another ghat in several quick paces. He leads her down the steps toward a wide canoe immersed half in the mud, half in the water. A man sits alone in the middle of it, facing away from them, his paddle across his lap.

Naveen calls out to him, asks in Bengali if the man will take them out for a little while.

No, no, it's too late. They'll just have to wait and see if anyone else wants to go. It's a big ferry. At least ten more people could fit. No one else will want to go. It's too late.

But this is important; it's a great favor he'd be doing. No one else is in sight. Only a miracle would bring five more people—how could they ever find ten? Please. Twice the regular payment. The girl is leaving the country in a matter of hours.

The man relents. Not because of the money, but because of the sincerity.

The vessel teeters as Bijou climbs in. She sits on a bulky burlap sack set in the middle of the boat. Naveen grabs a paddle, helps get the boat drifting away from the shore, asking that they maneuver the boat down the river, not across it. And not a long ride. The girl needs to go home soon, remember?

But Bijou isn't thinking of home, much less of leaving Calcutta. She doesn't know how she'll cry when they all drop her off at the airport, Naveen pressing a slip of paper into her hands with his address written on it. She doesn't know that in Paris, the two-hour layover will be doubled because of rain, and she will stand at the window by their gate, her palms and most of her body pressed to the window, that she will stand there watching the rain come down in silver drapes, and she will think, *Oh, this is rain,* and in remembering rain, she will remember Calcutta's lack of rain, and this will establish a pattern of shadow thoughts for the ensuing years. She doesn't know that she will stand at the window long enough to become conspicuous. She won't notice those around her, and even then she will not be thinking—because the idea will not come to her for years—that this moment, this part of a memory that will dictate the rest of her life, is not set in the shadow of sorrow but of a resolution still ahead.

She isn't thinking of all that, doesn't know it, as she gives

Naveen an embrace and he holds her dearly. As she looks over his shoulder, the shore shrinks behind them, and then they are parallel to it. The river is calm; it swallows the oar and releases it with a gush. Again. Again. And as they glide, she kneels, leans over the side of the boat, lets one hand dip into the water, leaves it there a minute before taking it out. She turns sideways and looks ahead. Naveen takes another turn rowing, continues to banter with the other man. They laugh, and she smiles. The boat keeps going as if magic keeps it afloat, and when she turns her gaze up, it is to catch a flock of birds taking flight from the highest branches of such old trees.

Perhaps the last memory to go will be one of his first, he contemplates one day, staring at the world outside his hospital window. Perhaps it will be this memory he still has of kneesocks and sandals, of being surrounded by giants, other boys teaching him to play marbles, and how he excels at it, shooting them like cannonballs across a patch of dusty playing field. Those sounds excited him. He hears again now the simple orchestra of teachers' chalk on slate in primary school. Those sounds used to arrest him the way he had seen temple chants arrest his father.

There is his father, then, statuesque with his eyes closed and his hard lips moving around long chains of Sanskrit: *Om Bhur Bhuvah Svah Tat Savitur Varenyam Bhargo Devasya Dhimahi Dhiyo Yo Nah Prachodayat.* His thumb against the base of his ring finger, then skipping up one of the three joints, and another—he is counting recitations; the next jump marks five—traveling like this across the other fingers until sixteen is reached.

Then the day when he lowers his head before his father as a sacredly spun filament is hung across his chest from his bony brown shoulder. He is about eight years old; this is the *paite,* his thread ceremony. Holy water falls like dew into his cupped hands, and he goes in circles around a small fire. His father takes him outside and directs him toward the sun. "Look, and keep looking. The light of the great sun pervades all things, and so should be your quest for knowledge."

He squints. Repeats after his father, as he has been told to repeat, *Into my heart, I will take your heart.* But already he is daydreaming. Already he is returning in his mind to a kite he wants to build, in the form of a Chinese dragon, with tails that will whip in the wind so loudly everyone will hear them, and wonder.

The kite is the first thing he remembers his father not liking about him. It was one thing to build it—he'd even helped—but another to waste so much time playing with it. His father works and prays; he wants Nitish to study and pray, and grow to be a stoic man who works and prays. Well, he studies. He passes his exams by wide margins, and his father says nothing. It is not what he does. Pride and flattery are for lesser people.

And, like yesterday, he can still remember how wide open the world felt to him upon entering college, how unrestrained and friendly. He hadn't made many friends until then. He hadn't known that so many people had left his father's principles in the dust, which is quite where he preferred them.

Or there is that vivid hot day months and months later in Darjeeling when Nitish stops hiking, dead in his tracks, and thinks he hears his old dragon kite, the same sharp fluttering and thrash. But it is instead a wild cat having some success in catching crows for breakfast. Wings mangled, and blood. Later, he'll turn to Ashok and say, "Have we made any progress?" Later, much later, he'll be mixing glazes in his Michigan basement and will smell a noxious element, like fertilizer and gas; when he makes a set of terra-cotta Diwali *diyas* for his wife, he remembers with what facility his hands had once assembled crude explosives.

Ashok's face burns out, blurs. There's no memory Nitish has

kept of his death. It's already been consumed; nothing is left. He sends letters to ghosts across the oceans. He hears news of his father's death, but his father never dies. He lingers all around him to this day, disapproving of his habits. Where will such habits get him? Certainly not to a place where he will ever make peace with Ashok's death.

Perhaps, then, it's the long passage by ship to Great Britain, days and nights of seasickness and constant thirst, at every port along the route telling himself to get off, to go back, to *get off the ship,* because he is sick in the head and the body, because there is a boy he has left behind to grow up fatherless, *because of his cowardice alone.* Just before dawn on the second day, he concludes that cowardice is the one thing no father should be so guilty of. So truly, he is doing the boy a favor, giving him a fighting chance at becoming a man, ego intact, confidence unshaken. Let the boy be loved, not made to feel frivolous and impotent. Let Kamla raise him with all her strength. Nitish cannot hold a candle to it. He stays on board, his own stowaway.

Another train, Dover; another ship, the English Channel, Calais, Le Havre, Gare Saint-Lazare all white light and stone and unlike Monet painted it. He remembers that. He remembers Gare Saint-Lazare, and knowing no one, no language like French, needing a shave, needing a bed, needing a hot meal, every need feeling criminal.

There is the first sight of Sheela, of course. He might remember the way she walks with regal posture, but when she sits, it is in a huddle, always girl-like, dizzying him. Her hair was piled high in the current fashion and fastened with mod barrettes she'd let her brother buy her instead of showy jewelry or clothes. She moves into his heart like a hand through water. She listens. Things are right, things are wrong; there is no gray area for Sheela, only clear-cut living. There is only *now*, and he needs someone who believes that, what with his past at his heels like wolves and the future seething in his face. He all but begs for her love. She reassures him. In so little time, they know all they need to know: that they can spend the rest of their lives learning the rest of it, together; it will all be good. It will take them far away from here.

Even now he believes that a life should be more than the sum of a few memories, and he is certain that he has left this problem unsolved. There is so much he will miss. When he is gone, and they go on, he won't be the one to advise the girls about the choices they will make in men, mortgages, motherhood, in golf or grief. Others will advise them, and he will never know who they are, those who will get closer than he is allowed. He does not know whether to hate them or love them.

Perhaps he will forget his last memory first. Is it here: these years of paralyzing rest. Will it be this recurring thought he tells not another soul, but turns over and over in his mind—*You have wanted to forget so much; well, now you will, now you will*—as disease eats away, feasting on him, showing him who is in control. Not him; never him. But no, it won't be this, nor will the last memory to go be his father's face set in rage, nor the cage of a jail cell that smelled like ashes and death, nor Ashok's voice when he asked, *Am I your prisoner?* The last memory to go will not be the night he left Calcutta, or Paris; not the first day on a new job, not the last day of an old one, not all the crushing free time in between, not a half-ruined kiln that sits in the backyard of his true home, where his wife will one day, without overt ceremony, place a bird feeder.

No, even when his wife's face reminds him less and less of his wife, when these two girls come to his bedside and he cannot remember their names, cannot speak, then cannot see, even then there is something else that won't be forgotten, and he rests assured that someday, someone will wake up on a clear morning, perhaps after heavy rains, and realize how much of life was not what you destroyed or what you took with you, not what you forgot or what you failed to recall, but what you left in place for others to discover, in themselves, and carry forth with their torches raised up higher than they ever had imagined.

X